# AS THE
# STAR LORDS ORDAIN...

*Even as I cursed myself, I cringed a little; I, Dray Prescot, cringed a little at the thought of what the Star Lords would do. For I had not disobeyed the Everoinye. I had done what the Star Lords commanded, through their spy and messenger the golden and scarlet raptor. But —for the first time on Kregen—I had failed the Star Lords.*

What would they do to one who proved a broken reed?

The thought of Delia drove mad phantasms through my mind. What if, through my failure, I was banished from Kregen forever?

The thought was impossible; I could not face it. I must recoup this situation, bash on, trample down any and everything that stood in my path . . . Better the ice floes of Sicce than being hurled back to the Earth of my birth and never more see my Delia of the Blue Mountains!

"The Miglas fought magnificently."

# ARENA
# OF
# ANTARES

By
**Alan Burt Akers**

*Illustrated by*
JACK GAUGHAN

# DAW BOOKS, INC.
DONALD A. WOLLHEIM, PUBLISHER

1301 Avenue of the Americas
New York, N. Y.     10019

Cover art by Jack Gaughan.

DEDICATION:

*For Kenneth-Laurence*

## THE SAGA OF DRAY PRESCOT

*The Delian Cycle*

I    TRANSIT TO SCORPIO
II   THE SUNS OF SCORPIO
III  WARRIOR OF SCORPIO
IV   SWORDSHIPS OF SCORPIO
V    PRINCE OF SCORPIO

*The Havilfar Cycle*

I    MANHOUNDS OF ANTARES
II   ARENA OF ANTARES

FIRST PRINTING, DECEMBER 1974

1 2 3 4 5 6 7 8 9

**DAW**st
BOOKS

PRINTED IN U.S.A.

# Table of CONTENTS

# List of Illustrations

# A Note on Dray Prescot

Dray Prescot is a man above medium height, with straight brown hair and brown eyes that are level and dominating. His shoulders are immensely wide and there is about him an abrasive honesty and a fearless courage. He moves like a great hunting cat, quiet and deadly. Born in 1775 and educated in the inhumanly harsh conditions of the late eighteenth century English navy, he presents a picture of himself that, the more we learn of him, grows no less enigmatic.

Through the machinations of the Savanti nal Aphrasöe, mortal but superhuman men dedicated to the aid of humanity, and of the Star Lords, he has been taken to Kregen under the Suns of Scorpio many times. On that savage and beautiful, marvelous and terrible world he rose to become Zorcander of the clansmen of Segesthes, and Lord of Strombor in Zenicce, and a member of the mystic and martial Order of Krozairs of Zy.

Against all odds Prescot won his highest desire and in that immortal battle at The Dragon's Bones claimed his Delia, Delia of Delphond, Delia of the Blue Mountains, as his own. And Delia claimed him in the face of her father, the dread Emperor of Vallia. Amid the rolling thunder of the acclamations of "Hai Jikai!" Prescot became Prince Majister of Vallia, and wed his Delia, the Princess Majestrix.

Through the agency of the blue radiance sent by the Star Lords, Prescot is plunged headlong into fresh adventures outwitting the Manhounds of Antares. After rescuing Mog, a high priestess, and Turko the Khamorro, and Saenda and Quaesa, Prescot brings them safely out of danger—when the giant bird of prey of the Star Lords appears once again to him. . . .

ALAN BURT AKERS

7

# Chapter One

## The Star Lords command

"What is it the Star Lords command, bird of ill omen?"

"That is better, Dray Prescot! You should know you have not completed your task. Not until the land of Migla is cleansed of the Canops and Migshaanu is returned to her rightful place—for a time only!—will your work be done."

"I am almost naked, I have no weapons, no money, two girls depend on me, the whole country is up in arms against me. You are hard taskmasters—"

"You have been naked before, Dray Prescot, and weaponless. You will do this thing."

With a loud and harsh squawk, a cry of triumphant rage, the raptor winged away into the fading suns-glow. Zim and Genodras, which hereabouts I should call with all hatred Far and Havil, sank in a smoldering angry blaze of jade and ruby, dropping down over the horizon. Darkness closed over the land of Migla upon the continent of Havilfar on Kregen.

Stunned at the enormity of the sentence passed upon me I went down to the boat.

In the darkness, before any of the seven moons of Kregen rose, I pushed off and in silence took the looms of the oars into my hands.

What I must do I must do.

Oh, my little Drak, my little Lela!

And my Delia, my Delia of Delphond—when would I see her again and hold her dear form in my arms?

The two girls, Saenda and Quaesa, ceased their silly chattering at sight of my face, and they shivered. Turko looked at me, hesitated, and did not speak, for which I was grateful. Turko had stood upon the bridge there in the great cavern of rushing waters beneath the citadel of Mungul Sidrath and had taken the crossbow bolts on that new shield of his. He was to become a good companion. His superb muscular development and the cunning khamster skills of unarmed combat were to stand me in good stead. But, just then, by remaining silent he did me the best service he could.

His ropy muscles moved with the ease and suppleness that all the bunched and massive bashing power of a warrior's hardened muscles might never match. He understood at once that we were not to escape easily down the River Magan away from this eerie town of Yaman in the land of Migla.

Out across the water lights moved in the starshot darkness. The armored men of the Canopdrin army continued to search for us. I pulled down gently, letting the ebb take us. Occasionally a hail floated across the water. The girls shivered in the bottom of the boat. If we were caught their fate would be horrible, worse than it would have been before I rescued them.

They were no longer my concern.

Those aloof beings, the Star Lords, had commanded me to erase the blight of the Canops from this land, and from the very first I had seen the enormous difficulties of that. I had no desire at all to involve myself in fresh fighting and scheming and planning; all I wanted to do was return home to Vallia or Valka, depending on where Delia and the children might be staying, and clasp them in my arms once more.

But if I refused to help the Miglas turn the Canops out, I would be seized up by the ghastly blue lambence of the scorpion-image and hurled back four hundred light-years to the planet of my birth.

That must not be allowed to happen.

Therefore I must begin at once to scheme and plan to aid old Mog the Witch, the old crone who was now the Mighty Mog, to regain her rightful place as high priestess to the all-powerful Migshaanu. Migla was dominated by religion. Mind you, if this Migshaanu was really all-powerful, then she would never have allowed her high priestess to be defamed, her temple razed, and her religion brought into contempt. If Mog or any of her friends and adherents thought of that, I guessed, they pushed the obvious consequences of the thought aside with the kinds of arguments that have sustained proscribed religions through the ages.

Lights glimmered upon the water and the two girls crouched down, frightened and shivering, and Turko

10

looked at me. All about us in the moonless darkness lurked danger. No hand would be raised to save us. Darkness and danger and the creeping sense of impending doom cast a shadow upon the boat, a shadow that had not existed only moments before, when I had gone up to the bank for the last time before pushing off.

Our whole situation had changed.

Now I must go boldly ahead into fresh dangers and new adventures, and never reckon the cost until the bidding of the Star Lords had been done.

All that had passed meant nothing.

This was a new beginning, a fresh assault upon the destiny that had brought me to this fantastic planet of Kregen beneath the Suns of Scorpio.

Lights moved upon the waters.

Our little boat drifted with only a faint gurgle and splash, a shadow among shadows.

"They draw close, Dray," said Turko, his voice a whisper in the gloom.

"Aye."

Plans and schemes tumbled through my head like a cloud of those infernal midges of the marshes men call kitches, cursing and swiping, and no plan was a good plan.

One of the three lesser moons of Kregen rose and hurtled low over the horizon.

That speck of light racing between the star clusters served only further to enhance my mood of restlessness, of unease, of a mindless shifting of forces I could not control or even come to terms with, and so hated and detested. Water splashed nearby and a voice cursed, the deep rolling cadences of a man who swore by Lem, the silver leem.

We peered in that scant and erratic illumination and made out the dark loom of a boat, ghosting along, low in the water. I could feel the hard lenk of the boat's gunwales beneath my hands, and I gripped tightly, feeling the frustration choking me. I have told you many times that on Kregen a man must possess a weapon and be skilled in its use if he wishes to survive, and this is no less true for the marvelous skills of the Khamorros, the khamsters famed for unarmed combat, like Turko. I had not revealed all my mind to Turko on the subject of unarmed combat against edged and pointed weapons, and would not do so unless Zair commanded in a moment of intense danger, and so I fretted that I did not grasp a sword or a spear or

11

a bow as that creeping dark boat ghosted over the water as we drifted down.

Those men over there, those Canops, hard tough fighting-men from the devastated island of Canopdrin in the Shrouded Sea who had invaded Migla and made the land their own and subverted the peoples' allegiances, they would not scruple to kill unarmed men. And I knew they possessed the skill to slay even a great Khamorro like Turko.

Our boat drifted, and I, Dray Prescot, peered over the gunwale at that other craft, and I cursed, and I was very conscious of my shame.

"She of the Veils will be up soon," said Turko. He spoke low on two counts, as I well knew. One, so that the armed Canops should not hear, and, two, so that Saenda and Quaesa should not hear, either, and begin a frightened squeaking.

"There are more of these Opaz-forsaken cramphs about than I had bargained for, Turko."

"They slink like leem."

"A leem may be slain with a sword."

"Morro the Muscle faced and breasted and slew a leem, Dray. It is not left for mortal men."

"Maybe not."

He cocked an eye at me sharply. Some of his old quizzical appraisal of my prowess showed through. He must clearly have wondered if I spoke thoughtlessly, or boasted emptily, or—but he could not know of the existence of Sanurkazz and the Eye of the World even as he had been unaware of the unarmed combat disciplines of the Krozairs of Zy.\*

For a space we drifted silently and the Canops' boat angled away from us, with an occasional faint splash. The torchlights dimmed. This would not do. I was acting as though I intended to take the two girls to safety, either to the land of Cnarveyl to the north or to the land of Tyriadrin to the south. I had to see them safe. That was a task I had laid on myself, for all their bitchiness and squabbling and their lofloolike hitchings and squirmings. They were just two silly girls, whom I had happened to rescue

---

\* This is intriguing. It seems to imply that Prescot did fight a leem barehanded before—or possibly after—he had become a Krozair of Zy on the Eye of the World. If so, it is just one more fascinating story lost to us in those tapes, as recounted in *The Suns of Scorpio.*
A.B.A.

12

from slavery and the Manhounds of Antares, and they could not weigh in the scales against what the Star Lords had commanded me to do.

A faint pinkish wash of light sifted above the eastern horizon, away across the mudflats and rushes fringing the River Magan. The river runs generally in a northeasterly direction into the Shrouded Sea; but in its sluggish windings a reach opened up due east, and She of the Veils rose and cast her streaming pink light full along the length of water.

I was looking up, watching the pinkly glowing orb as it rose, and I saw a black and angular silhouette for a moment flitter before the moon, dark and sharp and ominous, and as suddenly flicker away and vanish.

Turko sucked in his breath.

The two girls had not seen, and so were silent.

"Tell me, Turko."

"By Morro the Muscle! A volrok, Dray. A yetch of a volrok."

Many and various are the beast-men and men-beasts of Kregen. Away in The Stratemsk and the Hostile Territories I had encountered monstrous flying animals and reptiles, and here in Havilfar there were many beasts of the air. I kept a wary eye open aloft, and took up into my hands the boat hook. It was a poor thing, with a clumsy bronze point and hook; but it was all we had.

The thing had seen us, that was sure, and it must have correctly surmised we were a small party. In a rush of wings and a harsh clacking cry, it was upon us.

Now Turko had called the volrok a yetch, which is a Havilfarese term of abuse generally used for a human being, and this should have warned me. I was not facing a flying beast.

I faced a flying man.

The volrok had intelligence, and quick wits, and a supple sinewy strength for all that he was lightly built. He was no impiter, no corth, no fluttrell; he was a man, a halfling. His wings beat against the starlight and I caught the gleam of a weapon. She of the Veils threw down a fuzzy pinkish radiance, and in that glow I saw his eyes, glaring at me, as he circled and dived.

"Watch his feet, Dray!"

I grunted and leaned away from that first vicious onslaught. Wings buffeted air and I smashed the boat hook up and caught the descending blow of a long spearlike

13

weapon, something after the fashion of the Ullars' toonon, and so deflected the blow. The encounter had given me a closer look at the volrok.

He circled, screeching, and his wings folded, and he dived again. He had evolved from an eight-limbed stock, for his back bore real wings, wide and narrow, sharply angled, wings that enabled him really to fly. His arms held the toonon. His third pair of limbs consisted of legs—real honest-to-goodness legs—with attachments that made of them ghastly weapons of destruction and not honest or good at all. His remaining pair of limbs had fused in a fan to form a tail.

Turko brandished an oar above his head.

The volrok dived, and swerved, and the bronze head of the boat hook clashed against the toonon and then I saw the truth of those legs. On each heel had been bound a long and wickedly curved blade, like twin scimitars, and as the volrok screeched and rose so the blades whickered down toward my head. I ducked. I felt a grazing blow across my scalp.

Turko prodded with his oar.

Saenda and Quaesa were screaming. There was no time to do anything about them.

The volrok swerved there in the level air, turned, and I saw his narrow head peering down to regard us more closely. He wore a tight leather tunic, much decorated with feathers, and a belt from which hung a sword in a scabbard whose lockets held it so that it kept out of his way when flying. His legs scissored and the deadly wink of those scimitar blades made me dash the blood from my eyes and take a fresh grip on the boat hook.

The cut I had sustained in Mungul Sidrath had opened again and the bandage could no longer hold back the blood.

Turko was swearing on about the Muscle and swords and spears and devilish flying man-monsters.

The volrok folded his wings and plummeted.

This time I had to ignore his toonon. The spear had to be slipped, as Turko and I knew how, and I had to get those scimitar blades of his in good sight in that treacherous illumination.

I switched grips on the boat hook.

Instead of holding the sturm-wood shaft with my left hand forward, like a spearman, I held it right hand forward, like a swordsman.

A wooden longsword had been used before. This time it was of unhandy length, of ridiculous length; but it had a bronze point and a bronze hook. The volrok dropped down and I had time to realize the scimitar blades had been strapped to his heels to give a straight-line strength and control from his legs; had they been strapped to his feet or toes he would not have been able to deliver the same power. He would not have been able so easily to drag the blades free and lift off after a strike, either. As it was, he couldn't stand up easily for the blades curved to form a continuation of his legs.

The dark form swept in toward us. The glitter of the spear meant nothing. He would jerk his legs forward in the last moment of his dive, impaling me, or slicing my head open, and then fly on, trailing his legs, and so wrench the scimitars free.

With a yell to Turko, "Get down, Turko!" I ducked and let the toonon go past. It cracked the lenk gunwale of the boat and skidded on. Then I swung. The boat hook circled and smashed with awful force against the volrok's thighs. Both his legs broke. The blades abruptly dangled.

He shrieked.

In that tiny moment I was able to drive on and up, hard, and the bronze point tore up into his body.

Turko's oar battered his wings.

The volrok screamed. His wings churned the air as he sought to drag himself away. The boat hook had caught him. I leaned back, savagely dragging him down. The oar smashed down now on his head. With a convulsive effort, which tore his insides in a shower of blood, the volrok broke free from the bronze hook. He rose unsteadily, shrieking, and his wings beat feebly, and wavering and lurching, he flew away in the moonlit shadows. I was not content to let him go, and cursed.

"We could have used his toonon, and those vicious blades."

"He was a fighter—"

"Oh, aye, he was a fighter."

"Vicious, the volroks." Turko turned back and looked down into the boat. "Stop yelling! He's gone."

The girls yelped into snuffled wailings.

"Do they hunt in pairs, Turko, or singly?" I ignored Saenda and Quaesa. This was something a fighting-man had to know. "Or—in packs?"

"It depends entirely on which town or province they

15

come from. I do not claim to recognize all their markings. But, they are men, they have intelligence—"

"I see."

I scanned the night sky with the warming glow of She of the Veils spreading out upon the dark waters. Our noise had attracted attention. Lights moved across the water, waving, clotting into a bunch, growing in size, nearing.

"They've spotted us, by the Muscle!"

"Aye!"

I dropped onto the thwart, chucked the boat hook along the bottom boards and was rewarded by a shriek from one of the girls, and unshipped the oars. Now my training as an oar-slave aboard the swifters of the inner sea and the swordships prowling up along the Hobolong Islands would come into full use—not to mention my early years as a seaman of Earth's late eighteenth century wooden navy.

The blades bit deeply. Water surged. I put my back into it, uncaring of the blood that clotted on my forehead and stung coldly in the night breeze. I pulled for the north bank. It was the nearer of the two. Coming up fast from astern the long low shape of a galley, a liburna, hauled into just a prow upflung against the stars and what appeared a single oar, rising and falling, each side, starboard and larboard.

I pulled.

But those whipped Miglas slaving aboard the liburna pulled too, and the galley foamed along in our wake, closing.

"Where away ahead, Turko?"

He jumped for the bows, past my back. In a moment he called: "To the left—that is your right, Dray—"

"Aye."

The little fishing boat, a mere dinghy, in reality, surged ahead. If any more volroks attacked now we were done for. We would be done for, too, if I did not reach the shore with time for us to leap out and escape into those alleys of darkness between the mudbanks and the mudflats. I pulled. We had passed a quiet day, and rested, and my strength was restored. I would not tire yet; but there was little chance of a single man in a clumsy boat like this outrunning a galley crewed by oarsmen at forty oars, at the least.

"By the Muscle! Volroks! Scores of the yetches!"

I did not waste effort looking up. I pulled. The water

16

splashed and hissed and at each stroke the boat leaped. The liburna following cleft the water with a fine pink-tinged white comb in her teeth. She gained. I pulled. The boat leaped as Turko, waving his oar, for there were two pairs aboard, leaped and slashed wildly above his head.

A wing buffeted me over the head and for a moment a dark haze dropped over my eyes; but I fought it. I had to. This was no way for Dray Prescot, Krozair of Zy, Lord of Strombor—and much else besides—to die.

The girls were simply huddled together and screaming in mindless fear. The galley smashed her way after us. And the volroks descended in clouds from the pink-tinged darkness about us.

"This is the end!" shouted Turko, bashing with his oar. "We're done for!"

# Chapter Two

## Obquam of Tajkent keeps order

Neither the Star Lords nor the Savanti had made any attempts to save me when I stood in mortal peril of my life in obeying their aloof commands. I could look for no help from them.

There seemed no hope.

If the Star Lords moved the volroks, I did not know then and I do not know now.

But the cloud of winged men swirled up, their wings an evil rustle in the darkness, the pink sheen from their weapons rising and swinging, their eyes glittering, and then, in a single close-bunched mass, they swooped upon the galley pursuing us.

In an instant all was commotion and pandemonium aboard.

I did not cease from pulling.

"By the Muscle . . ." breathed Turko, in awe.

Any ideas I might have entertained of remaining in the boat and of slipping past along the river were banished as more galleys appeared, pulling up with the kind of individual precision obtained by a smart whip-deldar and drum-deldar, and a skipper who knew his business. A brisk little action was being fought back there. The volroks, of whom I was to learn a great deal later on in Havilfar, had flown in from their aerie towns far to the north and west. They had a plan. Although I could only guess what their schemes might be, I did know they would aid me in my own.

The conceit appealed to me.

One of the galleys had hauled around the main area of conflict. I knew they could still see us, as we could see them, a dark blob against the pink sheen along the water. The galley ignored the fight off to her side and settled

18

down to a strong steady pull. We would reach
first, I judged; but it would be a touch-and-go af

Now it was just a question of a long stron
the ebb toward the bank. Rushes and reeds
enough to shield us for a space, enough to giv
cross the mudflats and so escape into the shadows.
us, and full in my view, the clustered galleys were putting
up a doughty fight against the swarming clouds of volroks.

Arrows skimmed upward, their tips chips of glittering
light in the pink glow; crossbow bolts also, I guessed,
would be loosed among the flying men. Many I saw fall.
One of the galleys swayed drunkenly out of line, her oars
all at sixes and sevens, reeled into a second. Her upper-
works, which were, in truth, low enough to the water,
were dark with the frantic agitated forms of volroks, like
flies upon jam.

Now the Twins edged into the sky, and the two second
moons of Kregen, continually orbiting each other, shed
sufficient light in their nearly full phase to pick out details
with that pink and typically Kregen semblance of fuzzy
ruby clarity. Neither the galleys nor the volroks were winning, I judged. The galley pursuing us must be constrained
under the most severe orders to recapture us to leave the
fight. I pulled and went on pulling as I watched that furiously waged fight, clamoring and shrieking into the night.
We had traveled in our flier from the west coast of Havilfar clear across the narrow waist to the northwestern tip
of the Shrouded Sea. We had soared over a mountain
range. In those peaked valleys, I guessed, lay the towns
and aeries of these volroks, these flying men of Havilfar.

The boat's keel felt the first kiss of mud. The boat shuddered; but with a few long, powerful strokes I forced her
on until the keel grated unpleasantly on gravel and coarse
mud.

I grabbed Saenda. Turko grabbed Quaesa. Also, with a
semblance of a grimace that might be called a smile, I
seized the boat hook. It was our only weapon.

Over the side we plunged, thigh-deep, and at once the
water roiled and clouded with disturbed mud. We staggered on.

Wasting breath, but considering the waste justified to
cheer my comrades, I said: "This shallowness of the bank
side will hold the galley farther out. We have a better
chance."

Saenda, her fair hair streaming over my shoulder, her

...s and legs wrapped about me in a clinging grip, ...outed: "You'll be sorry for all this, Dray Prescot! By the Lady Emli of Ras! What you've done to me since we—"

I chose at that moment to stumble over an old tree stump half buried in mud and water, and recovered reasonably quickly; but Saenda went under and took a mouthful of that mud and water, and her sharp complaints changed to a choking gargling, in which I caught her attempts at further swearing and promises of the dire things that would happen to me when I took her home to Dap-Tentyrasmot. If ever there was a time for chuckling this night, I suppose that was the time; but I did not chuckle. I simply blundered on up the bank, slipping and sliding in mud, hearing the mud slop and suck at my legs, hoping that I would not fall into a patch of quicksand or that the mud leeches would not get a good grip on my naked legs. For I wore only that old scarlet breechclout. Saenda, for her part, wore a dead Canop guard's breechclout and a piece of cloth hung around her shoulders, and the leeches would relish the fine blood they would discover beneath that fair skin.

Quaesa, with her darker skin and jet hair, would also provide luscious blood-sucking territory. So it was that I was most thankful to blunder out on top of the bank and slip and slide down the other side where the rushes grew wild and in great profusion and leave the sluggish and highly unpleasant River Magan behind.

"They stuck, Dray, just as you said," said Turko as he followed on. His breath came as evenly and his chest moved as smoothly as though he had not plunged into muddy water and carried a girl up a slippery bank at top speed.

"But they'll wade ashore, as we did. Let us *move!*"

That old devilish crack whiplashed in my voice, and the girls jumped, and Turko chuckled, and so we put the girls down and we ran as best we could through the reed beds.

The harsh and mystical training through which I had gone with the Krozairs of Zy—a period that would never really end, for the krozair usually makes time to return and refresh not so much his physique but his mental attitudes to life and the secret disciplines—enabled me to push on quickly enough and to assist Saenda. The Khamorros, too, taught physical and mental disciplines that enabled Turko to forge on with Quaesa. This was lung-bursting, thew-tearing, heart-hammering effort. Some people when referring to what I have called unarmed combat talk about bloodless combat. There is such a thing, of course, and is what, really, the Khamorros do in practice—most of the time. But the unarmed combat man is seeking to down his man, and blood will flow then just as though he had sliced him with a sword as hand-chopped his ear so the blood gushes from his nostrils and mouth. There is nothing bloodless about the kind of unarmed combat Turko the Khamorro and I, Dray Prescot, Krozair of Zy, shared.

So we were able to outdistance the pursuit. Soon we ran across a road, muddy and full of potholes, but, nonetheless, a road, and here we saw the beings waiting for us to emerge from the reed beds.

Turko stopped with a low hiss of indrawn breath.

The two girls began to squeal—and two hard and horny hands clamped across their soft mouths. Turko knew as well as I the importance of first-footing with strangers, especially strangers encountered on a lonely road at night with the pinkly golden light of Kregen's moons glinting back from the muddy ruts and potholes and throwing details into a hazy blur.

Often and often has the understanding been brought home to me that this kind of situation is what life on Kregen is all about: This continual headlong advance into danger; this confrontation with the unknown. These beings might turn out to be friends, attracted by the commotion on the river and waiting to see what manner of men or beasts emerged from the reed beds. They might choose to be hostile, and so demand all Turko's skills and a measure of hefty thwacks from my boat hook. They would act according to their natures, and, of a surety, Turko and I would act according to ours.

"Llahal!" I called, using the nonfamiliar form of the universal Kregish greeting.

"Llahal," responded the leader, a being who stepped a little in advance of the others.

There were ten of them, and I saw the gleam of weapons; but I fancied that if Turko and I were quick we might see them off. Certainly I would not tamely submit. I had been trying, as you can bear witness, to quell that hasty and violent streak of mine that will not tolerate oppression in any form. I had been trying, you might say, to

21

talk first and then strike, rather than the vice versa method to which I had been accustomed.

"We come in peace," I said.

I know this does not sound like the Dray Prescot you may think you have understood, listening to these tapes spinning through the recorder; and I know I told a blatant lie if we were not received in peace; but I meant it. I had more important concerns than a brawl on a muddy path in the light of the moons. The being advanced cautiously. He looked not unlike a volrok, having long narrow wings, neatly folded, but there was about him a difference that marked him out. Those differences could best be described, perhaps, by saying that if a volrok was equated with a Latin of our Earth, this being would be equated with a man of Nordic stock. But the same eight-limbed original body-form was there, with the upper limbs extended into wide narrow wings, the two arms forward—and holding weapons!—the two legs and feet on which there were no scimitar blades, and the rear pair of limbs fused into a tail fan.

"We, too, seek peace. You have been fighting the volroks?"

Turko laughed and started to say "By the Muscle! We've fought the—" when I kicked him in the shins. He said, instead, "—The whole wide world in our time. Do you, then, fight the volroks?"

Another flying man pushed up from the pack. In that light it was difficult to tell them apart. But there is one curious fact that I own to with a certain silly pride, and that is with every successive season I spent on Kregen I was able to pick out more clearly and with greater certainty one halfling from another. Men of one race on Earth will say that all men of another race look alike to them; this is natural if regrettable. Rapechak, for instance, the Rapa mercenary with whom we had fought in Mungul Sidrath and whom we had lost when we escaped into the River Magan, had looked like Rapechak to me, and not like any other Rapa.

This second flying man said: "They are apim. I say we do not trust them."

"And I say," said the leader, in a fashion I admired, "that I will stick you if you do not keep quiet, Quarda."

"We are apim," I said. "But we are not Canops."

The leader laughed. It was a good belly-laugh, rich and round and boiling up from a well-filled stomach.

22

"We know that, dom. Had you been Canops you would have stepped upon the road as dead men."

"That's comforting to know."

He thought I meant it was comforting to know we had not been killed. What he did not know was that I scented allies here in the struggle to come against the iron men from Canopdrin.

One of the other flying men in the pack shouted: "The Miglas will be here soon. There was enough noise and torches on the river—let us kill them and be gone."

The leader did not turn.

He said, "Quincher—hit that onker Quilly for me."

There came the sound of a blow and a yelp from the dark mass of flying men. The leader nodded, as though satisfied. I rather liked his style.

"You tell me who you are, dom," he said. "And then we will decide to kill you—or not."

I am not given to idle boasts. "Tell me who you are."

He spoke in a very reasonable tone. "You are unarmed. We have weapons, of bronze and of steel. Surely, you must see it is in your own interests to tell us first. After, I will be happy to tell you, and, by the Golden Feathers of Father Qua, it would sadden me to slay a man without weapons in his hands."

I glanced at Turko. He did not betray his thoughts, but they were clear enough.

"What you say is indeed reasonable, dom. This is Turko, a Great Kham, and these are two foolish girls, Saenda and Quaesa, who live on the opposite shore of the Shrouded Sea."

"And you?"

The dark eyes regarded me with a closer intent.

"My name is Dray Prescot."

A buzz of conversation from the flying men, which told me they had not heard of me or of Turko, was followed by the leader bellowing for order. He took a few steps forward, his tail high and arrogant in that pink moonlight.

"I am Obquam of Tajkent. I seek for a certain cramph of a volrok called Rakker—Largan Rakker of the Triple Peaks. Know you of this vile reaver and his whereabouts?"

"No, Horter Obquam," I said at once. There was no sense in beating about the bush here. "We were attacked by the whole pack of volroks and escaped only because

23

they attacked the Canops in the galleys. This Rakker—he has done you an injury?"

"Aye! And more, may the black talons of Deevi Quruk rip out his entrails and strip his wings so that he falls into the Ice Floes of Siccel"

For the moment I had learned all I needed to know. Local detail could be filled in later. At any moment the commotion which had attracted so much unwelcome attention would bring a patrol of Canops to the scene. There was light enough still to see the wheeling flock of volroks above the galleys, although they were hidden from direct view. I fanced there were fewer flying men over there. I put it to this Obquam of Tajkent.

"If the one you seek flies with that pack there, why do you not wing over and discover the truth for yourself?"

He drew himself up, not so much with hauteur as with offended pride. I had suggested blatantly enough. Turko shook his hands and arms, loosening up, readying for the fight he thought must be imminent.

"Look there, apim!" Obquam pointed.

Out over the river the volroks were in turmoil. Their thin screeching reached us blown on the wind. Now among them appeared the larger and bulkier shapes of men astride flying beasts and birds, flutsmen astride fluttrells, as I thought then. The gleam of weapons turned to a bright glittering. I saw volroks falling, and fluttrells, too, with their riders pitching off to dangle by their clerketers all the way into the water.

The aerial battle raged and drifted away from us.

"The Canops from the galleys will be ashore now," I said. "If you seek this Rakker you had best follow, Horter Obquam."

He gestured. "I am a Strom, Horter Prescot. You really should address me as Strom of Tajkent."

"If it pleases you. But as for me and my friends, we are for Yaman, and the streets will not be friendly at this time of night, so we will take our leave now."

I could feel Turko's brisk brightening at my words.

The girls, whose mouths were now free of our hands, let our gasps of surprise and annoyance and, as was inevitable, fear.

"I am not going back there, Dray Prescot!" yelped Saenda.

"Not for all the ivory in Chem!" snapped Quaesa.

24

"Then you are perfectly willing to stay with this Strom and his flying men?"

Their outrage was both pitiful and painful.

If this Strom Obquam of Tajkent tried to stop me I was fully prepared to deal with him and his flying band. As for the girls, I knew I would have to devise a scheme to get them back to their homes on the other side of the Shrouded Sea, and a good scheme at that. But Turko surprised me. I did not then understand why he wanted to go back to Yaman, the city of eerie buildings where Migshaanu had been contemptuously ousted as the Great Goddess by the Canops. He had no particular love for Mog, the old witch who had so surprisingly become Mog the Mighty, the high priestess, for all that she had doctored him and healed him of his hurts back there in the jungles of Faol.

So it was that I turned to walk off, and said rather sharply: "You understand what it is we are about, Turko? We are making a fresh beginning. We are going to Yaman in the full knowledge that we might never leave, that we might hang by our heels from the ramparts of Mungul Sidrath?"

"I know. I doubt it will happen, Dray."

I grunted, for I could find no words to express what I felt just then.

The flying man—I suspected these were people who would not welcome being called volroks—called Quarda, who had already spoken out of turn, stepped before me. He held a weapon very like a toonon. The short and broad-bladed sword had been mounted on a shaft of a bamboolike wood, with cross quillons also daggered. He held it as a man who knew his business.

"You do not walk away so lightly, apim Prescot."

I did not reply. I looked with a hard stare at the Strom.

He spread his hands, a gesture of resignation.

"In this, Horter Prescot, a matter of honor, I may not intervene. It is between you and Horter Quarda, now."

The distance from my left kneecap to Quarda's groin was almost exactly what one might have wished in the exercise yard. My knee smacked it with a crunchy *whop!* and Quarda stood for a moment, absolutely still, his mouth open. Then he dropped the toonon. His eyes began to bulge. They bulged quite slowly, and shone, a most curious sight. Slowly, he began to fold in the middle. I stood watching him, quite still, not speaking. Quarda put his

25

hands to his middle, moving with a slow underwater finning movement, and bending forward and over, more and more, and his eyes bulged and bulged, and the cords in his neck stood out like a frigate's sheets in a gale.

He rolled right over into a ball, and fell on his side, and his legs kicked for a moment. He had not vomited yet, and that showed he must have been in good control. But he could not yell, and what with the yell inside him that couldn't get out, and the stream that wanted to spurt out as well, he lay in a coil and twitched.

I turned to the Strom of Tajkent.

"Remberee, Strom," I said, quite cheerfully. "Maybe we will have the pleasure of meeting another day."

His eyes on me remained unfathomable.

"Remberee, Dray Prescot."

Taking Saenda firmly by the upper arm, as Turko took Quaesa, I marched off.

Marched off along that dismal road toward the city of Yaman where waited horrors and battles and stratagems, were the other three, and I could not find it in my heart to pity them. As, of course, I could never find pity for myself.

# Chapter Three

## A wall beneath Mungul Sidrath comes to life

"Mag," said Mog, the high priestess. "Nothing can be done until Mag is found. The religion cannot be truly useful to us—to my shame—until Mag is freed."

"Unless," said Planath the Wine, "he be dead."

Old Mog surged up at this in her stiff and gorgeous robes, all crimson and smothered with gold lace and embroidery, the massive golden crown with its rubies toppling dangerously. She banged the great gold-plated staff upon the floor. She looked impressive and dominating and yet, remembering her as the mewling slave I had seen in the jungles of Faol, I felt the irony and pathos here. Her old face with the witch's beak of a nose and the boot-cap chin scowled most ferociously, and her agate eyes gleamed most furiously upon us in the back room of *The Loyal Canoptic.*

She might be an old halfling woman who had been defamed by the invading and conquering Canops, her temple razed and in ruins, her king and queen slain, this important Mag a prisoner or dead—but she cowed the assembled Miglas here. The tavern had seen many of these secret gatherings, but on this night the back room bulged with Miglas, more than ever before, collected together from all over the city of Yaman.

And yet they were a pitifully small number to pit against the might of the iron men from Canopdrin with their superlative drill and discipline, their bows and swords, their armored cavalry of the air. But I had had the task of creating a revolution thrust upon me by the Star Lords, so, therefore, a revolution there was going to be, by Zair!

"So we rescue Mag," I said, over the hubbub.

27

There was a great shaking of Migla heads, those ludicrous rubbery, flap-eared, pop-eyed faces like children's playthings all swaying in unison. Everyone wore a crimson robe; the men held their stuxes, the throwing spears of Havilfar. But, as I well knew, the brave crimson robes and the deadly accurate stuxes would all be safely hidden away before these Miglas would dare creep out under the radiance of the moons to slink home by back alleys and slippery stairs.

Turko sat back, his bright eyes on me, and, as always, I felt his quizzical glance and knew he weighed me up. A great Khamorro, Turko, a master of his syple, cunning in unarmed combat. He would follow me, for he had said so. But into what harebrained adventures was I proposing to lead him now?

The general consensus was that Mag must be rescued before any move against the Canops could be made. Even then, I wearily suspected, these Miglas were not the stuff from which could be forged a fighting force fit to stand against the disciplined ranks of the men from Canopdrin. I had seen a little of this occupying army, and I recognized their expertise.

But, first things first.

After we had rescued Mag, we could then weigh the situation afresh.

"He is of a surety imprisoned in Mungul Sidrath," said Planath the Wine. He looked troubled.

None of them had appeared surprised that I had returned with Turko, Saenda, and Quaesa. They knew I had rescued them from the citadel of Mungul Sidrath. They did not even show surprise at my announcement that I would help them in their fight against the Canops. Either they were too far gone in apathy, or they did not really believe, or they regarded this as merely a further happy result of the return of Mog the Mighty, their high priestess.

"Then it is to Mungul Sidrath I must go."

Turko lifted his head. But he did not speak.

I said: "How am I to recognize Mag?"

At this old Mog the Witch cackled. She bent her forefinger and pointed it at her nutcracker face.

"You have seen me, Dray Prescot. Therefore you have seen a likeness of my brother."

We were drinking beer, a thin and rather bitter stuff I did not much care for, although the Miglas lapped it up smartly enough. Now a man stood up, splayed on broad

28

feet, his ears flapping, beaming the idiotic Miglish smile. He lifted his blackjack, beer slopping down the dark cracked leather.

"A toast! A toast to Dray Prescot who will go in the safekeeping of Migshenda of the Stux."

"Aye," rumbled from the assembled Miglas, and they stood and lifted their goblets and glasses and blackjacks, and drank.

It was a pretty gesture. But that was all it was, a gesture.

As the Miglas resumed their seats one man remained standing. He lifted his pewter mug to me.

"I will go with you, Dray Prescot."

I looked at him.

Apart from the facts that he was a young man, that he looked fit and healthy, that he held his chin high, there was nothing to distinguish him from all the others.

"You will be killed for sure, Med Neemusbane!"

"Oh, no, Med!" A girl leaped to him, clasped her arms about him. He stood there, and for all the ridiculous appearance of the typical Migla morphology, an aura of dignity and determination made him not ridiculous at all.

Planath the Wine said, again, "You will be killed for sure, Med Neemusbane. But if you must go, we will pray for you."

"Aye," said the others. "At the temple, among the ruins, we will pray for you."

"Oh, Med!" moaned the girl, clasping him.

I had no desire to push this youngster into a danger he probably did not understand. I knew from his name that he had already won fame. A large proportion of the economy of Migla revolved around wild-vosk hunting in the back hills. From the vosk came rich and succulent joints, and supple voskskin, and this Med Neemusbane must be a hunter of great repute.

He said, "I shall go."

Turko said, "A neemu is a most vicious and beautiful beast, a machine of destruction. Even a leem will not willingly encounter two full-grown neemus."

"So be it," I said. I had a plan for this headstrong youngster. "And the thanks of us all, Med Neemusbane."

Although as you know I had figured in a rebellion before, when I had led my old vosk-skulls against the overlords of Magdag, I had been cruelly wrenched away from that final victorious battle by the Star Lords. The rebellion had had no time to flower into a revolution. The time when, as the great song, *The Fetching of Drak na Valka*, says, I had cleansed my island of Valka of the slave-masters and the aragorn did not really count as an organized rebellion. That had been a people aroused in a just anger against rapacious oppressors who raided and reaved. Here, in Migla, the Canops had taken over every aspect of the country and had settled in as the masters. I had no real experience of revolution as I knew it must be handled here. But, as in my avowed way, I would learn.

The problem of returning Saenda and Quaesa worried me; but Planath the Wine assured me he could arrange travel for the two female apims, one to Dap-Tentyrasmot, the other to Methydria, without too much trouble, provided they did as they were told. They had become accustomed to doing as they were told during their period as slaves, when they were being readied to run as quarry for the Manhunters of Faol. Just lately, after our escape, they had tended to revert to their usual hectoring and fault-finding ways. I spoke to them and I deliberately put that old vicious cutting rasp into my voice.

They quailed as I spoke.

"You both claim to be high-born ladies. You have prated on about the kools of rich grazing land and all the merchant agencies your fathers own. This may be so. But if you wish to cross the Shrouded Sea and return to your homes, you will do exactly as Planath the Wine tells you. He is a man to be trusted. If you give any trouble at all, I'll clip your ears, by Vox, and send you back for sport in the fangs of the Manhounds of Faol!"

"Oh, Dray!" wailed Saenda.

And, "Oh, Dray!" wailed Quaesa.

A vivid image flashed into my mind.

I saw myself in a muldavy with her dipping lug of the Eye of the World, and I heard myself cutting the Lady Pulvia na Upalion down to size. I hate and detest berating women. It is a cowardly pastime. But, here, these two silly gigglers demanded no less than a real honest-to-Zair tongue-lashing. I spared them. I recognized my softness and weakness; but they had suffered, by Zair, and I thought they would understand and respect the risks Planath and the Miglas were taking for them.

"You will need many golden deldys, Planath. These I will secure tomorrow."

"Hush, Dray Prescot! We will be happy to furnish all

the lady apims may require. Also—" Here Planath the Wine rubbed his chin and squinted up at me. "Also, if you knock any more Canop guardsmen on the head and steal their money the whole city of Yaman will suffer."

"Sink me!" I burst out. "I wouldn't want that—but, equally, I would not wish to sponge on your charity."

After a long and pleasant wrangle, during which a great deal more of the beer was drunk, we agreed that Planath and his friends should outfit the girls and buy them passages aboard the most convenient ship or voller traveling to the eastern shore of the Shrouded Sea. There would have to be matters of disguise, and secrecy; all that I left to the Miglas. It was no part of the plans of the Star Lords, I thought, to become embroiled with these two silly gigglers.

The frowning pile of Mungul Sidrath waited.

In order to rescue Turko and Saenda and Quaesa I had dressed myself up as a Canoptic soldier and marched in boldly. The commandant had been slain; I guessed the new commandant would have tightened up security so that it would be fatuous to suppose we could break in that way again, and, of course, Med could never disguise himself as a Canop, I thought. During the rest of the meeting there was talk of ways and means. I suppose because he looked more and more agitated as the night wore on I took stock of an ugly old Migla called Malkar, who kept rubbing a bald spot on his head, and pulling his flap-ears, and burying his hooked nose in his blackjack, and coming up spluttering to wipe the thin froth away. He had been the old boy charged with the duty of cleaning the drains in the temple. Now the temple of Migshaanu lay in tumbled ruins.

At last Malkar got his courage up, as I thought, although in that I did him an injustice. He took a huge draft of beer, spluttered, choked, and then bellowed so abruptly that everyone fell silent.

"May the divine Migshaanu forgive me, for she will understand why I speak! I know the drains and the sewers, for that is my work, and I joy in serving Mighshaanu the thrice-bathed. But—I know more! There is a—" He paused here, screwing himself up to the point. He was, in his eyes, betraying a secret which he should never have known. "I know! Often and often have I seen the king and queen, may Migshaanu enfold her golden wings about them, come to the temple from their palace by the secret way—"

"Ah!" said Turko, leaning forward.

"Yes! There is a way, a tunnel, dark and dangerous, and guarded in a most horrible way I do not know. The king and the queen knew. But they are dead, slain by the Canops, by the foul and rast-loving King Capnon whom the yetches call King Capnon the Great."

"Show us the entrance, good Malkar!" said Med Neemusbane. He spoke with a quick eagerness that warmed me. If there were other brave young men like him among the Migladorn, the chances of a successful revolution were greater than I had surmised.

So it was arranged. Turko and I said Remberee to the two girls, Saenda and Quaesa, and they were suitably tearful at parting. They were not the shishis they had been called. They were simply two young girls who had fallen on evil times and had tried to retain their sanity by clinging to their own old ways. I was in no real position to pass judgment on those ways, for all that I knew they involved slave management, and, as is notorious, women are infinitely more cruel to slaves than are men.

We slunk through the night streets of Yaman, with the eerie old houses, tall and narrow, crooked against the stars, hemming us in. The ruins of the temple glimmered in the hazy pink light of She of the Veils. The Canops had thrown down the columns and the walls and the roof had fallen. Malkar led us past a black hole that stank of sewage. We penetrated down past stone blocks with weird hieroglyphs incised on their hewn surfaces; but we had not lit our torches and so the secret and magical inscriptions were only fitfully revealed in the pink moonlight. When a stone overhang brought us into deep shadow, Malkar whispered and his voice rustled and echoed among the tumbled stones.

"You may light the torches now, Horter Prescot."

Flint and steel clicked and scraped, the tinder caught, and a torch flared. I held it aloft. Before us lay a narrow flight of stairs, hewn from the rock, leading down into inky darkness. Weird and ungainly forms of animals and birds crawled in the light across the walls. The atmosphere of decay and of doom hung about this shattered temple, dedicated to gods of a halfling race.

With a screech and a great rustle of membranous wings a Kregan bat fluttered madly in the light. The woflovol chittered and flew in crazy zigzaggings, seeking the darkness. I put my foot on the first step. Turko closed up. Med, also, began the descent.

Malkar hung back.

"It is down there, Horter Prescot. A great bronze-bolted door. And, after that, Migshaanu the All-Glorious alone knows!"

"I thank you, Horter Malkar. Now get you gone in safety."

"Remberee," he called; but his voice dwindled and faded, for he was already scuttling back and away from this place where, if I allowed myself the fancy, eldritch horrors awaited us.

We three pressed on, descending that narrow stair in the flare of our torches.

I wore my old scarlet breechclout, for the weather was mild. I carried the thraxter and the crossbow and a quiver of bolts we had earlier relieved of those who had no title in the higher warrior-justice to them. If this sounds a high-handed judgment I stand condemned. I knew what I knew of overfed, pampered, and decadent people who hunted other people with crossbow and spear.

This land of Migla stood on approximately the same parallel south as the parallel north running through the Black Mountains of Vallia. I wondered how Inch was faring. But the dark hole yawned beneath my feet and the steps, greasy and treacherous, trended downward inexorably to that massive bronze-bolted lenken door. I suppressed the instinct to hammer on that portal of ill-omen with the thraxter and I kept the sword in its sheath.

Turko, as was his custom, was unarmed. That is to say, he did not carry weapons of steel, edged and pointed. While he had his hands and his feet and his head, he remained a most formidable fighter, a Khamorro and therefore a man to be feared. Med carried eight stuxes in an interesting gadget. From a flat disc of wood eight near-circular notches had been cut around the edge. Each notch had a small spring of carved horn which, when a stux shaft was pressed into the notch, held the stux in place. A simple jerk would flex the spring and release the weapon. There were two discs, and the heads of the spears were so arranged that they staggered downward to give clearance to each fat wedge-shaped blade. A carrying strap could be attached to this stuxcal, when necessary, so that it might be slung over the shoulder and be ready for instant use.

33

Also, Med carried a large hunting knife similar to a scramasax.

The shadows clustered thickly and fled reluctantly before the flare of our torches.

Each individual bronze bolt head of the lenken door gleamed at us like a single malicious eye.

"There," said Turko, and, stepping forward, seized the sliding bolt. I saw the way his muscles slid and bunched, roping like great cables as he drew back the bolt. It had not been used for some time, and verdigris made that drawing difficult. A stale and musty odor puffed out, fetid with unnameable miasmas. Med coughed. Turko grunted. I stepped in, holding my torch high.

"Malkar prated of a great and horrible danger, Dray. Best tread warily."

And, as he spoke, Turko moved up and attempted to take the lead.

I simply increased my stride, plunging headlong into the tunnel beneath the ruins. Sink me! I was still young and foolish enough to think it not pride but a proper sense of martial valor that I should go first. Turko muttered something about a Muscle-bound onker, but he fell in to my rear. Our torches threw ghastly shadows fleeting before us, contorted phantasms from jagged edges of rock. I kept up my brisk advance, for I was not willing for Turko, all unarmed as he was, to take the lead.

We were all breathing lightly, tensed up, cautious, and yet anxious to be through this melancholy tunnel with its aroma of death and decay.

Little echoes from disturbed stones beneath our feet chittered ahead, reverberating tinnily, disquietingly. I stopped.

"Let us move quietly, my friends," I said. "As though we hunted leem."

The way grew warmer. The fetid breath on the air near choked us. Presently the sound of rushing water trembled nearer, until we came out to a cavern where steaming water, boiling and bubbling, spouted from a cleft in the rock and ran, hot and angry, in a channel cut alongside the path. The channel continued into the tunnel, and steam rose about us, slicking upon our skins, so that we gleamed and sweated as though passing through the baths of nine.

Through the steam I tried to espy what lay ahead. I could hear nothing above the boiling rush of waters. Our torches twirled their flaming hair, dampened and fading,

"Something waited for us at a bend in the tunnel."

so that the shadows closed in. Was that a movement there, up ahead along the tunnel wall? I slowed down and moved forward warily. Yes . . . that *was* a movement. Something waited for us at a bend in the tunnel, something I could not make out, something lethal and horrible and waiting to pull us down.

Now I put each foot down soundlessly. The torchlight wavered along the slimy walls. White-yellow vegetation grew here, and at the very corner of the bend a gap in the rock ceiling revealed a chink, and a thin streamer of pink light falling through. We were near the surface, then. I advanced.

Med's voice, whispering, reached me.

"Dray—there, by the wall! By Migshenda! A syatra!"

The wall writhed. Many thick and fleshy tentacles sprouted from a central trunk, corpse-white, spine-barbed, rippling and writhing and seeking us. I saw the barbed leaves of the trap opening, ready to snap on its victim. Each Venus's-flytrap would gobble a grown man. The steam rose bewilderingly. The tendrils swayed and writhed like beseeching arms, like the serpent-hair of the Gorgons. But this syatra was no Medusa; rather, it must be one of Medusa's sisters, Eurale or Sthenno. It lashed its tendrils about and its spined trap yawned, barring our way along one side of the tunnel.

I edged forward on the other, the sword in my fist, the crossbow slung over my back.

The tunnel widened a little. The horror opposite lashed its tendrils at me. I ignored them. Until they reached me I would refrain from smiting.

A few bones crunched underfoot.

I pressed on, the steam swirling confusingly in my face, the swishing, thrashing sounds of the blind tendrils seeking those who passed whistling by my ears. Turko closed up. Med followed.

The shadows gyrated madly. Crimson torchlight bounced from the corpse-white trunk and tendrils. The leaves of the trap, like doors hinged flat, quivered. I felt a light sliding glance on my arm and halted instantly.

But—Turko!

The wall at our side had opened. In some way the tunnel was wider still and a second syatra growing from the wall, its roots seeking the hot water, flailed its tendrils above us. We were directly between the two. Their tendrils locked and closed about us. Turko yelled. Two tendrils wrapped around his body were pulling him two different ways, toward the two opposite traps.

In scant seconds Turko would be torn in half.

# Chapter Four

## The Miglas demand
## revolutionary vosk-stuxing

Instinctive reaction lifted my sword arm. I was ready to slash through the tendril nearest to me. Then I, Dray Prescot, paused. Sheer blind bloodthirsty passion had almost condemned my new comrade Turko to death. Instinct to action here was useless. If I slashed through this near tentacle, then the other would have nothing holding it and so could spring back with all its hideous power and snap Turko into the barbed coffin of the trap.

Turko's magnificent body strained. His enormous strength concentrated in resisting the twin pulls. His body was being torn in half, but his training, his discipline, and his muscles fought every inch of the way.

One tendril cut would be followed instantly by the springing of Turko into the trap. The coffin-leaves would close and the spines bite, like a vegetable Iron Maiden, and perhaps a thin trickle of Turko's blood might seep past those clenched vegetable lips.

Instinct had been quelled, and thought had taken over; but to tell you all this has taken ten times longer than the facts of action. In almost the same moment the tendrils lapped Turko and he yelled—I had seized his body in my left arm, throwing the torch to Med and trusting to his quick-wittedness to catch it, had reached across and slashed the tentacle and almost had my feet pulled from under me, so savage and powerful was that force pulling from the opposite syatra. There was time—but only just, only just!—for me to follow that swiping swing with a second and sever the far tendril.

Turko was on his feet in an instant.

"By the Muscle! Burn the monsters!"

He thrust his torch at the nearest syatra and the thing

went crazy. Tendrils lashed and writhed, the torch went spinning, to plunge to a fizzing extinction in the boiling water. Med yelled. He was slashing with a stux, not the most handy of weapons for the business, managing for the moment to keep clear of the Gorgon's hair. My thraxter was circling and hacking and hewing all the time, leaving a growing heap of dismembered tendril tips scattered on the floor about us.

This whole scene was awry. How could the old king and queen of Migla have come walking through here in secret to their devotions in the temple? In the ceiling, erratically lit by the two remaining torches—Med had flung mine back—I could vaguely make out a straight line crack, some six inches or so wide. Now if . . .

I whirled the torch in that crazy steamy atmosphere. The king and queen would have brought samphron-oil lamps. I saw the long lenken lever protruding from the wall well past the syatras and a look back showed its counterpart. We had missed it in going past, an easily done thing in that treacherous light.

With a wild yell I whirled the torch at the near syatra, slashed more of those tendrils away, hacking and slashing, jumped for the lever. A tendril lapped my thigh as I reached the lenk. I ignored it. I felt the vegetable strength of the thing, horrific, dragging me back. With a single last heave I laid my hand on the lever and dragged it down. It resisted and I used all my strength, and with a clashing of gears and a great groaning, the lever fell.

"Look out, Dray!" Turko yelled savagely.

I whirled.

A single stroke from the thraxter severed the tendril around my thigh; but the stroke was unnecessary. From those two six-inch wide slots in the ceiling, one on each side of the tunnel and parallel to it, vast slabs of slate descended smoothly, their massive weight in some way counterpoised behind the walls. As they slid downward so the tendrils wriggled backward, bunching, coiling, avoiding the descending edge of slate. The last corpse-white wriggling tentacle slipped back beneath the slate and the two edges struck the ground with a hollow and reverberating clank.

The running water which gave sustenance to the syatras also must power the counterweight mechanism.

Turko peered over his shoulder, frowning. He never did like having his body ripped up—well, no one does, of course. But for a Khamorro the sanctity of his own body is very close to his heart.

"By Migshenda the Stux!" breathed Med. "We were nearly cast adrift on the Ice Floes of Sicce then!"

"Aye," said Turko. He breathed deeply and flexed his biceps gingerly, testing. Everything seemed to be in order, which put my mind at rest. "By the Muscle! They were strong kobblurs."

Trust Turko for a comment on the aspect that affected him!

We advanced, relighting the torch after some trouble, and found no less than four more levers and slate barricades which, descending with a rumbling roar, walled off the voracious syatras. Although I had not previously encountered this famous plant of Kregen, I had heard of it. It liked hot damp climates in general, and I understood Chem was choked out with the things. No doubt the builders of the temple and Mungul Sidrath had thought it a capital scheme to employ them when they had a ready supply of hot water. The cracks in the roof were not casual cracks at all but carefully constructed ventilation tubes, and no doubt their upper ends would be concealed in innocent-seeming masonry of an innocent-seeming building.

During the day the twin Suns of Scorpio would shine down here for a space sufficient to sustain the syatras.

We padded on and were thankful to leave that tunnel of dark and dank and danger to our rear. We came up into a shaft around the inside of which a narrow spiral stair led upward to—to more darkness and danger, for a surety.

We had, of course, no idea where Mag, twin brother of Mog, would be imprisoned. We did not even know if he was still alive.

Many and many a time have I crept into a fortress, a naked brand in my fist, bent on one nefarious scheme or another. This time I was out to rescue an old Migla and take him back so that the religion of which his twin sister was high priestess might regain its former glory and puissance. Then, if we were lucky, we could turn the Canops out of Migla. We padded through the lower levels of Mungul Sidrath and we were not gentle with those whom we met. We did not run across that dolorous cavern of the waterwheels, where slaves heaved and struggled to hoist water up to the high towers, so that the nobles and lords and ladies of the occupying Canoptic army and court might bathe and wash and refresh themselves. I took the time to don a Canoptic soldier's uniform, the white kiltlike lower garment, the greaves, the lorica, the helmet, and I took up his shield. As he had done before, Turko ignored the weapons, but he took up a shield and slid it up his left arm. I remembered what Turko had done with his shield on that fragile bridge above the rushing waters of the cavern, and I own I felt greatly more happy about life with Turko at my back with his shield.

And, of course, as you must guess, Turko soon became called Turko the Shield.

Presently a Jiktar, sweating, frightened clean through, the point of my sword drawing a bead of blood from his throat, was only too happy to tell me what we needed to know. I knocked him senseless, for that was his due, and we prowled on along the dungeon-lined corridor he indicated. Men and women crowded to the bars. Hairy and whiskery faces peered out, arms beseeched us through the iron bars, a wailing chorus of utter despair which senses that utter despair may be ending screamed at us as we passed.

"When we return, Med," I said, hard and unpleasantly.

"As you will it, Horter Prescot."

I did not blow up at his formality, taking it as a reproof.

"Take your formality to Makki-Grodno, Med! I have been Dray to you—there is no need for 'Horter.' We will release them when we return, for otherwise they will raise the citadel about our ears."

He glanced at me, and away, and gripped his stuxcal. For a Migla he had a spirit I admired. He must have had, for since when did I, Dray Prescot, the Lord of Strombor, condescend to explain my every order?

These were political prisoners, which in Migla meant religious prisoners.

A Deldar, arrogant in his brilliant uniform, strutted down toward us as we reached the end of the corridor where an iron-barred gate concealed the final cell. Med hurled his stux. The squat wedge-shaped blade smashed into the Deldar's lorica, punched on to lodge fatally in his heart. Gouting blood from his mouth—for the wide blade must have severed all his veins and arteries there about his lungs—he toppled without a scream.

"Stupid calsany," commented Turko.

The final cell yielded up Mag.

41

Mog had spoken truthfully. The oldster after the fashion of very old people was hard to differentiate as to sex. He looked just like Mog. The same beaky nose, the same rat-trap jaws, the same toe-cap chin. He blinked as the torches glittered across his eyes.

This was where Med Neemusbane proved the value of his coming with us. He was able with quick words and the right and correct references to the religion of Migshaanu to convince old Mag that we were friends, come to take him to freedom. The Canops no doubt had plans for him, for they could not be absolutely sure they had crushed the religion, and old Mag, with suitable encouragement of a kind I would not seek to dwell on, would have been a pawn to reimpose their will. We helped him back along that dismal corridor of incarceration, and we opened all the barred doors on our way, swearing vilely at the inmates to be silent. Like released slaves from a swifter, they could not contain their joy, and they ran about, some picking up weapons, others kicking prostrate Canops, others falling to their knees in thankful prayers.

"Mag!" I shouted. "Tell this rabble to follow us. And, by the diseased left armpit of Makki-Grodno, if they don't stop that caterwauling they'll have the whole Canoptic army at our throats."

Mag tried to calm them, but I saw he never would, and as my duty was to him I hustled him away. Turko and I hefted him between us, and he whistled through the air, his feet six inches off the ground and flailing.

We had to put him down half a dozen times to deal with isolated parties of Canops come to investigate the uproar. We noticed that none came upon us from the rear, and from this we took heart. The released prisoners were fighting, then.

Some came with us. Men hardy enough to want to get out with Mag and begin the struggle from the outside, when they were prepared, and not to idly throw away their lives in here.

At one point one of the Miglas, who looked just as stupidly flap-eared and rubbery as any of the others, but who had a rolling muscular look about him, hesitated as we were accosted by a detachment of Canop soldiers. A Migla next to this one, whose name was Hamp, screeched as a crossbow bolt thunked into his belly.

Hamp held a stux he had picked up from a dead Canop.

"Imagine they are vosk, Hamp," I said. I spoke quietly, without drama, reasonably, as though discussing an abstruse point of their own religion with him. "Hurl with Migshenda's skill."

The idea struck him as novel. "Vosk!" he shouted. I loosed and hit a Deldar in the mouth. Hamp bunched up, poised, and threw. His stux battered away the shield of a Canop soldier and slashed out the side of the fellow's face.

"It is done!" Hamp shouted. His curious Migla face looked dazed. "Canops are vosk, to be stuxed!"

Looking back, I saw that was the crux of the problem.

The Miglas *had* sought to fight off the Canoptic invasion, but I had put down their complete failure against what were so few men as being due to the superb organization and military discipline of the Canops. But the reasons ran deeper than that.

Here on our own old Earth the East has a tradition that only certain races or tribes are warlike. Others are never reckoned as being of martial spirit, as being of any use as soldiers. Certain developments in the last few years have undermined this belief. In Europe we are a warlike lot, it seems, for the West does not have the same tradition. So the Miglas were a religious nation, and warfare something with which they were unfamiliar. For the Canops, the army represented the ideal. The Canops, with a few regiments and a tiny air arm, had subdued the whole country of the Miglas. Now they sought to maintain their conquest.

With more Miglas like Med Neemusbane and Hamp, I judged, the task I had considered almost insuperable might have a solution that was one I could accept. We reached the open air and climbed back through the tunneled stair and so came out into the ruins. The Maiden with the Many Smiles shone down on us. We made our surreptitious way back to the tavern leaning so crazily on the bank of the River Magan. *The Loyal Canoptic* buzzed with activity that night. I worried over that. The two girls were gone, having been sent on the first stage of their journey home. *The Loyal Canoptic* was a sarcastic name for Planath the Wine's tavern. Before the time of tragedy it had been called *The Loyal of Sidraarga*. Now I fretted that Canop patrols, or any of the mercenaries they employed, would hear the sounds of merrymaking and investigate.

If they did so, of course, every man of the patrol would be dead. But that would only stir up fresh trouble.

The tangled skein of politics in Havilfar, and the delicate balances of power, I found fascinating. The Canops had been able to carry out their conquest of Migla, their own island of Canopdrin in the Shrouded Sea being made uninhabitable by the volcanic activity there, because no one wished to fight them on this issue. The Canops were no more powerful now than they had been. This was not an empire-building conquest. On the other hand, there were many countries around the Shrouded Sea which would welcome the downfall of the iron men from Canopdrin. Their army discipline and organization, I discovered, was not peculiar to them, or remarkably exceptional. The Canoptic army was a fair representative war machine of most countries of Havilfar.

Against that war machine we must pit only religious-minded halflings with vosk-hunting experience. In the normal course of events we could not hope to win; but I held ever in my mind what had been accomplished with the slaves and workers of the warrens of Magdag, and I did not lose hope. I had no right to lose hope, for that would have displeased the Star Lords, and my overriding duty was to stay on Kregen—no matter how.

A camp was established in the back hills of Migla and here collected disaffected halflings prepared to fight. They came in, in small numbers; but as the message was spread by word of mouth throughout the land that both Mog and her brother Mag were returned the stream of recruits thickened. The full rites of Migshaanu were celebrated every sixth day, as was proper on Kregen, and due observances were restored every day also.

I was kept very busy.

A small cadre of dedicated Miglas gathered about Turko and me. Hamp, as one of the better potential officers, and Med also, could be trusted to carry out orders faithfully. I spelled out various of the difficulties to them as we watched Miglas struggling to stay in line and advance shoulder to shoulder over the slope of a hill.

"We face a number of problems," I told them. "One is the absolute absence of hand-to-hand fighting experience here. Not only are you deficient in the art, you do not even have the weapons."

"I have this," said Med, ripping out his big knifelike

44

scramasax. "My veknis has slit many a vosk throat—aye! and a neemu's also, into the bargain."

They solemnly nodded their heads, these ugly little Miglas.

"Aye, Med Neemusbane, you speak the truth."

Whereat Med lowered his head, and looked away, ashamed of thus boasting of his prowess and calling attention to the deed for which he was both famed and named.

"And," I said cuttingly, "what of your little veknis against a real sword? Answer me that!"

I was harsh about his scramasax, for that Saxon weapon is a knife built like a sword, and is very ugly and deadly, although of beautiful shape. But a thraxter, the cut-and-thrust sword of Havilfar, would deal with the veknis with ease.

They shuffled their feet and the Miglas in the line advancing up the hill weaved about like those tendrils sprouting from that horrific syatra in the tunnels beneath Mungul Sidrath. I looked up. At least, the Suns of Scorpio still shone.

"We need shields, and bows, and we need the skills to use them."

Here there were no masses of slave workers skilled in all manner of arts and crafts, as there had been in the warrens of Magdag, as ready to produce a bow or a shield as to produce a statue or a decoration for the megaliths of the overlords.

Mog waved her arms. She insisted on attending every planning meeting, and this was her right, I suppose.

"We must collect all the money we can. All the deldys my people will give—aye, and more. Then we can hire mercenaries. I am told Rapas are very good, for I do not think we could afford to hire Chuliks. There is your answer."

They could do this, of course.

"You can do this," I said. "But who holds the treasury of Migla now? Who controls the state chest in Mungul Sidrath? Can you outbid the Canops in hiring soldiers? For every Rapa you hired they would hire two Chuliks. And, I tell you, for I know these things, no mercenary likes to be hired to fight for a side so obviously doomed to lose."

That, I realized at once, had not only been a tactless thing to say, it had been also offensive.

I went on bluntly and offensively: "Until you learn to

fight for yourselves, you will not regain your own country."

"We will fight!" yelled Med Neemusbane. He jumped up, waving his stux. "We will fight!"

"Then learn, you wild neemu! Learn!"

Turko said, in the hush that followed, "If we fight and begin to win, will not the Canops then hire more mercenaries?"

"If they do that, good Turko, they admit defeat. Then, I would be happy to see contingents of Rapas and Brokelsh and Fristles landing in Yaman. For then we would be winning!"

One important fact I must make clear at this point is that I felt myself cut off here in halfling Migla. I was a Homo sapiens, as was Turko; apim. We were the only apim among all these halflings, people whom I would have dubbed, when I first moved among the races of Kregen, as beast-men. I knew a little better by this time. But the oppression of being stuck away here in this backwater of Havilfar, when all I really wanted to do lay across the Southern Ocean, filled me with a haziness as to my proper course for the immediate future. Building up an army seemed to me the only sensible course to follow. The army grew slowly, and shields were produced, and I hammered out a system of tactical combat that I felt would serve its purpose on the day of battle.

We had the advantage of numbers. But, had I been a Canop Chuktar commanding my brigade of regiments, I would have chuckled and in the old uncouth and savage way have said: "All the more targets for my fellows."

As far as the numbers opposed to us were concerned, I was amused to notice how the oddly intricate mensuration of Kregen hampered estimates. Kregen measures in units of six and also in units of ten. In the ancient and misty past we here on this Earth used to measure in units of six; but the decimal system ousted that, and a last rearguard action was fought when shillings vanished and twelve pennies were no longer a unit. There were eighty men in a Canoptic pastang. Six pastangs formed a regiment. With ancillaries like the standard-bearers and the trumpeters and grooms and orderlies and cooks and others of the unglamorous duty-men necessary in every army, there would be, I judged, something like five hundred and fifty men in a regiment. The commandant in Yaman held no less than twelve regiments, of crossbowmen and of footmen. With extras here, also—say between seven and eight thousand men. He had an air wing also, of which I knew nothing, tough aerial cavalry mounted on mirvols and not on fluttrells as I had previously thought. There was a ground cavalry force, riding totrixes and zorcas, and I had been told that here in Havilfar the half-vove also was used.

In addition there would be the Canop Air Service, flying vollers, those airboats which were at the time manufactured solely in certain of the countries of Havilfar.

All in all we faced a formidable fighting machine.

They hadn't understood my reference to being glad to see contingents of mercenaries, and I had to explain that I meant that these would be mercenaries we hired, for then they would be happy to come to join the winning side for booty and glory.

I had for the moment discounted various Canoptic regiments stationed outside the capital city, for I meant to make the decisive struggle in and around Yaman itself. By the time those regiments scattered throughout Migla arrived they would march into a debacle and could easily be dispersed and captured.

The air of impatience among the Miglas grew with every new bunch of arrivals. They were excellent spearthrowers. I told them what I wanted, what, indeed, I could see as their only chance.

"Shield-bearers will protect your flanks and your front and the stux-men must hurl as they have never hurled before. By sheer weight of flying stuxes you must beat down the Canop shields and slay their bowmen. Then, once you can charge into close quarters, you must use your veknises to strike savagely upward and in, past the edges of the devils' armor. That is your only chance." I stared at the group of Miglas I had chosen as officers, not finding it at all strange that they and Mog had allowed me to take overall command. "I shall show you how to create a new kind of stux that will strip a man of his shield. It will be hard and bloody work. But with a continuous supply of stuxes"—and, Zair forgive me, I did not add, 'and a continuous supply of men'—"you should beat down their strength and their will and so slay them as you slay a wounded vosk."

That, too, was not a clever image, for a wounded vosk is atrociously dangerous, the time when vosks lose their usual placid stolidity and become fighting mad. But, then, the image was correct, after all, for the iron men of Canopdrin were far more dangerous than any vosk, wounded and raging.

And as well I must not lose sight of the fact that Med and his fellows hunted wild vosk out here in the back hills. The domesticated vosk is the stupid sluggish animal of story and legend, and I recalled how we had used them and their appetites in the Black Marble Quarries of Zenicce. The wild vosk, as I discovered, was another kettle of fish altogether. They were wild. Their horns would impale a man and his totrix together given half a chance. The Miglas prized them, though their meat was stringier and tougher than that of the domesticated vosk, because their skins were infinitely more supple and strong, and the export of voskskin had been of great economic value to Migla. The Canops were altering that, as I knew; but for us, here and now training up an army in the back hills, the wild vosks had served to create men—Migla men—with unerring eye and aim, and muscles that could drive a stux with deadly accuracy.

More and more Miglas joined the growing army and shortly a vociferous claque began to demand we march instantly to Yaman and smash the Canops in fair fight.

However much I tried to explain the truth, the hotheads would not listen. They were the victims of an old illusion. Once a man joins his regiment and puts in a little training his whole life changes, he knows he is fitter and tougher than he has ever been, and possessed of fighting skills he had not dreamed existed. He sees his comrades all in line and charges valiantly with them against straw-filled dummies. He believes he is then a soldier. He imagines he is ready to fight.

They would not listen.

Mog and Mag, ugly old twins, whipped up the passion for immediate action. The crimson of Migshaanu appeared everywhere.

I did what I could to depress this premature enthusiasm; but everyone, including Turko, looked at me askance, and could not wait to march.

As promised the new spears were made under my instructions and issued. All I had done was to tell the smiths to convert a stux into a pilum. This was simply done, and in the crudest of fashions, by inserting a rivet halfway along the shaft which, when the spear bit into a shield, would bend and snap and so allow the pilum to droop. The trailing shaft on the ground would impede the soldier

48

and drag down his shield. He would not be able to drag it free for the barbs, and he would be unable to cut it away with his thraxter for the metal splines running down the forward portion of the shaft. When the pila flew shields would be cast away—or so I hoped.

The men were divided up into regiments, and shield-men, stux-men and pilum-men formed into units for the tactical plan.

We had a small totrix-mounted cavalry force, mostly of young Miglas who had been shaken from the placid lethargy of their elders by their resentment of the Canop-tic invasion. The totrix, a near relative of the sectrix and the nactrix, is a somewhat heavier beast than either of those and will carry an armored man more easily. They had nothing of the fleetness and nimbleness of zorcas, and nothing of the smashing power of voves, but we had our-selves a cavalry screening force.

Of course, it was not easy. I had to be everywhere and superintend everything, and I own I was tired in a way strange to me, enervated and depressed and struggling vainly to whip my enthusiasm up to the giddy heights of all those around me.

We possessed no aerial cavalry whatsoever.

Hamp was a transformed man.

"They are vosks, Dray Prescot! You said so yourself!"

"Yes—but, Hamp, we are not ready—"

"Look!" Hamp waved his hand at the men who now ran forward steadily in long even ranks, hurling their pila, the air filled with the flying shafts. The stux-men threw, hard and accurately. Then the whole mass drew their veknises and charged, whooping and skirling and roaring. They made a brave sight.

"Not ready," I repeated. My face was ugly.

"You cannot be afraid, Dray Prescot," cackled old Mog. "I saw you at work, in the jungles of that Mig-shaanu-forsaken Faol. You perhaps fear for the lives of my young men?"

"I do."

"We are happy to give our lives for Migshaanu the All-Glorious!" yelled Med Neemusbane, waving his knife.

"Aye, you are happy. But I am not. Suicide is no way to find Zair and to sit at his right hand in the glory of Zim."

"Heathen gods, Dray, heathen gods!"

I had to bite down my angry retort. I was, as you would say in this day and age, losing my cool.

Despite what many men—aye, and many women!—have said, I, Dray Prescot, Krozair of Zy and Lord of Strombor, am a human being. I am only human. I was tired in a way that irked me. If I let the decision slip away, if I did not fight them more forcefully, I own the fault is mine. Worry and concern pressed in on me, and I gave way. Their enthusiasm and confidence were treacherous pressures. I should not have allowed it. But, to my shame, I did.

"Very well! Give me two more sennights. Just two. Then, by Vox! Then we will march on these men of Canopdrin!"

I was a fool.

The Miglas would not wait twelve more days.

Hamp was the ringleader; chosen by me as a commander, he took full control, actively encouraged by the twins Mog and Mag. Med Neemusbane was his enthusiastic lieutenant. The Migla army, a creation wholly new to them, and a thing not seen in Migla for many and many a season, marched out.

They marched singing.

They carried their shields over their backs. Their stuxcals were filled. Their pila were ready. Their veknises were sharp. They sang as they marched and the long winding columns of crimson, with the great staff of Migshaanu borne at their head, rolled down from the back hills and took the road to Yaman.

Turko and I sat our totrixes on a little eminence and watched them go.

"Fools!" I whispered.

"They are brave, Dray. They will fight well, for you have taught them."

"I have sent them to their deaths. . . ."

"They chose to go."

"Aye. And I cannot let them go without me." I shook out the reins.

Turko lifted his great shield, specially built and strengthened, behind my back. The Suns of Scorpio streamed their mingled red and emerald light about us as we trotted down from the hills, our twin shadows moving with us. All this was happening because of the direct orders of the Star Lords. I did not much care for the Everoinye then. We trotted down from the hills and so rode with the Migla army for the city of Yaman and for disaster.

50

# Chapter Five

## Turko the Shield and I sup after the first battle

That disaster did not strike exactly as I had imagined it must.

The raw army of recruits of Migla fought well.

I fought with them. The memories I retain of that battle are scattered and fragmentary, of the charges and the falling spears, the glitter of armor and weapons, the clouds of crossbow bolts, the solid chunking smash of masses of men in close combat. The fliers astride their mirvols rained down their bolts from above, and the Miglas lifted their shields, and the crossbowmen afoot loosed into them.

But the pila dragged down many a shield, and the stuxes flew. The Miglas fought magnificently. They outnumbered the army of Canopdrin. They did not consider their own losses. They charged again and again, their veknises gleaming crimson with blood, and again and again they were hurled back. Yet still they charged. The supplies of stuxes I had arranged to be brought up by wagons were late arriving, and when they did at last reach the field, which lay in wide meadows about a dwabur west of Yaman, there were pitifully few hands to grasp them.

I had four totrixes slain under me. When there were no more riding animals to be had I charged afoot at the head of the Miglas. I found the thraxter to be a useful weapon, used with a shield, and I also discovered—as I had always known—how inordinately powerful a shield wall could be if it remained intact.

The Miglas broke two shield walls.

They toppled two Canoptic brigades into rout.

But the supreme efforts spent their strength and the remaining two brigades were able to drive in, charging in their turn now under showers of bolts, and tumble the Miglas back into destruction.

Trapped in a close-pressing melee Turko and I were tumbled back with the rest. Yes, I do not recall many of the details of that battle, which, from a windmill nearby owned by a Migla called Mackee, was henceforth known as the Battle of Mackee; but one scarlet memory stands out and runs like a thread through the whole conflict.

How strange it was, I thought, not to have to worry over my back!

For, where I went, there went Turko the Shield.

With those lightning-fast reflexes of the Khamorro he picked up the flight of a bolt and interposed the shield between it and my back or side. He hovered over me, an aegis through which no single bolt, no single arrow, no single stux could penetrate.

And—more than once a Migla, inflamed by the homicidal fury of combat, seeing in Turko and me two hated apims, would hurl at us. Turko's muscles roped and twined as he held the great shield up, its surface bristling with shafts. Whenever he could he took the opportunity of ripping them away. He had the Khamorro strength to rip a barbed bolt out where a normal soldier would have no chance of doing the same.

A pilum smacked into the shield. I remember that. I remember seeing Turko hoisting the shield up, seeing bolts glancing from it, seeing the way he held it despite the dragging effect of the pilum. For a space we were clear of the press. Dust and blood and the shrieking screams of wounded and dying men created that insane horror of a battlefield all about us.

Turko bent and ripped the pilum away—

And then I remember looking up at the night sky and seeing the Twins eternally revolving one about the other sailing across the sky, cloud wrack driven across their faces giving them the illusion of movement. Turko at my side lay senseless, blood clotting his hair. He wore a red band around his head now, as a reed syple, and I knew why.

All about us the horrid moaning of hundreds of wounded men, Migla and apim, rose into the cool night wind.

Occasionally shrill shrieks burst out, to sputter and die away. Canops were out with lanterns searching among the dead. I discovered the blood dried along my head. All the famous bells of Beng-Kishi rang in that old head of mine;

but my skull is a thick one, and I had bathed in the pool of baptism in the River Zelph in far Aphrasöe, and so I was able to hunch up and get Turko on my back and stagger away from that awful and tragic field.

There was nothing to be done here, the disaster was on so great a scale, that all there was left for us was to save our own skins. Then, I vowed, then we would come back and do properly what we had so signally failed to do this day on the field of Mackee.

A voice hailed.

"Over here, dom."

Armed Canops, with samphron-oil lamps and flaring torches. If I ran they would split Turko and me with accurate bolts. I took Turko across to the fire. Many Canops lay on blankets around the fire, and I saw Canop women tending them. The smoke drifted in the cool wind.

"Let's have a look at you, soldier."

This Canop, this one with the lined haggard face, the haunted eyes, must be a doctor. In mere seconds he had stuck his acupuncture needles into Turko and so could banish my comrade's pain while he tended the gash on his head. My own wound needed merely cleaning and poulticing and bandaging.

"A nasty crack that one, soldier." The doctor handed me to a Canop woman, a mere slip of a girl with dark hair and eyes I knew would be merry in other circumstances. Her long slim fingers bandaged my head. We were apim; therefore we were Canops. We were not Miglas, we were not the enemy.

The situation was not without its piquancy.

Turko breathed easier now. We had both been wearing armor taken from Canops, and we would pass.

We were put down carefully on blankets in a ring around the fire, and broth—good vosk and onion soup—and a rolled leaf filled with palines were handed to each of us. We drank and ate with relish. Later there was wine, rough army issue wine; but refreshing and invigorating at the time.

"Those old cham-faces," said a soldier next to me, who had a bandage covering most of his stomach. "They stuck me in the belly. But I feel sorry for 'em."

"Sorry for 'em?" I was genuinely surprised.

"Well, look at the crazy onkers, charging us like that." The soldier moved and suddenly, unpleasantly, he groaned and I saw his face go set into drawn haggard lines.

53

"Nurse!" I called, and the girl hurried over. She knelt, her yellow tunic and skirt, not unlike the kilts worn by the men, glimmering warm in the firelight. There were many fires over the battlefield, each with its ring of wounded. She looked cross.

"Have you been drinking, soldier?"

He winked at her.

"You silly onker! You've been cut up in the belly—no more wine until the doctor orders. Understand?"

She had given one of the needles sticking in him a twirl and his pain receded. He looked properly subdued. "Orders is orders, nurse. But I'm fair parched."

"Suck palines, soldier."

When she had gone in answer to a muffled scream from across the ring of wounded men, I returned to the source of my puzzlement. "Those Miglas. They were out to kill—"

"Well, wouldn't you be? If your land had been taken from you?"

The disorientation of all this could not be explained merely by his mistaking me for a soldier and a comrade. The soldier next along lifted on an elbow. He had a broken leg which had been expertly set and splinted. He spoke over the man with the stomach wound.

"How much do we get out of it, then, I ask you? We do the fighting—aye, and I'm proud to fight for Canopdrin. But I'd like a little more booty."

These men I had already summed up as soldiers fighting for their country, not mercenaries, and therefore urged on not by cold greed but hot patriotism. They talked on, quietly, and I came to understand the viewpoint of the Canoptic soldier much better. A rough lot, like soldiers almost anywhere, they enlisted for enormously long periods and expected hard fighting, for they had had a long-standing feud with a neighbor island of the Shrouded Sea. When Canopdrin had been made uninhabitable they had welcomed the decision of the king and his pallans to make a new home in Migla. But, as was usually the way, the high-born reaped most of the benefits.

The man with the belly wound, whose name was Naghan the Throat—he was always thirsty—rambled and muttered and I feared that he would be gripped by a fever and so taken off. He suddenly tried to sit up, his eyes wide and brilliant, and he cried: "I fought, by Opaz! I fought!"

Then the man with the broken leg, one Jedgul the Finger—I was too delicate to inquire why he had acquired the name—sat up sharply and dragged himself toward Naghan's blanket and took Naghan and thrust him down, his hand splayed over the face.

"Quiet, you onker!" He spoke breathily, quickly, and then, in a louder voice: "By the Glorious Lem, you will live!"

The picture came clear to me in those few words. Lem, the silver leem, was the supernatural being worshiped by the Canops, and his statue was everywhere, for a soldier most noticeably in the form of a silver leaping leem atop the standard. This leem cult had broken the religion of Migshaanu. But Naghan the Throat had cursed in his delirium by Opaz, the great twin deity, invisible and omnipotent, that represented the major religious beliefs of the peoples of Pandahem and of Vallia and of many other civilized places besides. So, I reasoned, Lem, the debased silver leem, had ousted the followers of Opaz before he had started in on Migshaanu. Now I have made no attempt to outline the beliefs or practices of the religion of the Invisible Twins, of Opaz. I have told you of the long chanting processions streaming in torchlight through the cities and all chanting "Oolie Opaz, Oolie Opaz, Oolie Opaz." The stresses come on the first syllables of the words. It is always "*Oo*lie *O*paz!" over and over again.

But—there is a very great deal more to it than a mere chanting procession.

Jedgul the Finger looked at me over the prostrate form of Naghan and I saw his eyes glittering in the firelight.

"Naghan the Throat is a good comrade of mine, dom. You are a soldier. You would not betray him?"

"Never," I said.

Jedgul slumped back, as though relieved.

"It's all the fault of the officers," he said, his voice low, grumbling. This is so common a complaint in every army I would have taken no notice of it; but Jedgul added, "They think themselves so high and mighty. A common ranker may never enter their shrines to Lem. Everything of the best is always theirs. I bet you your officers are doing what ours are now, drinking themselves silly and pestering shishis. . . . You didn't say what your regiment was."

I had seen his shield, with the embossed image of the leaping leem at the top, below that a black neemu, painted on, with the figures eleven and one. He was of the first pastang of the eleventh regiment of foot. At the beginning of the battle I had made it my business to make a note of all the regiments arrayed against us, and now was able to choose one on the opposite wing from the eleventh. Also, in choosing this particular regiment I could exhibit a little hard-won knowledge.

"Third," I said casually. And added, "Hikdar Markman will be occupying two shishis, if I know him."

Jedgul chuckled.

"Aye, Nath," he said, for I had told them I was called Nath. "And King Capnon can sleep safe in his bed this night."

"Better get some sleep yourself. Here comes the nurse."

"Aye," he said, yawning. "Paline Chahmsix is a sweet kid. Her old man ought to be proud of her."

"Six" is one of the common suffixes denoting daughter, as "han" often denotes son. The nurse, Paline Chahmsix, came up, tut-tutting, and bid Jedgul and I sleep as soundly as Naghan. "Lem keep you," she said, which is a way of saying good night.

Jedgul answered with a snore.

I turned over and closed my eyes. When the light tread of her little feet had gone I rolled across to Turko and shook him awake. The sounds around us were dying. The wounded were finding peace in sleep. Tomorrow would see the collection and burial of the dead, with their memories dedicated to the greater glory of Lem, the silver leem.

"We have to leave now, Turko. And don't make a sound."

He was awake quickly enough. He touched his bandaged head and checked the needle. "What—?"

"A doctor attended you, and a charming little girl not really old enough to be out here at night with all these desperate soldiers. We've been lucky, Turko. Now let's get out of here without a fuss. I wouldn't want anything to happen to little Paline Chahmsix."

His glance contained all that old quizzical appraisal; but he rose, and together we silently crept away from the glow of the fire out into the moon-drenched shadows of Kregen.

Late on the following day we caught up with what was left of the army of Migla and with these sorry remnants we returned to the camps in the back hills. We had lost a sorrowful lot of men. Hamp and Med had both been wounded; but they were unrepentant when I started to tell them a few home truths.

"We were not ready, as you said, Dray. But we have learned. We know now we can beat them next time."

"There will be no next time," I said. I was savage and cutting and angry and contemptuous—of myself. For, I, too, had seen my own crass stupidity. "There will not be a next time until I give the word."

Mog waved her arms about at this, and quieted Mag, who had been about to try to say something, and she yelled: "I am the high priestess! We must strike, and strike again!"

"Agreed. But we do it my way. The common soldiers of Canopdrin are just ordinary men. They are driven into fighting by their masters, who crack the whips over them, and who dazzle their eyes with statues of Lem, the silver leem."

As I spoke these words Mog and Mag and the others shuddered and put up their hands, warding off the evil of that foul name.

"Opaz," I said fiercely, proddingly. "Aye, Opaz is known among them and some still love the Invisible Twins. They would welcome you of Migshaanu if a way could be found."

"They would cut us down with swords if we tried," said Med.

"Agreed. You cannot face them in battle, not for a long time. You must accept this as a truth. But there is a way, and I shall take that way, and bring you help. You must wait here, recruit more men, train them up as I have shown you. When the time is ripe Turko here, or one bearing a message from me, Dray Prescot, will come to you. Then, my friends, strike at Yaman!"

They jabbered on at that; but all I would say—for fear I should fail—was that they must prepare themselves for the day. When that day came, they would be told.

And, even as I cursed myself for my own stupidity, I cringed a little at the thought of what the Star Lords would do. For I had not disobeyed the Everoinye. I had done what the Star Lords commanded, through their spy and messenger the golden and scarlet raptor, the Gdoinye. But—for the first time on Kregen—I had failed the Star Lords.

I had not failed them in Magdag but had been too successful.

I had not disobeyed.

I had failed.

What would they do to one who proved a broken reed?

The thoughts of Delia, and our twins, drove mad phantasms through my mind. What if, through my failure, I was banished from Kregen forever? If the Star Lords had no further use for me? The thought was impossible; I could not face it. I must recoup this situation, bash on, trample down any and everything that stood in my path. Oh, I did not relish my avowed intent, there in that ring of hills in backward Migla. But—better the Ice Floes of Sicce than being hurled back to the Earth of my birth and never more see my Delia, my Delia of Delphond!

Never before had I failed in what the Star Lords had set me to accomplish. This was no time to start.

Turko would come with me.

I bid Remberee to Mog and Med Neemusbane and Hamp, and set off for Yaman. We traveled secretly and by night, and I wore my old scarlet breechclout and carried weapons, and Turko wore the scarlet band about his forehead that was his new reed syple, and a shield strapped on his left arm. And so we came under the moons of Kregen into the ruins of the temple within the grove of trees sacred to Sidraarga.

Shadows dappled the stone where lichens already stained and obscured the sacred symbols. The moons rode the sky above and the pink moonlight flooded down. I moved into the shadows beneath the trees, and my brand gleamed naked in my fist.

The flier was still there.

This was the voller that had brought us out of Faol and away from the slavering if human jaws of the manhounds.

Turko said, "I have never inquired why you had to bring old Mog home, Dray, being content to follow you. And, now, I am filled with joy that I may lift a shield at your back. But—"

"And much do I value that, Zair knows!" I climbed up into the airboat. "In me, Turko the Shield, you behold a great and misbegotten fool! An onker of onkers, a get onker."

"If you say so, Dray, I would be the last to correct you on so weighty a point."

He was laughing at me again, this muscular Khamorro!

I checked over the flier and saw she was intact and ready to go. I would not give Turko the satisfaction of rising to his sarcasm; for all that we owed each other much, I still had that prickly feeling that he weighed me and sized me up at all times. I had proved to him through the disciplines of the Krozairs of Zy, of which he had never heard, that I was as good as any Great Kham produced by the Khamorros, and I had earned his shocked "Hai Hikai!" But, still, he wanted to know more of me. You could not fault him for that, I did realize, somewhat ill temperedly; for I own I am a great shambling bear of a fellow when it comes to human relations and I know what I want to do and say and, Makki-Grodno as a witness, I say and do the exact opposite. I have overcome that defect a great deal in later years; but it is a burden many of us bear.

With a finicky delicacy on the controls I edged the voller out from under the trees. Mog had truly said no one would venture into the sacred grove. We cleared the last boughs and I looked up ready to haul the lever into the ascent position, when I saw the black shape of the Gdoinye hard-etched against the glowing pink and golden face of the Maiden with the Many Smiles.

For an instant the accipiter hung; then it vanished.

No mistake was possible; that had not been some nocturnal, completely ordinary bird of prey. The Everoinye watched over me, watched me in my failure!

"Where away, then, Dray?"

"Do you know where lies Valka?"

"No." Then he added, "I've never heard of it, I think."

This did not surprise me. Kregen is a world where rapid transport by flier rubs shoulders with quoffa carts, where men in one continent cannot be expected to know very much of another continent, and that in the other hemisphere. And yet one expects travelers, businessmen with overseas agencies, military personnel, and, above all, the men of the air services, to be aware of vast numbers of names and places scattered across the islands and continents in this part of Kregen.

"Valka lies a trifle west of due north." At this time on Kregen the magnetic variation was approximately naught degrees naught minutes and ten seconds west—which was very handy for calculation—and a due north course would serve admirably. "It must be something like two thousand or more dwaburs which, in this excellent voller, are a mere nothing."

I said no more.

Around me in the flier a blue nimbus spread. I was aware of outside sounds slipping away, of Turko's light voice fading. The blue radiance grew and began to coalesce around me into the gigantic form of a scorpion.

This was idiocy.

This was sheer lunacy.

Were the Star Lords then so abysmal a pack of cretins?

The blue radiance closed around me.

"You idiots, you onkers of calsanys of Star Lords!" I roared. "How will taking me back to Earth help you now? I am going to Valka and to Vallia to raise an army to fight the Canops and to free Migla! As you commanded! Are you so stupidly dense as not to see that?"

The blueness wavered, not thickening; but not thinning, either. I sweated. Would these lofty Star Lords heed my impassioned call? Or were they truly less than perfect and blind to my purposes? I had fooled them before—or, rather, not so much fooled them as twisted their motives to my own ends. "I have to raise an army somewhere, and the Migla money will not serve against the Canops' control of the treasury!"

Familiar falling sensations swung me and I felt the faintness overcoming me. They were not listening! They were contemptuously hurling me back to Earth! This was unlike that other time I had struggled against the Everoinye, there in the courtyard of the Akhram as the Star Lords and the Savanti had through the agencies of the raptor and the dove sought to determine if I should stay on Kregen and to which side of the Eye of the World I should venture. I had gone eventually to the green north, to the land of the Grodnims. Who was to say what my fate would have been had I gone to the red south, to the land of the Zairians?

So, again, I struggled. I roared and raged and cursed and pleaded. The blue glow about me wavered uncertainly.

"If you banish me back to Earth now, you Opaz-forsaken cramphs, you will never free Migla! By the Black Chunkrah! Let me go to Valka and raise my own men. Then we will see how the army of Canopdrin fights!"

The scorpion leered down on me, at once surrounding me in the blue radiance and also hovering over me, that arrogant tail upflung as the constellation of Scorpio flings its tail across the night sky of Earth. I felt the beginnings of a fading, of a lessening of power and of a lightening of that lambent blueness. The glow blinded me. All I could see, suddenly and with a shocking clarity that told me the vision came from within my mind, the face of Delia blotted out everything else in the world of Kregen. But I did not utter her name aloud. Even then, onker that I am, I kept my wits about me. Instead, cunning with the cunning of the desperate, I screamed: "Let me go to Valka and there raise an army to fight for you, you—you Star Lords." The thought had occurred that cursing them might not help, either.

The blue radiance rippled, as a pool ripples from a flung stone, trembled, and—instantaneously—was gone.

Turko was looking at me quite normally and saying, "I agree this is an excellent voller. We can make about fifteen db* and with stops to pick up supplies should be there in three and a half or four days."

As far as he was concerned nothing had transpired. He did not know I had fought as hard a battle over my fate, dangled between two worlds four hundred light-years apart, as ever I had done—but not, Zair rot the Star Lords, as I was to do, as you will no doubt hear in due time.

Whatever their mysterious purposes were they clearly wanted me to reinstate the religion of Migshaanu—and her twin brother Migshenda the Stux, who was in something of a decline even compared with Migshaanu—pretty badly, enough to allow me to call them a bunch of onkers and calsanys and many another vile word I could put my tongue to. The voller drove up past that grove of trees sacred to Sidraarga and sped out over the face of the land spread beneath the moons of Kregen.

I was on my way home—home to Valka and to Delia.

* db: Dwaburs per bur.

# Chapter Six

## A stowaway and I
## part on the field
## of the Crimson Missals

Delia held me fast and would not let me go.

She clung to me, not sobbing, holding me tight, her arms wrapped about me, her dear form pressed against mine so that I could feel the beating of her heart.

And I held Delia, my Delia of Delphond, my Delia of the Blue Mountains—and, now, to our eternal glory, Delia, the mother of the twins, Drak and Lela.

We could have stood thus, breast to breast, locked in a thankfulness and a joy that was a mutual rapture, until the Ice Floes of Sicce went up in steam.

But, eventually, outside forces broke in as the Emperor strode testily into that inner chamber in the high fortress of Esser Rarioch overlooking my Valkan capital of Valkanium. The room was low-ceiled, and tastefully furnished with sturm-wood and tapestries, with rugs of Walfarg weave and silks of Pandahem strewn upon the low couches, and in the corners vast jars of Pandahem ware with many colorful and scented flowers springing in a blaze of beauty. On the windowsill sat a flick-flick in its pot; but it was likely to go hungry here, where the very cleanliness and beauty of the place must repel flies.

"Well, son-in-law, so you deign to return home to your deserted wife!"

Reluctantly, I released Delia. She wore a sheer gown of silk—not Pandahem silk but silk from Loh—of a pale glimmering laypom color, and her brown hair with that outrageous auburn tint shone in the mingled streaming radiance from Zim and Genodras shining splendidly in the sky of Kregen. I had taken time to wash myself after that mad dash across the skies in the voller with Turko. I would not voluntarily present myself before my princess in any other condition than of utmost cleanliness; but there had been no time to take the baths of nine. I wore my old scarlet breechclout, still, and a Havilfarese thraxter swung at my waist.

How Delia had shrieked when I appeared in the door, thrusting impatiently past guards and attendants and footmen. We kept no slaves, Delia and I, on any of our estates. She had shrieked once, and then thrown herself into my arms and held me—and now her father, the puissant Emperor, was here and demanding explanations I could not give him.

"Well, Dray Prescot," said Delia. "Am I your deserted wife?"

"Alas, my heart, to my shame, you have been." How much could I let the Emperor know? Delia already knew of my absences so inexplicable to her, absences which she met with the sturdy resources of a loving heart. She must be told the truth, and I knew that even if she could not understand—as, by Vox, neither did I understand myself—she would not call me a madman and run for the guards.

"I have been away on business near to us all," I said. And then I plunged. "I have brought back a voller—an airboat—that I do not think will break down or fail us."

"That I cannot believe."

"Indeed you would not, and I do not blame you for that. But I have been in Havilfar—"

"Havilfar!" They both said the word, astounded.

"Aye. There are secrets to be learned there it much behooves Vallia to learn."

"That is true, Dray, by Vox!" The Emperor scowled as he spoke. Every Vallian resented the dependence on the manufacturers of Havilfar for the supply of airboats that continually failed.

"How are you here, Emperor?"

"That daughter of mine—she insisted we bring every resource into looking for you. You vanished on your way from Valka to Zamra. We have combed every stew, every alley, every barracoon—although, Delia and you, between you, are closing the bagnios so fast you'll bankrupt us all."

"We will not talk of that, my father, at this time."

"As you will, daughter, as you will. Come, where is

wine? I would like to drink a toast to this wild leem of yours, who swings a sword and pulls my hair."

This was the man who had yelled a harsh command to his men to cut off my head—instantly. Well, times changed.

The twins were thriving wonderfully. Delia was blooming. Seg Segutorio and Thelda, his wife, the Kov and Kovneva of Falinur, were here also, aiding in the search for me. Inch, too, the Kov of the Black Mountains, with all his seven foot of height, was here. How we chuckled at these titles, for had we not all, at different times, been foot-weary nomads wandering with only our swords and our wits between us and destruction?

Also I saw my elders and council of Valka, and assured myself that everything ran smoothly. As I told Tharu ti Valkanium: "I warned you, Tharu, that I might be taken away on business. I am happy the island prospers so under your wise direction."

To which he replied: "I have the help of the elders and of fine young men like Tom ti Vulheim, Prince. We shall not fail you."

That evening in Esser Rarioch we caroused and sang in the Valkan way. The songs burst upward to the rafters, all songs we knew and loved. And, to my intense surprise, I found my Valkans singing that notorious song, "The Bowmen of Loh." Since I had introduced an honor guard of Valkan Archers to the imperial court, and since Seg had proved by deeds as well as words that he was a true friend to Dray Prescot, Prince Majister of Vallia and Strom of Valka, the Valkans accepted the Lohvian bowmen as equals. Seg and I exchanged wry smiles at this; but we kept our thoughts to ourselves.

"Crossbows, it is, in Havilfar, mostly, Seg."

"We can put ten arrows into the air while they wind up their monstrous contraptions."

"We will have need to. We cannot take all the men I would wish for."

I had conceived that the Emperor would prove a problem, and had not been altogether pleased he was here on my island of Valka when I would have thought him safely back in his capital of Vondium in Vallia. But since the abortive revolution had been put down, as I have told you, he was a much freer man. Now he surprised me by wholeheartedly flinging himself into preparations for the venture to Havilfar. He would be the mainspring that would enable me to collect airboats and men and to transport them to Migla. If he questioned why we must go to Migla and aid a halfling race against the Canops, who were apims like ourselves, he did not mention it. He did say, however, that the Miglas did not manufacture airboats, did they, Dray?

And I said they did not, but that they would be useful allies to us for the future.

He had a long eye, had the Emperor of Vallia. He nodded and set about collecting men and weapons and fliers.

If this was a confidence trick I was pulling on the empire of Vallia, it was on a gargantuan scale, and I was gleeful at my thoughts.

Vomanus, who was my half-brother-in-law, was away in Port Tavetus at this time, on the eastern coast of Turismond, no doubt drinking and wenching in his reckless way, and so was unavailable to come with us. Korf Aighos was in the Blue Mountains. But with Seg and Inch I wanted no other companions. Except for Nath and Zolta, my two oar comrades, those two rascals I had not seen for long and long.

In all this preparation Turko wandered like a man in a dream, dazed, and every time he saw me he would say, "Prince Majister," and shake his head. Then he would flex his muscles and so I would know he was all right. He would get on with my comrades, with Seg and Inch, for all that they were Kovs these days.

The day dawned when our preparations were ready. In the end his Pallans persuaded the Emperor it would be folly for him to go with us, and grumbling and reminding us of how he had fought the last bloody remnants of the third party led by Ortyg Larghos outside his own palace, he gave way. I felt relief.

Seg was bringing three thousand of his Crimson Bowmen of Loh. Tom ti Vulheim was bringing a thousand Valkan Archers. There were five thousand of my old Valkan fighters, men I had trained myself in the arts of war and with whom I had thrashed the aragorn and the slave-masters and so cleansed my island of Valka. Many of them still addressed me as Strom Drak. I did not mind. It was a name of honor.

We did not take a single mercenary. I had no desire to lead Chuliks or Rapas or Fristles up against the apims of Canopdrin. I had received a new insight into them, on the battlefield of Mackee, around the fires, among the wounded. They were men. We must deal with their noble masters, and then, I devoutly hoped, we could come to terms.

By the Emperor's express commands we collected an impressive fleet of fliers. They might fail us on the way. We had to accept that. The Vallian Air Service, trim in their blue uniforms and orange cloaks, would do all they could to bring us through. Chuktar Farris, the Lord of Vomansoir, would lead. I was pleased, for although we had met and got on well, our paths had not crossed as often as I would have wished.

We even had a few commercial airboats, and I was amused to see a couple of ice boats there, gray and ugly—but fliers, able to take a platoon of men into Havilfar.

So it was that under the light of the Suns of Scorpio we took off, a great aerial armada of better than a hundred and fifty fliers, slanting up against the rays of the suns, heading due south.

I had bidden farewell to the twins, Drak and Lela, and wondered what they made of this ugly-faced old graint of a fellow, who claimed to be their father. I could not find Delia. This was odd. I raged about the high fortress of Esser Rarioch, shouting, and maids and servants and guards ran hunting, but she was not to be found. My flier, which should have been up there leading the host alongside that of Chuktar Farris, waited on the flight platform overhanging the sea.

Then I slapped my gauntlet down on my thigh.

I should have known my Delia!

Seg and Inch had left, each leading his own contingent, and Inch had brought eight hundred bonny fighters from his Black Mountains, for we had not called on Korf Aighos for any of his Blue Mountain Boys. We were remiss in that, as Delia had prophesied, and the Korf followed us, in what fliers he could scrape up, swearing and cursing and his fingers itching for plunder.

So I vaulted up into the flier, and nodded to young Hikdar Vangar ti Valkanium, who had been a Deldar when I had been in most desperate straits in Vondium, and who now commanded my airboat. He saluted and started to yell his ritual orders to cast off, for he had seen how I had observed the fantamyrrh as I came aboard.

In the aft cabin, and hidden beneath a great pile of silks, I saw a rounded bottom in tight buff leathers only half concealed. I did not slap. The itch was there, but I did not.

I hauled her out.

She came, laughing, joyful, her gorgeous face glowing with fun and pleasure, that marvelous hair tumbled about her, her glorious brown eyes filled with the light of love.

I stood back and looked at her, and I put an expression on my face that would have cowed a leem and she laughed—she laughed!—and shook me and kissed me and so I was done for.

She wore buff leathers, and a brave scarlet sash around her waist, so narrow, so slender, so beautiful. Her form was something to take a man's breath away. She wore buff boots of supple lesten hide, reaching to the knee. At her side swung a rapier, and opposite the Jiktar she wore the Hikdar, the main-gauche. Her face glowed upon me.

"You did not think, darling Dray, that you could escape me again?"

"I had thought to leave you mewed up, in Esser Rarioch, to care for the sewing and the darning, the pot-washing and the clothes-scrubbing and the floor-cleaning. They seem fitting occupations—and the twins?"

This was a serious note.

"They are safe and cared for as no other children in all the world, my heart. Aunt Katri is there, and Doctor Nath the Needle, and there are so many nurses and handmaidens the children will never remain unwatched. And, Dray, they are so young! And, too, there is my father...."

"All right, you female schemer. But, remember, as soon as we have freed the Miglas from the Canops—it is home for us!"

"Amen to that, my heart."

So we pressed on through the air levels. Due south we drove, keeping mainly over the open ocean and retracing the course taken by Turko and myself. We passed the Koroles, the group of islands extending tonguelike from the eastern seaboard of Pandahem. We kept a lookout, for the Pandaheem do not buy airboats from Havilfar, but they had a few examples, all the same, and we wished for no trouble from the ancient foes of Vallia. I wondered how Tilda the Beautiful fared, and her son Pando, the Kov of Bormark, an imp of Satan if ever there was one. And Viridia the Render—was she still pirating away over there up the Hoboling Islands?

Over the northern coast of Havilfar we passed, crossing Hennardrin but too far east to see the White Rock of Gilmoy. Now we crossed the vast plains and the enormous areas of cultivation, until we sped above the wild lands. We avoided that area where no flier would go—but not by much—and we saw only a few spots in the sky to indicate we might be observed. We understood the risks we ran. More than one flier had to descend because of these infernal faults of the airboats supplied to us by the manufacturers in Hamal. We pressed on, and those left behind carried out repairs and so took up the chase again. Straight to the northwestern shore of the Shrouded Sea we flew, independent of air currents or winds, and so swung away to the west and gave Yaman a very wide berth, to land within the circle of the back hills of Migla.

The Miglas greeted us in stupefaction.

Hamp and Med Neemusbane gaped, their ears flapping, their eyes goggling. Only Mog retained her composure. She cackled and her old nutcracker face snapped at me.

"I always knew you were no ordinary man, Dray Prescot. You conjure an army out of thin air—"

"An army I should have brought at the start. Then you would not mourn so many of your dead."

"Migshaanu the All-Glorious counts the cost. We who serve her do not. Go out to war, Dray Prescot, and the light of Migshenda the Stux shine upon you."

Which was all very nice and magniloquent; but the idea still rankled that I had allowed these cheerful flap-eared, rubber-toy Miglas to march off singing to a war which was quite outside their experience. I knew those gathered here would be by far a fitter and more efficient army than that first one; but the cost came high, too high for me, I fear, and thereby I betray just how soft I had become.

That evening as the final plans were made and the Miglas caught a little awed insight into the way my fighting-men of Valka and those other fighters from Vallia behaved, Delia and I stood looking up at the last of the suns' glow.

The giant golden and scarlet form of the Gdoinye swept over us. I pretended to ignore it. The Star Lords were observing me and making sure they received their pound of flesh.

"That bird, Dray. I have seen it before."

"Possibly. It is of no consequence—"

She put her arms on my shoulders and forced me to

look into her face. How sweet she was, clean and fresh and smelling so delectably of all the fabulous perfumes of paradise!

"Do not put me off, Dray. We both know the strange things that have happened to us—we have only to think back—"

"There is little I can tell you, dearest heart. I am constrained by forces I do not understand. I love only you. I love only you, and yet I love the twins, and I love this beautiful and cruel world of Kregen. I would not choose to leave all this—"

"How could you leave Kregen—unless you were dead? Oh, Dray! I did not mean to speak like this, on the eve of a battle."

I kissed her, a long, long kiss, and so silenced her.

When we drew back, I said, "Remember always, my Delia of Delphond, my Delia of the Blue Mountains. I love only you. Whatever I may do, that is why I live and breathe, that is why I am anything at all. If what I do seems strange, think only that I love only you."

I could not go on. I would have to tell her something, but I quailed from opening my weird story to the one person in two worlds from whom nothing should be hid. I would tell my Delia, one day. . . .

The sound of laughter and loud voices heralded the arrival of Turko, Seg, and Inch. Turko had been telling them of the Canops, and of the Battle of Mackee, and of how the army of Canopdrin used the shield. I, also, had told my men of the uses of the shield. But, as I have earlier told you, the men of Segesthes and Turismond, as of Vallia and Pandahem, rate the shield as a cowardly weapon, something to hide behind. I knew they would find out differently in the morning, and I prayed the discovery would not come too high in blood.

The plans were laid. If the Canops scouted us with their aerial cavalry, we would deal with them. Seg had the skills for that. We had both watched an army cut to pieces from the air, when the impiters of Umgar Stro destroyed the army of Hiclantung in the Hostile Territories. Now, we had bowmen who would do more damage than a hundred stux-men.

Of shafts the Emperor had scoured his empire and we had brought so many arrows that I had devoted all the draft animals and all the totrixes we could spare to bring them onto the field. Our fliers were equipped with efficient varters, varters and gros-varters made in Vallia. They would not fail us.

The Miglas with their shields were apportioned to the various formations from Valka. I bore down all opposition. I told them, in a very high and mighty fashion, that I was the Prince Majister of Vallia. I was also Strom of Valka. My men *would* be shielded by the Migla shield-bearers.

"If I see a man wantonly exposing himself to the Canops' crossbows, Seg, and you too, Inch, I will be most severe." And to Tom ti Vulheim, in command of the Archers of Valka, I said the same things. "We use our superior rate of discharge, and we swamp them with shafts. When we get to close quarters they will be shot to pieces. Then your rapiers, daggers, and glaives will have to stand against thaxter and shield." I didn't like that bit of it at all. But I showed my officers a few passes that would serve, and the Jiktars passed these on to the Hikdars, who in their turn instructed the Deldars. The Deldars with their brazen lungs bawled it out to the men, and I fancied that at least some of the instructions would penetrate those blockheaded if valiant warriors of mine. One day I would forge an army that was an army, here on Kregen. . . .

The day dawned brightly. She of the Veils had risen late and her pale orb gleamed bright pink against the blue, fading as the suns climbed, but remaining. I pointed this out to the men as an omen of good fortune. The ranks formed up after breakfast was eaten. My cavalry scouts informed me that the Canops, who I was sure had not spotted the fleet of fliers, had scouted the camp and that the main force, confident of an even greater victory than the last, had marched out. They would be breaking camp at about the same time as we were, and would be marching west as we marched east. I frowned. The suns would be in the eyes of my men.

Orders were given to the Vallian Air Service to prevent any aerial scouts from observing our movements. We saw one or two skirmishes in the hazy distance, dots swarming and sweeping about our fliers. The Canoptic vollers put in an appearance and were quickly seen off.

I said to Seg, "Take over the command, Seg. Keep them moving, but slowly. I do not want to engage with the suns in our eyes."

"Aye, Dray."

Hikdar Vangar had my airboat ready. She was the voller

70

we had taken from Faol and flown to Valka and back. We rose into the air and swept toward the army of Canopdrin. From up here I was impressed by the dressing and alignment of the Canops. The silver gleam from their standards, where Lem, the silver leem was flaunted, splintered into my eyes. Their whole mass advanced with a steady tread, perfectly confident. They were disciplined, professional fighting-men. My Bowmen of Loh were professionals too, but of the rest of my army all were rough and ready warriors, some drilled and trained by me, but ever ready to let warrior passions inflame them. Oh, we were not a wild undisciplined body of men claiming to be an army, as my savage clansmen were. We were a drilled army. But Vallia has been famed for her navy. She has always hired mercenaries for her fighting. This was, as I knew, the first time since beyond any memory, when Vallians themselves had stepped onto a foreign field in such numbers to do battle.

When I had seen what I needed we slanted back to the army.

I sent a messenger to Seg, telling him to trend his men away to the north. Along there a valley lay athwart the path of both armies. When I saw Seg reach the crest on the western side and halt I knew we had, for the moment at least, achieved a considerable advantage.

By the time the Canopdrin army formed up on the opposite crest the suns had risen enough to satisfy me, and, because we were in the southern hemisphere of Kregen, the suns would circle the heavens to the northward, behind us. I felt a little more pleased, then. A cavalry scout came in to report he felt sure the Canop king was with his army. He could not be sure, but . . .

If King Capnon, whom his nobles called the Great, was really with his army we might finish the thing in three hours of hard fighting.

Now the suns were high enough so that they formed no hazard to us at all. I lifted my sword. As you must guess I was carrying that Savanti sword I had taken from the dying hand of Alex Hunter. I wore Vallian buff, with a great scarlet sash, and sufficient armor to protect my vitals. Turko was there, at my back, a great shield upraised. Seg and Inch had both given me looks when Turko, unspeaking, unsmiling, had thus positioned himself. I had said, "Turko the Shield follows me," and they had nodded,

71

pleased, I liked to think, that they had someone else to keep me out of harm's way.

The sword slashed down.

The whole army advanced.

The Canops must have been puzzled. For instance, where had all these vollers sprung from? They did not recognize the markings. And now, an army of men—apims—marched toward them. But they were soldiers. They obeyed orders. And, led by King Capnon, their masters urged them on. With a great brazen roar from their trumpets, and with the silver leems high, they charged.

At once Seg halted. The Bowmen of Loh lifted their weapons.

Well, it is all a long time ago now, and so I shall not go into every gory detail of that battle. It took place along that valley, called the Valley of the Crimson Missals. Crimson missals are very rare, for the trees usually carry white and pink blossoms, and the valley was thusly famous and well known throughout Migla. So the Battle of the Crimson Missals began with the Crimson Bowmen of Loh, shielded by the crimson-clad Migla shield-men, shooting in a long series of controlled discharges that tore huge rents in the ranks of the Canops.

Powerful and deadly is the longbow of Loh. Those steel bodkin-tipped clothyard shafts, expertly fletched and flighted, skewered through the Canops like—well, to liken that sound and that sight to anything is to lessen it. The Lohvian longbowmen tore the heart out of the Canops.

Here was where Seg was able to show beyond dispute the superiority of the longbow over not only the Canoptic crossbow but the Valkan compound reflex bow. My Valkans raged, and led by Tom ti Vulheim, they raced forward, brushing aside the Migla shield-men, got themselves into range so that they too could join in that sleeting storm of shafts.

The Canops, although dreadfully stricken, did not lose their formation or their dressing. They closed up and charged, shields high, straight for our bowmen.

Many and many a Canop went down. I had to harden my heart, and I suffered. I remembered what Mog had told me of the devilish practices of these iron men of Canopdrin. Now their iron was of no avail against those withering shafts pouring down on them from the sky. A few soldiers reached our ranks so that our rapier-and-dagger

72

men could get to hand grips. The lines swayed and roiled, and then it was all over.

The crossbowmen had been shot down, their splendid weapons tumbled into the green grass. The crimson missals glowed in the light of the suns above them, and clumps of Canops formed in the shelter of the trees. They formed a shield wall and the branches deflected the arrows from them. The Miglas were yelling and prancing. So many men were involved that complete views of the scene were impossible without taking to the air.

I had a mind to let the remnants of the Canops alone, to survive. I remembered Naghan the Throat and Jedgul the Finger. They might be safe in the hospital in Yaman. But there were other men like them in that army trapped among the trees. Also, there were officers like Hikdar Markman ti Coyton. The face of Kregen would smile more cleanly if they were removed.

The decision was not too difficult, for there was a precedent.

"Tell Seg—tell the Kov of Falinur—to leave off now."

The message was taken by one of the small corps of aides I had quickly organized from young men anxious to play a part. His totrix bounded away. The Miglas were inflamed. This was their first heady taste of victory. The field presented a dreadful spectacle and I wanted to get in touch with the Canoptic hospital organization and arrange a truce so that the wounded might be speedily treated. We had brought doctors and medical equipment with us, but the Miglas were ill prepared. And the Miglas were inflamed. I caught a glimpse of crazy old Mog, wearing all her regalia, her golden staff lifted high, racing across the field astride a totrix, yelling blue bloody murder, thirsting for the blood of every Canop alive there.

Another aide was dispatched to bring her back.

I had done what the Star Lords commanded, but in my own mind this was only a beginning. Now must begin the harder task of reestablishing Migshaanu and of integrating the Canops with the Miglas. Failing that, I would find them a country they might make their home without bloodshed or dispossession of the people native to that land.

It seemed clear to me that the task must begin with the banishment of their king, if he still lived, and of the reversal of roles between common soldier and noble—judging by the examples I had met.

An attack made by armored Canops astride mirvols was beaten off with an ease that made me think back with some savage self-contempt to the way the mirvollers had ripped up that first raw Migla army. I thought I caught a glimpse of the scarlet and golden raptor, among the whirling bodies of the mirvols; but the glimpse was too quick for certainty. It would be like the Star Lords to keep this close an eye on what went on.

Delia rode out to me, her totrix an old nag and well worn down; but she had refused anything better, saying the best animals were needed by the fighters. Her presence thrilled me as always. She rode with a free fine grace. She hauled up, dust kicking from the totrix hooves, and she was not laughing.

Rather, she said, "This is a terrible business."

"Aye. But it is over now. Now we begin to put everything back in place."

"Those poor men—the arrows are so cruel."

"Some deserved it, some did not. Seg is ordering a cessation. We will get help for the wounded."

We dismounted, for her totrix threatened to keel over any minute and I wished to talk seriously to her. We went a little apart from the others, from my dwindled group of aides, from Mog and Mag, from the trumpeters and the standard-bearer. Oh, yes, Delia had not forgotten to bring a brand-new and impeccably stitched flag with her. My own old flag—the yellow cross on the scarlet field, the flag that fighting-men called "Old Superb"—had floated over our victory.

Turko the Shield gazed after us, but he had sense enough not to intrude.

"We have won a victory, Delia, my heart. But you must wonder why it had to be, why I became involved with this backward country in Havilfar which is generally more advanced than other places—"

"Really, Dray!"

"I know what you think. But Vallia cannot produce fliers."

"No. But Father says this is a first step in the right direction."

"So it is. But I would like to tell you why, my Delia."

She looked up at me, perfectly aware of the seriousness of the moment, her soft lips half parted, her brown eyes brilliant upon me, waiting for me to speak. A little movement scuttled in the dusty grass at her booted feet.

"We have won a victory, Delia."

And now I must relate a thing that seemed impossible to me at the time, and still strikes as strange and weird as anything I encountered on two worlds.

For Delia looked down sharply, and without screaming or starting, said, "Oh, Dray! A *scorpion*!"

I looked.

The reddish brown scorpion scuttled past Delia's boots. It halted before me and that damned arrogant tail lifted. I did not move. Delia, with a single glance at my face, remained silent.

And then—Dear God!—the scorpion spoke to me.

I thought I was hallucinating again, as I had done in that first dreadful attempt to cross the Klackadrin when the Phokaym had captured me. I put a hand to my head, staring at the scorpion.

"Dray Prescot," said the scorpion in a reedy and shrill voice not unlike a buzz saw ripping through winter logs. I did not think anyone else might hear that baleful voice.

"Dray Prescot. Perhaps you are not so great a fool as we thought." The Gdoinye had spoken to me. A bird had spoken to me. Was a scorpion any the more strange in this weird and wonderful, beautiful and horrible world of Kregen? "You have done what you were commanded to do. We acknowledge your deeds. Now you have our leave to depart from here, to Hyrklana—"

I shouted in my old savage, intemperate way. "I am not going to Hyrklana!"

Just how it was done I did not know, could not know. But, on the instant, black clouds roiled across the sky. Huge raindrops began to fall, gouting the dust into fountains, spreading and joining and coalescing into rivulets trickling down into the Valley of the Crimson Missals. In a twinkling the darkness of the clouds shut off every other person from my sight. Thunder boomed.

"Delia!" I shouted. "Delia!" I screamed it out, spinning around, lost and shut away and condemned. "*Delia!*"

"Dray!"

I heard her answering call, but faint, faint. "Dray! Where are you, dearest heart?"

"Delia! Here—I am coming to you!"

I blundered in the direction of her voice.

"Dray! It is dark and I cannot see— Oh, Dray!"

The shape of a terrified totrix reared above me in the gloom, his hooves wicked.

I ducked and heard a faint and dwindling cry: "Dray—"

And then the blue radiance swamped down about me and that greater representation of a scorpion caught me up in its ghastly blue embrace and I was falling and spinning and tumbling away into a long blue tunnel of nightmare.

## *Chapter Seven*

### Of the descent
### of a slate slab and
### a scarlet breechclout

Yells of panicking men and shrieks of terrified women burst all about me as I sat up, cursing, and looked upon a bedlam. Trust the damned Star Lords to pitchfork me headlong into frantic action. I knew why I was here— wherever here might be. Someone was in danger. Someone was in deadly peril and the Star Lords wanted them rescued—so, send for Joe Muggins, Dray Prescot. He'll land flat on his back, stark naked, unarmed, and he'll sort out the problem, never you fear.

Oh, yes, I cursed the Everoinye to the Ice Floes of Sicce and gone as I climbed to my feet and started to sort out what the hell now the Star Lords had chucked me into.

I stood in a cavern carved from virgin rock, the marks of chisels sharp and distinct upon the walls and roof giving no indication of the age of the place. It was clean and only a little dust puffed as the crazed mob of people ran and struggled madly from the square-cut opening through which streamed the mingled streaming rays of the Suns of Scorpio.

I could hear brazen lungs yelling orders out there, and the harsh blocky silhouettes of halflings in armor packed the entrance. Men and women ran screaming past me and plunged headlong into a farther opening, smaller, in the back wall. About twenty people were left to struggle through, away from the armored halflings raging to get at them. These people wore decent blue robes and dresses, had sandaled feet, combed hair, clean faces and arms. Most of the women wore bangles and bracelets of cheap imitation jewelry: Krasny ware, but pretty in their way. Now every face was a mask of horror. There were a few children there also, running fleetly between the legs of their elders, skipping for the far opening and safety.

Then I saw the smooth slab of slate descending. It dropped smoothly and slowly down over the exit and when it touched the floor it would wall off the way of escape from the halflings and give safety to those who had passed through.

But there were still these last twenty to pass through. And the descending slab would shut them out of safety, shut them back in this cavern with the swords and spears of the halflings, who, I now saw, were Rhaclaws, most savage and unpleasant. So I, Dray Prescot, pawn of the Star Lords, must rescue them.

"By Zair!" I said feelingly. At my side on the floor—and next to an overturned sturm-wood bench and a gilt cup still rolling and spilling its dark wine across the rock, a positive indication of how suddenly and how recently all this panic had begun—lay a length of scarlet humespack. I grabbed it on my way toward that descending slab of slate, wound it roughly about my loins. People tended to get in the way as I ran, trying to thrust their way through the narrowing opening.

"Out of the way, onkers!" I roared, and barged on. I got my fingers under the hard edge of slate and then my shoulders. I braced my legs apart. I could feel the weight coming on. It grew and grew and pressed me down so that I felt my feet would puncture the rock of the floor.

Men and women flung frightened glances my way, but they did not stop, and scurried past me, to left and right, as I stood there like poor old Atlas, chained by the weight of Kregen.

I could feel my muscles cracking. I bent a little—I had to—and the massive slate slab inched down. Now there were barely ten people left, and I heard a woman—a short but plumply rounded woman with a tumbled wealth of dark hair falling across her face and the shoulders of her blue gown—calling to her son and daughter, as I judged.

"Hurry, Wincie, hurry, Marker! This great paktun is holding the door! It will not crush you!"

The children squealed and the little girl, Wincie, all disarrayed black hair and long naked legs and flickering petticoats, dived between my legs. Those legs of mine corded under the strain. Sweat ran down my body, and my muscles bulged, my chest arched and resisting, backbone taut. I knew I could not hold much longer, for the weight of the slab was immense. But now there were only five people left, and then three and then one.

This one halted, ducking his head to pass by my left shoulder. The edge of the slab pressed cruelly into the flesh, denting it to the bone. My fingers were bone-white as I gripped the slate, heaving against the dead weight.

"I would not believe it possible, my friend," he said. He was a well-set young man, with quick direct eyes flecked with green. His blue robe had been tucked up into a lesten-hide belt from which swung a small, curved, overly ornamented dagger. His brown hair clustered in curls. "You must let go or you will be caught, too."

A stux pranged off the slate above our heads and I said, "By Vox! Get inside, onker, and run!"

His handsome face flushed and he stepped past me.

Another stux barely missed my side.

I had to now let go this monstrous thing bearing down on me, and somehow summon the strength and agility to dodge backward and so let it rumble all the way down and bar off those blockheaded Rhaclaws. I was breathing in jerks and gasps, and specks and shards of fire splashed across my eyes. Sweat stung and near blinded me. Another stux nicked my calf and I cursed and tried to move my hands away and found they would not obey my will.

I could not move my body!

So great had been the pressure bearing down on me my body had locked in defiant resistance. Now I could not move. The gigantic slab of slate trapped me as a silversmith traps a bangle in the jaws of his vise.

Yet if I did not drag myself free those Opaz-forsaken rasts of Rhaclaws would be able to pass under the slab and so enter the escape tunnel. Then all my efforts would have been in vain. The halflings would be upon the terrified fugitives, hacking and cutting and capturing. I fought with my own body, there in a rocky cavern, trapped between a massive descending slab of slate and the rocky floor beneath my feet.

I felt a nudge in the small of my back.

A voice said: "I am Mahmud nal Yrmcelt, oaf, as you must very well know. And I do not take kindly to being dubbed onker." His finger jabbed me in the back again.

80

"But I will condone it now, for you are a remarkable man. Now, oaf, let me take a part of the slab—"

I managed to speak. I truly felt if I had not interrupted he would have gone prattling on until the Rhaclaws were upon us. They were advancing more cautiously now, and I guessed their eyes had not fully adjusted to the interior of the cavern from the brightness of the suns without.

"No." I hacked the words from a corded throat. "No. I cannot move—so you must push me."

"My oafish friend! You will fall into the rasts!"

"There is no other way—you cannot pull me—*push*!"

A woman screamed shrilly and most distressingly from somewhere in the greater darkness at his back. He did not hesitate more. "May Opaz the Mighty and All-Beneficent have you in his keeping, and may the Invisible Twins smile upon you—" And he put his booted foot against my back and thrust.

At the same time I summoned up every last shred of willpower I possessed and forced my body to obey. I got my hands free and moved my feet and then Mahmud nal Yrmcelt's thrust kicked me clear. The slab smashed down with a great and horrible thunking, so that slate chips flew from the bottom edge.

Hands caught me as I sprawled forward. My body felt as though it had been knotted and starched and then unwound, aching inch by aching inch. I shuddered and drew huge gasping breaths. I tried to twist my arm away. Slick with sweat as it was it should have sprung away easily. But the locked grip of the Rhaclaw held fast. My limbs trembled. I felt a trilling vibration all through my poor abused old body and I knew I wasn't going to clamber to my feet and bash a few skulls for some time yet.

Mind you, I promised myself as I was swiftly carried out into the sunshine some skull-bashing seemed an inevitable prospect.

Once more my duty—imposed and arbitrary—to the Star Lords had flung me headlong into danger and perils of a kind I could not then conceive, but which were to become hatefully familiar in the succeeding days.

Assuming two things—one: that my transit here from the battlefield of the Valley of the Crimson Missals had followed immediately in time, and I was not caught in another of those weird and damnable time loops of the Star Lords (and, as you will hear, that was a mistaken assumption); and, two: the weather had not changed drastically—I fancied I was not very many dwaburs nearer the equator. The suns gave me that impression. Of course, as Kregen swings about the Suns of Scorpio they will appear to change in size, and their size changes are visibly greater than that of old Sol from Earth. The air had a warmer feel, and there were unfamiliar scents from the trees and flowering bushes surrounding the entrance to the cavern.

Twin shadows fell from my horizontal body as I was hauled out.

I was dumped into the back of a quoffa cart. Above me reared a craggy cliff face, its fissures dappled with the glowing colors of rock plants and the green of shrubs. A fringe of thorn-ivy grew in a level line I did not think natural about a hundred feet up that cliff. I had the hope that the terrified people would escape from secret exits tunneled into the rock.

The quoffa were whipped into action. I frowned. Of all the animals of Kregen the quoffa least need chastisement. With their huge, patient old faces and their perambulating hearth-rug bodies, they are docile and obedient and completely lovable and dependable. The carts creaked and moved forward. There were seven carts and each was stuffed with half-naked men and women and halflings, all bound with thongs, and most groaning and crying and sobbing and lamenting.

No need to inquire what was going on, or who we were.

I was partially wrong in that instinctive assessment, as you shall hear. But the difference was, if Zair will forgive me, a difference I was to welcome.

The fact that I was also bound made little impression, for my muscles seemed still locked in the stasis caused by holding up that damned great weight. The thongs were of a kind and thickness—they were not lesten-hide—I would have snapped by a single muscular surge.

We bumped along and I took in the new sights and impressions around me as a matter of course. That length of scarlet cloth I had picked up in the cavern worried me. It hung around my hips now, and I was as respectably dressed as many of the slaves. Always—so far—the Star Lords and the Savanti had brought me to Kregen stark naked. The Star Lords dumped me down into diabolical situations naked and unarmed and with only my wits and strength and cunning to get me through. I had understood that I would think less of them as they of me had they provided me clothes and weapons, a helmet, and a spear, say, a sword and shield. But this time a damned scorpion had chittered words at me, and called me by my name, and in this new emergency I had found a length of scarlet humespack. Was that coincidence? Or had the Star Lords decided to give me a little more assistance than they had ever done before?

We bumped along between the trees and so came out onto a reasonably good road, dusty but firm. On either hand stretched vast fields ablaze with flowers. Soon this purely decorative agriculture gave way to crops thriving under the suns. I saw marspear and sweet corn—which I detest—and crop plants of kinds unfamiliar to me then. Because I could see out only backward, like the man who always sits with his back to the engine, I had no idea of where we were being carried. The fields opened and I saw good quality fat cattle grazing, with men riding zorcas among them. We passed occasional hamlets with small cottages made from honest brick with thatched roofs, and a village well. The procession wound on and I felt hungry and thirsty; but we stopped only once to be given sips of water from huge orange gourds, and a mouthful of palines each. The palines were thrust into our open mouths by skinny, gaunt lackadaisical girls with stringy hair, who ministered to the Rhaclaws. Then we creaked and groaned on our way.

This was a rich land. That was very clear.

We passed a gang of slaves digging ditches, and I marked the Fristles who stood guard, as well as Ochs who wielded the whips.

Suddenly there came a bustling commotion and the old quoffas were lashed to the side of the road, the wheels of the carts slipping into the drainage ditch. I heard the crash and stamp of metal-studded sandals.

A column of infantry passed. I thought, at first, they were Canops. But no pagan silver image of Lem, the leaping leem, crowned their standards. These soldiers with their tall helmets, tufted with feathers from the whistling faerling, with their scaled and plated armor, greaves, shields, stuxes, thraxters, and crossbows, marched following a golden image of a zhantil.

If I thought of Pando, boy Kov of Bormark, then, who can blame me?

Of almost all the wonderful wild animals of Kregen, I might have chosen a zhantil for my standard.

We were hauled out of the ditch and went on, and a bur or so later, again were driven off the road by the passage of a brilliant body of zorcamen. They were resplendent in armor and gems, silks and embroideries, their lances all slanting at the same angle, their helmets ashine under the suns. They trotted past most gallantly. I wouldn't have minded ripping each one from his ornate saddle and breaking his back across my knees. But I, Dray Prescot, still felt the effects of that damned great slate slab. By the time we passed under an archway and I heard the muted roar of a great city all about me, the stiffness was wearing off. The suns hung low in the sky and the horizon sheeted in emerald and crimson, opaz colors filled with a dying radiance. Then towers and ramparts and roofs jagged against that sky glory and the shadows dropped down.

The carts pulled into a flagged courtyard and the Rhaclaws yelled commands. Torches flared. Stone walls, frowning and somber, rose about us. We were hauled out and pushed and prodded into line. Although the stiffness had quite worn off now, and I had bulged my muscles and found to my satisfaction that my battered old body responded once more to my will, I fell down and lay on the stone flags. I was kicked. I continued to lie there. I was looking for the man in command.

Then I saw him. A Jiktar, he strutted out, rather paunchy as to waist and puffy as to feature, but a fighting-man for all that. His armor glinted redly in the torchlight.

"Won't get up, Notor," reported the Deldar in command of the slave detail.

"If he's damaged goods he is of no use to us." The Jiktar's words carried a nasal whine. He glared down on me.

This, I felt, must be the time. I had suffered a very great deal. I had been kicked and prodded and mauled, and I was bound with thongs and I was destined for slavery. Well, someone would be sorry for all that before I was finished.

I broke the bonds with a single convulsive jerk.

I stood up.

The Rhaclaws began to yell at once.

The Jiktar took a step back, and then I took his pudgy throat between my fists. I did not kill him. I threw him at the nearest bunch of Rhaclaws. They are a stocky lot, the

84

Rhaclaws, with two arms and two legs, and heads that are so large and dome shaped that, lacking a neck, their chops seem to rest on their shoulders and, as Zair is my witness, are almost as wide as those shoulders. I say they do not have necks; this is not perfectly true. They do have a small disclike neck that enables their massive domed heads to swivel. Now their two legs apiece did not stop them from toppling over in a muddle as the Jiktar struck them.

"Seize him!" someone was yelling, as there is always someone willing to shout those easy words rather than to dive in.

I picked up a Rhaclaw who was driving in with his stux low at me, and whirled him about my head. I yelled, then, like a fool: "Hai, Hikai!"

The huge domed head of the Rhaclaw cut a swath through his fellows. I forged on. Things were becoming interesting. One or two of the slaves were beginning to jump up and down, and at least three of them had freed themselves from their bonds. We might make a tasty little party of this yet.

The gate lay open. No one had thought to close it on a rabble of cowed slaves. The Rhaclaw-club in my fists cleared a path. I aimed for the gate. Torchlight spattered the scene with drops of ruby radiance. Shadows writhed at the gate and I saw a Hikdar—he was apim—hurling his stux.

A quick roll of the wrists interposed my human club and the Rhaclaw made no sound, for he was already unconscious, as the stux penetrated his chest.

I bashed my way on, and dodged two more flung stuxes, and then a Rhaclaw came at me with a thraxter. He was smashed to the side. His great domed head struck the gate, burst, and blood and brains splashed out, vivid in the torch glare.

I felt sorry for him. But then, he should never have hired out as a mercenary had he not envisaged some such bloody ending.

"Run with me, comrades!" I roared at the slaves.

Some responded. I saw a burly fellow with a shock of villainous black hair slashing about him with a thraxter. He handled the weapon as he would handle a cutting knife in the cane fields. Others ran to follow me.

Swinging back to the gate I started through, and this time I draped the senseless Rhaclaw over my back and so heard the individual sick chunk of three stuxes as they smashed into him, poor chap, instead of my naked back.

I was through the gateway.

The torchlight dimmed, but the Maiden with the Many Smiles floated serenely above, a little cloud drifting across her smiling pink face.

Fresh torches blazed before my face. A group of men riding half-voves halted and the glitter from their accouterments near blinded me. I shook my hair back and glared up at them.

Their leader stared down, remote, in complete command, with a haughtiness I recognized and loathed.

"Hai, Jikai!" I roared, and swung the dead Rhaclaw and let fly at this supercilious rast astride his half-vove. He ducked. The Rhaclaw flew past.

The half-vove rider spoke in an icy tone of voice.

"Take him alive!"

The half-voves closed in.

Well, they were tougher opponents, but I could handle them.

From nowhere a net descended about me, enveloping me. I had no knife, no sword. I fought the strands, the smothering folds tangling and obstructing. Men dropped from the high saddles of the half-voves and closed in. Their thraxters gleamed most wickedly in the confused lights of the torches and of the Maiden with the Many Smiles.

I took two strands of the net into my fists and wrenched, and wrenched two more, and so tore a hole in the net.

I thrust up through the net, kicking it from me.

The first man was upon me.

I slid his sword, chopped him across the neck, took his sword away, and parried the immediately following onslaught from three of his fellows.

They sought to strike me with the flat and so knock me senseless.

I used the edge, for I cared nothing of them.

They wore armor and billowing cloaks, very romantic in the streaming moonlight. I was near naked, clad only in an old scarlet breechclout I had had no time to fasten properly.

That I, Dray Prescot, Krozair of Zy, Lord of Strombor—and much else besides—should be laid low by a breechclout!

And—my own old scarlet breechclout, at that.

I sprang and leaped and fought and beat them back and so took stock of a fine half-vove and readied myself to leap upon his broad back and so urge him away with those special clansmen's words that only we and the voves may understand.

I leaped all right—but I was heading downward instead of upward.

The scarlet breechclout had finally untwisted and fallen about my legs. Tripped, I pitched headlong.

In the next moment something extraordinarily hard and heavy sledged alongside my head and there was no time for a single chime from the bells of Beng-Kishi.

# Chapter Eight

## In the Jikhorkdun

Nath the Arm glowered on the recruits as we stood on silver sand in the wooden-walled ring, blinking in the suns-light, shuffling our feet. We were coys, for anything that is young and green and untested on Kregen is often dubbed a coy, with a sly laugh, and we screwed up our eyes and stared up at Nath the Arm as he looked down on us from his pedestal.

"Unequal combat is the secret," he roared at us. "That is what pulls the crowds. You'll be unequal, and if you live, maybe you'll be unequal the other way." Nath the Arm chortled, his massive black beard oiled and threaded with gold, his wide-winged ruby-colored jerkin of supple voskskin brilliant with gems, his kilt a splash of vivid saffron. He wore silver greaves. His black hair, graying at the temples, was savagely cut back around his ears.

The villainous fellow with the black hair who had thrashed about with the sword, back where I had chastised the Rhaclaws, swallowed and grimaced at me. "Unequal?"

"Silence, rasts!" Nath the Arm thumped a meaty fist onto the wooden rail before him. His face, leathery, whiskered, and lined, crisscrossed with old scars, loomed above us, the huge blue-black beard glittering with gold. "You talk when I tell you. You do *anything* when I tell you."

As though we had been faced with a victorious render crew we had been given the alternatives. We could become slaves and work on the farms or in industry or the mines. We might become fodder for the Jikhorkdun. We might, if we thought ourselves apt enough with a weapon, become kaidurs, beginning, of course, as coys. Or, we could be slaughtered, there and then, out of hand.

Some, who with a shake of the head said they knew of these things, had chosen to go as slaves.

88

Those of us here, in the small sanded practice ring hot and sticky beneath the Suns of Scorpio, had chosen to become coys and so perhaps, one day, if we lived, to become kaidurs.

Escape, we had been told, was impossible, and then, with many a sly wink and nod, Nath the Arm pointed out to us the wonderful advantages enjoyed by a great kaidur: the gold he received as purses, the girls who sighed and lusted for him, the wine he might quaff, the soft living between bouts in the Jikhorkdun where the maddened crowd showered him with plaudits.

The arena, Nath the Arm told us, was the life for a man.

Well, I had heard a little of the arenas of Hamal and of Hyrklana, and we were in the capital city of Hyrklana, Huringa, just as the scorpion had promised me.

Listening as Nath the Arm threatened and promised I had already agreed with myself that at the first opportunity I would test if escape was impossible or not. I needed to get back to Migla and discover what was going on there, after the great Battle of the Crimson Missals, and assure myself that Delia was safe. I shuddered more than a little, as you may well judge, at the thought that any of my comrades might discover how I had tripped over my own scarlet breechclout. How Seg and Inch would roar! How Hap Loder and Prince Varden would chuckle! How Turko would lift a quizzical eyebrow! How, in short, all my good comrades would think it a great jest that I, Dray Prescot, had been brought low by a breechclout.

Questions as to dates produced the same bewildering and conflicting replies as one would find over all of Kregen. Men called their days by names they fancied themselves, and sennights likewise. With seven moons floating in the sky the month—surprisingly moon-cycle mensuration was known and practiced—hardly counted. As for seasons, men dated the beginning of a seasonal cycle from many and various occurrences. Usually it would be from the founding of a city, as in the case of Rome on Earth, or a great game cycle, as of the Greeks and their Olympiads, or the birth of a great philosopher, or the travel of a seer from the place of his birth to the place of his ministry, very familiar to us on Earth. Hyrklana dated her seasons from the foundation of the Lily City Klana—the old capital away down in the south of the island, long since tumbled into ruin. By that reckoning this was the year

89

2076. A relatively new nation, on Kregen, then, the people of Hyrklana.

I wondered if I would meet Princess Lilah. That, I owned as I sweated through the drills prescribed by Nath the Arm, would be pleasurable. I was human enough to admit that a great deal of the pleasure would come from what I hoped would be her immediate adoption of me as friend and her instant removal of my ugly old carcass from the arena. But I knew, too, that the deeper part of that pleasure would be in the knowledge she had escaped successfully astride that fluttrell from the Manhounds of Faol.

We were afforded an early opportunity to see what occurred in the Jikhorkdun of this city of Huringa.

The suns shot their brilliant rays across the raked silver sand. Blood spots were covered with fresh sprinkled sand, raked and leveled. Deeply into the ground, in a great natural hollow, had been set the arena. Around it and sloping up the sides of the honeycombed hill rose tier after tier of seats and private boxes. Above these towered the walls, lofting high, carrying the terraced seating away up to dizzying heights. I have mentioned that the telescope is known on Kregen, and a spectator up there would have need of one when the combats were staged down in the arena. When the peculiar Kregan form of vol-combat was produced, then everyone had his or her own chance to see everything that might occur.

The coys clustered at iron bars covering the exit from an apprentice kaidurs tunnel.

I could see the opposite loft of the amphitheater. The spectacle presented a dizzying perspective of towering multicolored masses, of thousands of faces, mere white or tan or black dots, thousands of people, both halfling and apim, cheering and screaming and gesticulating, hurling down flowers or fruit rinds, old cheeses, rotten gregarians, hurling down golden deldys and silver sinvers and copper obs.

The roar, the noise, the sheer caterwauling bedlam of it all broke about our heads like a rashoon bursting in primitive violence.

"By Opaz!" breathed Naghan the Gnat, at my side. A little fellow, all gristle and bone, he stared out in great apprehension.

"No wild beast will wish you to fill his belly, Naghan the Gnat!" bellowed Lart the Stink. He was aptly named,

90

and we gave him a wide berth. We had fallen into a rough comradeship, these coys in this training bunch, about twenty of us. We lived and ate and talked together. We trained in the wooden-walled ring, one of many set in the complex of buildings and courtyards to the rear of the amphitheater. Now we were watching what we would be doing in a sennight or less.

Men strutted out there, their armor blinding in the light of Far and Havil, the twin Suns of Scorpio, named thus here in Havilfar. We saw the quick twinkle of swords, the bright gush of blood. We saw and understood what Nath the Arm meant about unequal combat, for swordsman was not pitted against swordsman; rather, the Hyrklanish relished a swordsman against a stux-man, or a rapier-and-dagger man against a shield-and-buckler man, a retiarius against a slinger. We saw the way the fights went. We sweated out all one long afternoon there, clutching those iron bars, hearing the horrid yells of the crowd and the despairing screams of the dying. As a final fillip a bunch of slaves who had not been selected for anything useful in the land were herded out, and wild neemus, black and sleek and deadly, devoured them with a great crunching of bones and a spilling of blood.

There were many things that went on in the Jikhorkdun of Huringa I will not mention to you, for we are supposed to be civilized people, and such things are abhorrent to us.

Yet was not the land of Hyrklana civilized? Did they not manufacture airboats? And was not that beautiful girl, the Princess Lilah of Hyrklana, one of the inhabitants of this island? Truly, civilization means many different things in the different worlds of space.

Naghan the Gnat said, "They will not get me out there!"

The Hyrklanish who organized the games for the arena employed Rhaclaws and other beast-men to control the kaidurs. They told Naghan the Gnat what would happen to him if he did not venture out upon the silver sand with us. He shivered; but he took his stux in hand and crept out with us when it was our turn, the day appointed for us to show if we could live through the unequal combat and so begin the long path of combat and victory that might lead to perhaps just one of us becoming a kaidur.

The amphitheater had been built in a classically oval shape. The lofting terraces had been divided vertically into four sections, each section, rather naturally, with one of the four full colors: blue, green, yellow, red. It fell to our lot to walk out onto the sand wearing red breechclouts, a red favor tied about our left arms, and a small leather helmet with tall red feathers. As you may imagine, I was not displeased that chance had brought me to fight once again under the red.

We each had two stuxes.

From the blue corner trotted half-men wearing half-armor, with blue favors and feathers, and carrying thraxters and shields. I frowned. This was unequal combat with a vengeance!

And yet there were twenty of us and only fifteen of the blues.

The beast roar from the crowded benches had to be ignored, to be rubbed away from the consciousness. We advanced over the silver sand and the suns burned down and the smell of beasts and the smell of human blood and sweat dizzied us. The blues formed a neat line and walked slowly towards us. We had been told what we must do. If we won, very well. But, as Nath the Arm had said, one thick hand searching his gold-threaded beard: "Whatever happens, you reds! Die well! Die like men! In dying show that you might have become kaidur!"

Each color had its own complex of training rings behind the amphitheater. I could not fail to understand Nath the Arm's passionate desire for the reds to do well. This utter obsession with the Jikhorkdun besotted almost everyone in the city. Huge bets were wagered. Enormous sums of money, and land, zorcas, and vollers too, changed hands every day.

Through that crazed blood-lusting thunder of voices we heard Nath the Arm's fierce last words.

"Fight well, reds! Fight for the ruby drang!"

The thought that for almost no extra reason at all Nath the Arm would leap out after us and join us in the fight was not an idle one. Nothing in Hyrklanan Huringa could arouse the passions as the chances and thrills and excitement of the Jikhorkdun.

The reds fought for the ruby drang.

The blues fought for the sapphire graint.

I knew that the yellows fought for the diamond zhantil.

The greens fought for the emerald neemu.

People were still crowding into the amphitheater, running down the steeply sloping stairs and edging along the terraces. This was still early in the day and the coys were put on as a mere appetizer, to keep the crowds amused before the main bouts. All the important combats would take place just before and during and after noon, so that the twin suns shining down would cast as few shadows as possible from the uplifting walls. After that, the spectacles tended more to the mammoth and bloodletting-in-droves style, with the skill and professional daring of the kaidurs over for the day. Usually—not always, as I was to find.

The blues advanced in their neat line. I judged they were apprentice kaidurs, just out of the coy stage. They were not apims. They were Blegs. If you have seen a representation of the face of a Persian leaf bat you may have some faint idea of the appearance of the faces of the Blegs. They do not possess the large and typical bat ears; their coloring is brilliant green and yellow and purple, with bright fur and skin patches; their lower jaws hang and the thin membrane there droops, to reveal a row of small, thin, and intensely sharp teeth. They have arms and shoulders very apimlike; their bodies are not unlike a man's; but they have four legs from which the trunk springs almost vertically, rather like a tower rising from a four-legged support. Over their backs lies an atrophied carapace and it is thought they once had the power of flight.

The Blegs are considered, on a planet famed for its prolific life, as among the most hideous of quasi-humans.

Like almost any species on Kregen, the Blegs may be found in any of the continents and islands; but they are more usually to be found on Havilfar. Given that wide spread of the temperate regions north and south of the equator that makes so much of Kregen comfortably habitable to intelligent beings, one would expect to find a wide spreading of life-forms, flora and fauna, particularly as through the use of fliers, seeds and spores and people may move relatively freely from landmass to landmass.

The beast roar of the crowd, the reek of thousands of people crammed together, the heat of the suns, the crisp sliding feel of sand beneath my feet—I can feel them all as though they happened this morning. Yet I felt no animosity toward these hideous Blegs. They were halflings, beast-men, and yet I was being forced into fighting them for the debased amusement of these decadent spectators massed around me in the amphitheater.

Naghan the Gnat kept close to me. His thin, wiry frame looked more scrawny than ever beside the massive muscle of Lart the Stink and of Cleitar Adria. These advanced boldly toward the Blegs.

If what I am about to tell you appalls you, makes you sick, gives you a strong sense that I, Dray Prescot, am a very beast in truth, I cannot blame you. We had been given wine before we stepped into the arena, a rough red wine much like vinegar, poured carefully by Fristle women from leather bags into our leather cups. We had drunk deeply, for the day was hot and we faced dangers we would rather not face.

Cunning are the ways of the managers of the Jikhorkduns!

Not only were the four colors pitted one against the other, in two, three, and four way combats, but the races and species were pitted one against another, so that it was rare except in special wagered combats to find apim against apim, Och against Och, Fristle against Fristle, Bleg against Bleg. The Jikhorkdun demanded a man fight against other men who aroused in him the deepest and most basic fears and furies of blood.

Among the ranks of the reds were Blegs, and they might on the following day be set against apims—men like me—wearing the blue.

But all that might be lived with. I was prepared to fight if that meant I might stay alive.

The subtle cunning of the Jikhorkdun managers—and, yet, not so subtle, not so cunning; rather, inevitable—saw to it that the wine was drugged with the crushed distillations of the sermine flower. Already I could feel a rage growing within me. I did not know then the wine was drugged. I did not discover this for some time. But I must mention it now, to try to explain why I did what I did.

Yes, I even felt a glow of prowess, as though I had performed a great Jikai! Deep was my shame, I acknowledge, for I had lived and others had died.

"Come, brothers," growled Cleitar Adria. His tanned skin showed a light dusting of golden hair; his braided hair had been caught up beneath his leather cap. He had told me he had been quoffa handler, until he had mentioned, when drunk, that the queen should be put down, and the king too. From that speech until his appearance in the arena his progress had been swift and inevitable. He had not been slave. Now he shouted and lifted his javelin. "Let us destroy these Blegs, and have done!"

And I, Dray Prescot, shouted, "With all my heart!" and so hurled the first stux.

The cast was shrewd. It slid between the shield and the armor of a Bleg and transfixed him, whereat he shrieked and writhed and fell.

With four legs, a Bleg was a difficult foeman to knock over.

With a series of bloodthirsty shouts, the two lines met.

We should have had little chance. The Blegs were apprentice kaidurs, growing skilled in the ways of the arena. They had passed through their coy stage. I kept the second stux, unwilling to deprive myself of a weapon at this pass, and so dueled with a Bleg who kept spitting obscene words at me through his funnel-mouth. His thraxter smashed against the cheap purtle wood of the stux-shaft, and that wood, poor stuff from the pine forests far to the south of Havilfar, splintered and cracked across. I seized the splintered end containing the steel stux-head and swung viciously and saw Naghan the Gnat, on all fours, thrusting his stux upward at the Bleg. He stuck the point in one of the fellow's legs. The Bleg yelped and swung his sword violently down at Naghan. I leaped. I put the stux into the Bleg's face with my right hand and with the left took his right wrist into my fist. I bent. He crashed over with me on top of him, and then I had the thraxter and was on my feet.

"The Invisible Twins!" screeched Naghan the Gnat.

Lart the Stink was down, his blue and yellow intestines greasily strewing over the silver sand in the glare of the suns.

A quick look about showed me that Nath the Arm had done his work well. Of our twenty, ten still remained on their feet, and six of the Blegs were down and one more went over, his four legs flailing, as a stux from Cleitar Adria took him full in that hideous vampire face.

Now the killing should in theory begin, for we had hurled all our javelins, and there were eight Blegs left to dispatch us.

"Gather up stuxes!" I roared at Naghan the Gnat. "And stay out of the way!"

A Bleg bore down on me and there was no time to snatch up a fallen shield. I leaped. I took the shield-rim in my left hand and parried off the sword blow and so dragged the shield down and thrust long and hard. This time I glared around malevolently, and I know my face

95

held that old devil's look of maleficent murder, as I stooped to pick up the shield. The next Bleg tried a clever series of overhand and underhand passes and I simply smashed my shield against his, upset him on his four straddling legs, and passed the thraxter through his eye.

A quick glance showed me four more of our reds down and Cleiter Adria taking a stux from Naghan and hurling it with tremendous force and accurate aim. I went after the rest of the Blegs, who fought well—oh, yes, they fought well, for had they, poor devils, not also been given the drugged sermine flower wine?

When I learned the secret of that anger-stimulating wine I understood why there was kool after kool of beautiful flowers growing in Hyrklana. And I had thought that meant the people were civilized, beauty-loving! We grew flowers in Delphond, gorgeous blooms, and they delighted our senses. I did not think a happy Vallian of Delphond would care for the uses to which the Jikhorkdun put the sermine flower.

"Behind you, Drak!" roared Cleitar.

Already aware of the Bleg heaving up from the sand at my back as I turned, I yet shouted an acknowledgment to Cleitar.

"By Opaz! A persistent fellow, Cleitar."

We stood upon that blood-soaked silver sand. The suns poured down their radiance upon that scene of horror. Stretched upon the arena floor lay the bodies of fifteen Blegs and seventeen apims. Only Cleitar Adria, Naghan the Gnat, and myself survived. With the fading of the effects of the drugged wine, Naghan vomited all over the sand.

"Brace yourself, oh Gnat!" said Cleitar. There was about his blond face a look that did not puzzle me. He had fought and he had won, and he was feeling marvelous. I suspected that the quoffa handler might have found his true vocation as kaidur.

The amphitheater was filling with spectators. We saluted the royal box, empty as yet, and marched back to face the wrath of Nath the Arm. Slaves ran to sprinkle and rake. The beast-howl of the crowd muted as we entered the iron-bound tunnels and so made our way back to our quarters. Nath the Arm looked at us.

"Three!" he said, shaking his head in wonderment. "I had thought the whole twenty of you marked for the Ice Floes."

"Maybe you trained us well, Nath," I said.

He looked at me, and his dark eyes swelled in their sockets—then he chuckled. "By Kaidun! You three may yet become kaidurs! A miracle, a veritable miracle, as the glass eye and brass sword of Beng Thrax is my witness!"

Cleitar Adria chuckled, flexing his muscles, the blood wet and slick upon his body, clogging the blond hairs. He was a man who would never need drugs to fight as kaidur; he had tasted the power, and he had found his vocation.

Naghan the Gnat winked and said, "Nath the Arm! Where are all the shishis sighing for our favors you promised us?"

"Cramph!" roared Nath, mightily outraged. "You are coys! When you are kaidurs! And then, oh puissant Gnat, who will care for your scrawny body, hey?"

"You'd be surprised," said Naghan the Gnat.

# Chapter Nine

## I fight for the ruby drang

Tilly peeled a grape most carefully with her long, slender golden fingers and popped the juicy squishy morsel into my open mouth. I lay on my back, supported by heaped silken cushions, clad in a light lounging robe of sensil whose touch is softer than the ordinary silk, a massive golden bracelet upon my left wrist, a trophy flung down by an admirer the day before. Around me the high-ceilinged marble chamber with its tall windows letting in the glorious rays of Far and Havil was crammed with trophies, feathers, weapons, gold and silver, flowers and laurels, the whole gorgeous and barbaric loot of a successful kaidur. A chest of jewels open at the foot of the couch spilled pearl necklaces, diamond rings, brooches and torques of a hundred varieties of gems.

Much of this lavish wealth, of course, had been won by wagers. A table whose legs were formed into zorca hooves supported a lavish display of wines. Needless to detail them all. Each was a superlative vintage. There was even a flagon of Jholaix. What that had cost I did not know, for commerce on Kregen follows common sense routes and parameters, and an importer will fetch his wine from only so far off, and an exporter will scarce wish to venture farther than he need to sell his wares.

"Enough of grapes, Tilly," I said. "Palines!"

She giggled. Tilly was a Fristle girl. I detested Fristles as a general rule, and yet—remembering Sheemiff—I had to admit I cared for their women. A cat-people, the Fristles, yet quite un-catlike in their social habits. Tilly had a golden body fur covering a shape that would drive most men's mouths dry. Remembering my Delia—a shallow and silly remark, that, for I would never be able to forget her, my Delia, my Delia of Delphond—I could still admit that Tilly was a most beautiful female. Her face with its wide

slanted eyes, its full moist mouth, and—even—her delight-
ful little whiskers, so unlike the Latin woman's heavy
moustache, all delighted me.

She began to toss palines into my mouth and I to suck
them down. I had respected her. I was a successful and, so
far, exciting new kaidur. I was not yet a great kaidur. Everyone said that would come.

I did not agree.

Escape for the slaves, the workers, the coys, apprentices, and kaidurs was impossible. All the working exits to
the warren of workrooms, rings, and barracks adjoining
the massive amphitheater were closely guarded. And there
was no way of climbing up into the lowest ring of seats
and escaping through the many exits used by the public of
Huringa. Only the greatest of great kaidurs were allowed
freely to stroll in the city. They had the scales weighed in
their advantage and they had everything to gain by
staying, and nothing to win by escaping. I did not think I
would stay around long enough to become a great kaidur.

So I could loll in my grand sensil robe and eat squishes
and palines and grapes and chatter pleasantly with Tilly;
for on this night I would escape from Huringa, and from
the land of Hyrklana, and return to Migla. If Delia had
left I would then fly to Valka. I own for a concern. It had
begun to rain through the diabolical interference of the
Star Lords on that field of the Valley of the Crimson Missals. A force of Canops had remained unbeaten. If the
rain prevented my longbowmen from shooting . . . But, I
felt, Seg would master that problem.

Nath the Arm strutted in then, his gorgeous robes worn
when off duty lighting up that already dazzling chamber.
He looked cheerful.

"I have had three more offers, Drak the Sword. And
one from that pimply idiot, the Kov of Manchifwell."

"You will accept, of course."

I had to let Nath the Arm believe everything went as
usual. These special wagers were a profitable source of his
income. Other famous kaidurs were already beginning to
measure their prowess against the strides made by Drak
the Sword. Nath had promised, with tears in his eyes, that
he would make me the greatest kaidur in all of Hyrklana,
aye, in all of Hamal, too!

The reds prospered, to the greater glory of the ruby
drang. Naghan the Gnat still lived, and was now, at my
request, not used as a kaidur in the arena but served as

our armorer. His sinewy strength was more adapted to the cunning blows required in the fashioning of armor than in the different skills of parting warriors from essential portions of their anatomy. Cleitar Adria, too, still lived, and was winning a renown for himself. There were a number of kaidurs in the barracks controlled by Nath who were still regarded as greater than I; this had no power to disturb me. I merely fought that I might stay alive. Well, in that, as you who have listened to my story may guess, I am less than honest. A fight is a fight. I have given you something of my philosophy of swordsmanship already, and I admit to a fascinated interest in the chance that each fresh day, each new challenge, would bring me at last face to face with a greater swordsman than I am.*

"There are also fifty coys all green and dripping."

I sighed. We needed recruits, for the reds were fighting many unequal combats on the silver sand of the arena. But I disliked the way we obtained our coys. Anyone who displeased the queen or any of her nobles was liable to be swept up to serve as fodder for the Jikhorkdun. Those people with whom I had been captured had been leaving a meeting called to discuss ways and means of bringing the queen down. She was, everyone agreed, a bitch. Her husband, the king, was a weakling, a mere cipher. She was, also, this haughty Queen Fahia, the twin sister of that Princess Lilah I had rescued from the Manhounds of Faol.

Many a time had I seen the queen sitting enthroned in her ornate box, covered by the regal awnings, decorated with flowers and vines and many banners, sitting there, chin on fist, gazing down as men and beasts, and beastmen and men-beasts, hacked at each other and gouted blood and died—for her pleasure.

Not once had I seen Princess Lilah. During every spare moment in the arena I had looked along the boxes and tiers of seats reserved for the aristocracy, searching for her beautiful face and golden hair among all the other faces there. I had made discreet inquiries, but no one seemed to know. More and more I was coming to the dismal conclusion that she had not made her escape astride the fluttrell, or had been taken by another slave gang of Havilfar, or, perhaps, had not even survived that mad escape attempt.

"As to the coys, Nath," I said. "Cannot you shield them

* See *Swordships of Scorpio*, Chapter Fifteen: "I give an opinion at Careless Repose."

100

from the demands of the arena? With a little more training—"

He shook his head. "Alas, Drak the Sword. I would like to, Kaidun knows! But it is impossible. We reds must put on our part of the show. Already, and despite the work you among our great kaidurs are doing, the yellows claim they honor the diamond zhantil the highest among the four quarters."

"The yellows have been doing well." I flicked Tilly's long golden tail away from where she had been slyly tickling my side. "That riot last sennight—have the terraces been repaired? And what is the latest count of broken heads?" I was always asking for news from the outside world. To Nath the Arm, the world was here in the Jikhorkdun, and, possibly, he would allow some interest to what went on in Huringa. Apart from that, the whole wide world of Kregen might not exist as far as he was concerned.

"Tilly!" I shouted. "Take your golden tickler away and pour wine for Nath the Arm—or, you fifi, you will be whipped."

She slid from the couch with a soft shirring of her silken gown, her long golden-furred legs very wanton. She mocked me, her slanted eyes wide, her lips pouting. "You would never whip me, Drak my master. You are too soft-hearted."

"Beware lest I chain you up at night with an iron chain."

She brought the wine for Nath, and she pouted her lips at me. "If you chained me, Drak the Sword, it would be with a silver chain."

Tilly, like me, was a slave, although I was a kaidur and therefore the object of considerable envy.

How many and devious ways there are in the world, to be sure, for a man to earn a living!

Cleitar Adria came in as Tilly was pouring again and at once he lifted a goblet and she poured for him, carefully. It was not unknown for Cleitar Adria, kaidur, to strike even a little furry fifi if she spilled his wine. Still, I was pleased to see him, for he brought news.

He occupied a chamber constructed in the marble fashion of splendor of the Jikhorkdun builders of Hyrklana, although perhaps not as grandiose as mine. We were prisoners, but we lived in highly gilded cages. Far below us groaned the great mass of coys and apprentices and common kaidurs, pent into their barracks and cells. We, at least, could see the suns in their glory and revel in the sweet air away from the fetid breath of the arena warrens.

"I fight twice today, Drak the Sword." He quaffed his wine, his golden hair done up in braids, finely twisted by one of his slave wenches, his color high, his eyes fierce. He wore a corselet of gilded iron, and silver greaves, and carried a thraxter. He would have a lad—not necessarily an apim boy—to carry his massive helmet for him. The helmet would be of iron, heavily chased and carved, gilded, and with a face mask with breaths and sights let cunningly into the metal. On everything about him—as about me and the rest of us here—the red color was flaunted in feather and sash and favor.

"My felicitations, Cleitar. I wish you success twice over."

He was not so far drunken with his own image of himself as to forget to thank me. Then he stared at me directly. I knew he had been jealous—to put no baser construction on it—of the bestowal of the tag "Sword" to the name Drak I was using. He wanted to ask something, and his own newfound kaidur pride rebelled. At last he drank again, wiped his lips, and said, "The first is with Anko, an ord-kaidur of the greens, a Rapa. I do not trouble myself over the outcome."

I nodded. "You are kaidur, Cleitar. One who has two more accolades to obtain before that will scarcely evade your sword."

"Aye. But the second is a graint."

Oho! I said to myself. Here is the rub. I said to Nath, "Has Cleitar fought a graint before?" And then, quickly so as to negate any imputations of hostility, I added, "He fights so often and so well it is difficult to keep track of his victories."

"No, Drak the Sword."

As you well know, I have fought graints. I have also fought them with swords that did not kill. But that was a fading dream to me, in those days as a kaidur, and the paradise of the Swinging City of Aphrasöe had never seemed so far distant.

After some more drinking and talking I managed to give Cleitar the benefit of my experience, and hoped he would take it. I had made no good companions as a kaidur. The tragedy of that course was all too apparent. A good friend in the morning might be merely a mangled corpse, dragged by the cruel iron hooks from the blood-smeared silver sand, by the time the twin suns sank in their opaz glory.

I scratched my beard. I had let my hair and beard grow unchecked and I was now a most hairy specimen, like a shaggy graint in truth. This was done for a set purpose.

Cleitar left, and Nath, also, and I called young Oby to help with my armor. Oby was short for Obfaril—first beloved—and he was an engaging imp, an apim boy, with tousled fair hair, a wide cheeky smile, and fingers as dexterous in the manner of stealing palines as of buckling up armor. He was slave and was, of course, mad keen to become a kaidur.

I, too, was fighting twice this day. A kaidur's life was not all lolling on silken cushions being fed palines by delectable Fristle fifis and quaffing winc and counting golden deldys and adding up the winnings. Today I faced a notable kaidur of the greens, a Rapa like the green Cleitar was to face; but a kaidur. That is, he had passed all the destructive tests of the arena from coy and now, with a string of victories behind him (a defeat was almost impossible for sometimes the defeated were allowed to live), was looking for the supreme accolade of being dubbed great kaidur. He, like myself, would be a trifle pampered by his manager. The backers with the money, nobles in consortia, business people, great merchants, and landed gentry, would wager more and more heavily upon him. He would be sought out for combats from his peers; he would not be chanced too often in the melee. He would, in short, be a prize kaidur. Like Cleitar. Like the other kaidurs and great kaidurs of the Jikhorkdun. We fought the combats in theory as unequals, as the blood-lust and the blood-curiosity demanded; but we were arena professionals, and we met and matched our skills rather than the mere differences of weapons.

If Cleitar was killed this day, then his ord-kaidur Rapa opponent would be one step nearer to being full kaidur.

I had little fear for Cleitar. He was of the manner of man to whom the arena had come as the real purpose of his life.

Between Tilly and Oby I was accoutered in a clean white linen shirt, a padded vest, a corselet of gilden iron, shoulder wings—scarcely pauldrons—golden greaves, and I buckled up two crossed lesten-hide belts over the scarlet breechclout. Often Nath the Arm would glare at that scarlet breechclout, and say: "But, Drak the Sword! By Kaidun, but the color is overly scarlet for the ruby drang!"

And I would say: "It has brought the ruby drang fair pickings, oh Nath the Arm! Would yóu offend, perhaps, the ruby heart of Beng Thrax?"

"By the glass eye and brass sword of Beng Thrax! Do you then mock me, Drak the Sword?"

"May Kaidun forfend!"

We went down to our assembly place where the coys shuffled away with many a long look, at once apprehensive, fearful, envious, at the kaidurs. Cleitar greeted me. So did Rafee the Render, a giant of a kaidur who had been a pirate before being captured and offered the usual alternatives. He was a huge ruffian and a great hand with his ax. With the other kaidurs of the red who were fighting this day we took our places on ponsho-fleece covered benches behind the iron bars where we might sit and quaff wine and swap stories and stare out upon the silver sand. One by one the combats took place. Cleitar disposed of his Rapa, as I disposed of mine. At this time there might be as many as fifty separate combats going on in the arena, and wherever the public might sit, strictly in the color-quarters they would support from the day of their birth to the day of their death, they would have a fine close-up view of the fighting.

The suns crawled up the sky. The wine we drank, that raw rough red stuff the kaidurs called Beng Thrax's spit, served to slake our thirsts. It was practically nonalcoholic. But—it contained the hidden drug distilled from the sermine flower.

The day wore on bringing the most important of the combats especially staged as wagers went on increasing. We lost a great kaidur, one Fakal the Sword, who slipped in a patch of sand-strewn blood and so recovered to stare at a thraxter as it plunged over the rim of his corselet into his neck. We yelled and rattled our swords across the iron bars and made the shrieks and ululations from the paid mourners, starkly dramatic in their black robes, separated in their special boxes, seem like thin chittering whistling.

"Ornol the Chank!" yelled Nath. "We have him marked, by Kaidun!"

Ornol the Chank was a great kaidur of the yellow, and we saw poor old Fakal the Sword's head offered up as a tribute to the diamond zhantil. Out of deference to custom we must remain mute while the observances were being made. But we all looked at Fakal's dripping head, and we all wanted to get onto the silver sand and cross thraxters with Ornol the Chank.

I checked in horror.

This night I had planned an escape. What then, by Zair, was I doing vowing to revenge our injured red honor by dealing with Ornol the Chank in the future? I had no future I wanted here in the Jikhorkdun. Rather, having established what position I had, I would reject it all as trivial for the realities of my life which were, as you know, Delia and—well, the rest might go hang. Delia, and little Drak and Lela were all I wanted.

So—why shout and rave and shake my sword at the triumphant yellow benches?

There was no denying the excitement of it all, the thrills and terror, the narrow escapes, the great shouts of triumph or of raging despair that roared up at victory or disaster. I was one of the reds. We fought for the ruby drang. Out across that sun-soaked arena of silver sand lives were staked. The huge sums of money and jewels and property were all behind the scenes. Here, in the blood and the agony, the swift clash of combat, here was where it all happened.

Oh, yes, I was caught up in it all. I was a kaidur, and conscious of that, proud, even, and I fought for the reds and as much as I joyed in my own victories I gloried in the victories of my fellow reds. I even think that a great kaidur, when at last he was beaten and so fell with his opponent's bloody weapon drinking his life blood, felt greater sorrow that his color had gone down in defeat than that he was losing his own life.

Eerie and powerful are the ways men may be twisted by systems and customs and the hot passions of blood.

The proud and remote land of Hyrklana gathered men from many other lands and nations and races to fight in the Jikhorkdun. The demands of the arena were insatiable. Of poor people to be used merely as fodder, to whip up the blood appetites, few might be found outside the criminal classes and the political opponents, and those betrayed by hidden enemies. But the land of Havilfar is wide, and there are very many different countries upon its surface, even if the wild lands in the central northwest are relatively barren. Slave dealers thrived. It had taken a mighty empire to support the arenas of our Earth's ancient Rome. But that empire, large as it was, could not compare with the resources open to the swift vollers of Havilfar.

Fighting in the arena were men from Pandahem, from Murn-Chem, from Ng'groga—their seven-foot height and incredible thinness could not be mistaken—men from Walfarg and Undurkor and Xuntal. Men like my good comrade Gloag from Mehzta who was not apim. There were the wild black-haired, blue-eyed men from the valleys and mountains of Erthyrdrin. There were men from Vallia, too. And, I believe, from Zenicce.

On a day before my plans for escape were complete, I had been engaged in the melee and the reds had been steadily wearing down our yellow opponents. The diamond zhantil remained in the ascendant over the red drang; but we were doing what we might to redress that balance. The four huge colored images on their movable staffs situated at one end of the gigantic oval of the amphitheater showed by their relative heights the state of the colors. If the reds emerged victorious we would lift the red drang another notch higher and bring the yellow zhantil a notch lower.

So, on this day, as we fought and I dispatched my man—for this was a skilled melee, where like fought like, and we were matched—I swung about to smash away a thraxter aimed at my back and so slew that one, also. Cleitar Adria was just stepping back from his man.

The yellow lay gasping on the sand, his face agonized. His oiled curly black hair in tight ringlets gleamed in the steaming light of Far and Havil as his helmet rolled away. Cleitar bent to finish him, as was proper, given that this was a fight-to-the-finish melee.

I saw the man lying there turn his eyes up. His face lost its writhing reflection of the agony he felt. He watched as Cleitar's sword lifted high against the suns. And then he spoke, quick, simple words, breathy and blood-filled. Words I heard in a kind of stupefied daze.

"I join you, my brothers, Krozairs of Zamu! I join you to sit on the right hand of Zair in the glory of Zim!"

Shattered, I sprang forward.

"No, Cleitar!"

I was too late. The sword slashed down. A Krozair brother had indeed gone to join his comrades in Zair. Aye, his comrades as a Krozair of Zamu—but, also, my comrades as a Krozair of Zy!

Cleitar bent to wipe his thraxter, there in the arena of Huringa in Hyrklana, so many many dwaburs from the Eye of the World and from Sanurkazz.

"What is it, Drak the Sword! What ails you? Are you hit?"

"It is nothing, Cleitar Adria."

But it was something.

I could not find another man from the inner sea fighting in the Jikhorkdun of Huringa in Hyrklana. I would ask, when I saw a man who looked as though he knew what a swifter was, who knew the difference between Zair and Grodno. But I never did find one, then.

So, now, on this day I was to escape, I watched as Cleitar Adria went out to fight his graint. He won. He managed to kill the great and noble beast. When he came back he was ripped and scratched and one arm hung useless. He stared at me, and licked his lips. His beard had been torn and bloody flesh showed.

"I did as you counseled, Drak. I took him, limb by limb." Cleitar looked all in. "I think—I think you counseled well."

I had to say it, for all that the words nearly stuck in my mouth. "You did well, Cleitar. Hai Jikai!"

I had never used those great words in the arena before. I considered the place and occasion base and unworthy. But Cleitar had fought well. He deserved the "Hai Jikai." "Jikai" is for warriors, I thought, hardly for kaidurs.

Nath the Arm had overheard. He glanced at me curiously.

"Now, by Kaidun, Drak the Sword! I had often wondered, but now I am sure. You have been a paktun—perhaps a Hyr-paktun."

A Paktun, as I have said, is a great warrior of fortune, a mercenary leader, or one who has achieved some feat of great renown. It has become a little debased in usage, and is often applied to any noteworthy free-lancer. But, to be a paktun is to be a leader of a free company, or a mercenary so famous as to be hired at the hightest fee obtainable. Many Chuliks were paktuns—and many were Hyr-paktuns, also; "Hyr" being a word for great.

"And if I have, Nath the Arm, does not that augur well for the ruby drang?"

He glowered at me and pulled his gold-threaded beard. He knew how I liked to mock him, and he could only take it, for we had become as friendly as men in our respective positions might. As to my references to the ruby drang, he could never make up his mind if I meant what I said, or merely mocked the more.

My own second fight followed, and it was a bloodthirsty affair which I prefer to forget. But I did what I had to do—had to do, for a kaidur who would not fight was a kaidur with a garrote around his throat and a stone lashed to his legs and a billet in the fast-flowing River of Leaping Fishes which pours around the northern side of Huringa.

After that I had no wish to sit further on the ponsho fleeces of the benches in the red quarter. Out on the arena stakes were being raised. Presently females of various races would be brought out, all naked, and lashed to those stakes. Their male counterparts would be let out, naked also, and armed with that very broad, very short two-edged sword the Havilfarese call djangir. Then, when all was ready and the crowds would be leaning forward in expectation, the wild bosks would be driven out, mad with hunger and rage. The bosk is piglike, and very good eating, and highly prized, a delicacy of Valka, as you know. The wild bosk has two horns upon its head, each at least two feet long, straight and sharp and deadly. It can lower its head and charge and skewer through good leather.

The men must defend their womenfolk, for the managers of the Jikhorkdun are most clever in this, and select married couples, or son and mother, or father and daughter, or lovers. The short djangir is scarcely the weapon with which to meet the wicked twenty-four-inch twin horns of the wild bosk.

But the spectacle affords amusement to the paying public of Huringa. . . .

# Chapter Ten

## A voller flight
## over Huringa

Soft and gentle and very skilled were the fingers of Tilly, the girl Fristle, as she clipped and combed my hair and beard and moustache. I like a short, pointed, damn-you-to-hell beard, and moustaches that, whether I will it or no, thrust upward arrogantly. Tilly sang a little song as she snipped. It was "The Lay of Faerly the Ponsho Farmer's Daughter." Young girl Fristles with their soft fur and their sweet cat-faces and their exciting figures are notorious for their knowledge of the arts of love. Perhaps I am unfair in using the word notorious. It would be kinder to say famous. Of course, this meant nothing to me, for only Delia could ever stir me; but it was undeniably pleasurable to have Tilly thus minister to my wants. She would wash and rub me with oil and ease the stiffness out of my limbs and clip my hair and comb it and sniff at me and say, cheekily, "You are a veritable apim graint, Drak the Sword."

To which I was honor-bound to reply, "Tomorrow I shall buy a silver chain."

To which she, in her turn, would toss her pretty head and flick her tail around to tickle my ribs, while she went on snipping and combing and singing about the lay of Faerly, the Fristle ponsho farmer's daughter.

All this was meaningless. By tomorrow, far from buying a silver chain, or even threatening to, as I did almost every day, I would be aboard a stolen voller and winging my way northward to Valka—or southwestward to Migla, for I still felt great unease about that diabolical rain shower.

I have said I prefer a short pointed beard. I had deliberately allowed my face fungus to grow inordinately. Oh, it had not sprouted into the great blaze of jet threaded with gold that Nath the Arm sported. But now, when Tilly finished her clipping, she sat back, curling her tail up, and said: "By the furry tail of the Frivolous Freemiff! You look so different, Drak my master."

She knew I didn't like her calling me her master.

We were slaves together. I frowned. She opened those wide slanting eyes of hers, so catlike, so sensual, and flicked her golden tail.

"I am no different, you impudent fifi. I am still Drak the Sword, a great hairy graint of an apim."

"Aye! That you are!"

So, that being settled, I packed her off to her bed in an adjoining room, where she was perfectly safe not only from me but from any amorous kaidur who might wander the corridors of this high barracks. Somewhere below in a courtyard a poor devil was being flogged. I could hear the meaty thwack of each blow and the shrieks that gradually quieted to a moaning and then to a more horrible silence, punctuated only by that devilish sound of a man's bare back being lashed raw.

The contrast between my condition up here, with all its luxury, and that poor devil below sobered my high spirits for the night's enterprise. Young Oby came in, cheerfully whistling a scandalous song. He wanted my authorization for him to collect our allowance of samphron oil for the lamps. I gave it to him, sealing it with the crude signet stamp allowed me in the form of a thraxter crossed with a djangir. I had not chosen that signature.

"Who is that below, Oby?"

"Why, master, the onker Ortyg the Sly. He was caught stealing wine—purple Hamish wine, too."

Well, stealing rum was a crime for which I had seen floggings enough in the navy of my youth. I dismissed Oby.

Then I set about dressing myself for the night's adventures.

A nobleman or a Horter—that is, a gentleman—of Havilfar might well walk the streets of his city wearing a sword. He would not ordinarily carry a shield. They favored the curved dagger here, and with its ornate sheath and grip the one I slung to my belt was a flashy toy. But the thraxter was a warrior's weapon, bloodied this day in the arena. I put on my favored scarlet breechclout—a new one specially procured and washed and ironed by Tilly.

110

Over this the white linen shirt and then a yellow jerkin, its shoulders and back a blaze of embroidery. The weather was too hot for trousers. I chose calf-high boots of a supple leather that would breathe, for I did not wish to wear sandals in the game I was playing.

A pouch contained a considerable sum in deldys and sinvers, and this I buckled to my waist. With due precaution I also wrapped a few extremely valuable gems into the scarlet breechclout. Around me in my marble chamber with its silks and feathers and furs lay a fortune I had won. All this must be left. It meant nothing. I wore a hat, one of the Havilfarese closely fitting leather caps, and could wish for one of the wide-brimmed Vallian hats with their jaunty feathers.

I knew nothing of the city of Huringa—save that its people liked to pay money to enter the Jikhorkdun and to wager if a man would live or die—and Oxkalin the Blind Spirit must guide me when I set foot outside the amphitheater. You may be sure I observed the fantamyrrh when I left that chamber, as I thought for the last time.

A stuxcal stood by the door, fully filled with its eight javelins. I had to leave it. A gentleman does not walk the streets of his city carrying stuxes, now does he? In a civilized city like Huringa? I thought not, judging by what I knew of Vondium and Sanurkazz and Zenicce.

Tilly and Oby were left. They had prepared me a good meal, and I had eaten well—roast vosk, taylynes, a pie of squishes and gregarians, rather too sweet, rich yellow butter and fluffy Kregan loaves, and—a triumph!—cup after cup of that fragrant superb Kregan tea. In my wallet I had stuffed a package of palines, and I carried two strips of dried beef, veritable biltong, which would sustain me for a long period.

Once past the corridors and passageways immediately adjacent to my chamber I was able to pass without notice. From my cap a great cascading mass of red feathers drooped and a red favor glowed on my left shoulder. These I planned to discard the moment I was out on the street and unobserved.

The success of my plan hinged on the evening entertainments of the Horters of Huringa. They would take their carriages, their sleeths, or their zorcas and ride up to the Jikhorkdun, unable, it seemed, to keep away from the blood-reeking place, to inspect the latest hyr-kaidur, or a newly imported wild beast, or to watch practices. Some of these Horters, I knew, fancied their luck and would don a kaidur's gear and venture into a practice ring. They would use rebated weapons—that went without saying. There must be many other entertainments for a pleasant evening in the city, I reasoned, taverns and dancing halls, dopa dens, even theaters. But the pull of the arena was stronger.

Down in a practice pit I saw a group of gentlemen watching a kaidur fence one of their number. The kaidur gave them their money's worth, letting himself be bested. The Horters laughed and joked, garish in fine clothes, flicking their thraxters about, sniffing from pomanders, chewing palines. Oh, yes, they were a brilliant parasitical lot. I joined them. I, Drak the Sword, kaidur, had the temerity to insinuate my way into a group of nobles and Horters from the city.

Had Nath the Arm appeared he might well have recognized me. I doubted that even Cleitar Adria would do so. I was confident that Naghan the Gnat would recognize me at once; he was a sharp little one.

So I had chosen a practice ring well away from the usual ones patronized by the coys and apprentices and kaidurs of Nath the Arm's barracks. I was jostled by a young Horter, who did not apologize but merely twitched his elegant shoulders away. I let him remain on his feet and with his senses intact. As in almost any group a natural leader led this one, a young man in the bright flush of youth whom the others called Strom Noran. He joked and laughed with them and yet quite clearly remained aware of his position.

"By Clem, Dorval!" he shouted to one of his friends, older and leaner and, I judged, looking for any opportunity to make money. "I'll wager a thousand Deldys you could do no better!"

"I would refuse to take your money, Strom Noran," replied this Dorval. "Callimark might be a kaidur himself!"

Callimark, the youngster who fancied he had beaten the kaidur in the practice ring, lifted a flushed face. Sweat stood on his forehead. "By Clem, Dorval! Don't get out of it like that! Come down here and fight me!"

"Yes, Dorval," said Strom Noran. "And a thousand on it."

"Now, by Flem, you do push me, Strom Noran."

"And by Flem I want to see it, Dorval!"

I stepped back. Their silly pride, their stupid wager, meant nothing. A great and horrid suspicion overwhelmed

112

me. These brilliant carefree, rich young men swore casually by Clem and by Flem—gods or spirits or saints of whom I had never heard, although with so many cluttering the pantheon of Kregen that was not surprising. But I had not missed the hesitation as they swore. If the first consonant of any of the gods' names was omitted, one was left with *Lem!*

Then I knew the evil cult of Lem the silver leem had penetrated in secret into this city of Huringa in Hyrklana.

As I was to find, the people of Hyrklana are a fiery-tempered lot, hasty with the sword, bloodthirsty as their love of the arena testified to me even then. Yet there were very good and pressing reasons for much of this fierceness, this predatory urge to supremacy and violence. All along the southeastern coastlines of Havilfar the populations lived in a constant apprehension of the raids from those strange beings from the southern oceans. I had already met and fought one of their ships. But I had had little direct contact and knew nothing about them, except that as reavers they were viler than anything I had known on Kregen—the overlords of Magdag could not bear comparison—and as reavers ought to be put down. So that Hyrklana, from her exposed and precarious position jutting out into the southern ocean from the eastern flank of Havilfar, received her fair share and more of these devastating raids. A viciousness of reprisal, a hardness of character, a streak of reckless daring ran through all of Hyrklana—aye! and many another country of Kregen, too. They clung to the belief that one day, someday, a final reckoning would have to be made with these reavers. They had so many differing and usually obscene names I have not bothered to give a single one; but one name they had given to them that chilled me by its implications was—Leem-Lovers.

From Quennohch in the south to Hennardrin in the north, the whole eastern flank of Havilfar knew and detested these reavers from the southern oceans. They came, this way around the planet, from the easterly southern ocean. Usually they limited their farthest advances to the sea areas around South Pandahem and the one we had fought must have been a loner. Not so very long ago they had captured and set up a base in the Astar group of islands approximately midway between Pandahem and Xuntal. Then a great Jikai had been called and they had been

113

hurled out, reeking with their own blood, as men from this grouping of islands and continents dealt with them.

"By Gaji's bowels, Strom Noran! Very well, then, and the thousand deldys will buy me a new zorca chariot!"

The lean dark Dorval had been goaded enough. As he threw off his ornate cloak and jerkin to stand in his tunic and kilt, Strom Noran laughed delightedly. The young man Callimark looked up, still panting from his previous bout, and he laughed also.

"Welcome to our circle, Dorval! It will be a pleasure to cross blades with you."

Time was ticking along and the suns were now almost gone and the idlers and rufflers were drifting back from the Jikhorkdun at last to their other evening pleasures. I stood shoulder to shoulder with the Horter they had called Aldy and watched the mock combat. The youngbloods of Huringa catcalled and whooped and whistled as Callimark and Dorval set to. The kaidur who had allowed this youngster Callimark to beat him had done so with skill, so that it appeared Callimark was something of a sworder. Now the saturnine Dorval cut him to pieces—or would have done so had the blades been sharp and not rebated.

At last Callimark threw his thraxter down, his face angry and near tears, puffed with chagrin.

"You have the devil's own tricks, Dorval, by Glem!"

Dorval turned his thin dark face up to the Strom.

"A thousand deldys, I think the sum was, Strom Noran."

With a curse concerned with the obscene Gaji, Strom Noran lifted his hand. "I will settle with Havil in the morning." By this he meant he would settle when the green sun rose above the horizon.

The raffish Horter next to me, Aldy, chuckled and half to himself said: "By Gaji's slimy intestines! The Strom must pay, the devil take him!"

Then he shot me a swift suspicious look, and I could guess he was cursing himself for so openly allowing his feelings to be known by a stranger. During the planning stages of my escape I had made it my business to inquire for a remote and almost unknown and certainly unfrequented part of Hyrklana. An oldster whose job it was to muck out after the totrixes told me he had come from a land far to the south called Hakkinostoling. This was a mouthful so that few people bothered to recall it, and the land being ravaged, its people were almost unknown. I

114

had asked old Wenerl about his home, plying him with wine, and with rheumy eyes he had obliged with a description of a place anyone would wish to leave. So it was that when this youngblood Aldy glowered at me, suspiciously, I was able to speak with a fine free assumption of bumpkin ignorance.

"I am Varko ti Hakkinostoling," I said, "and am but lately arrived in Huringa. Everything is strange to me, as you may well imagine, and I feel very lost."

"Get a bellyful of wine and you will find friends," Aldy counseled, and then yelled and dodged as Callimark came flying up out of the ring. Callimark landed neatly enough on the wooden edging; but then his foot caught and he pitched forward. I caught him under the armpits and stood him up. He was not at all pleased. He started to bluster, and Dorval, with his saturnine look, vaulted up after him, saying: "A fair fight, Callimark. You witness I did not wish it."

"Well, Dorval, by Gaji's bowels, you could have lost it then!"

Dorval chuckled and drew on his jerkin and cloak. "What! And lose a thousand deldys to a man who scarce notices them?"

So, arguing and expostulating, the crowd swaggered from the practice pit of the Jikhorkdun. Aldy mentioned my name to Callimark and Dorval, saying: "This is Varko ti Hakki-somewhere-or-other. He's drinking with us tonight."

They were a trifle rough and ready in a high-spirited way in their manners, not thinking much of the formal Horter, or of the Tyr or Kyr some of them ranked. Larking and shouting they made their way out of the Jikhorkdun past the watchful Rhaclaw sentries, out onto the broad patio fronting the amphitheater, and I, Varko, went with them.

Snug in the center of the group and talking to Aldy, I passed through the iron sentinel ring set around the Jikhorkdun. My red favors mingled with the flaunted red colors of the others. Maybe I would not have to dispose of them swiftly, after all. We swaggered down the long shallow flight of steps fully a hundred and fifty yards wide, thronged with people leaving the amphitheater. My escape had been comically simple. I think that somewhere, unknown to me at the time, above the clouds, perhaps, Homeric laughter was being roared out at my expense.

I could stare about me, enthralled, for was I not a bumpkin oaf from the backwoods? The outside of the amphitheater could never match the interior for grandeur, for a great deal of the seating was sunk in the ground; but the place reared up, all right, tall and imposing, with facade after facade of architecture rising on arches and colonnades. I looked where we were going. A wide boulevard led off southward. Three other boulevards led off to the other three cardinal points, but I discovered that no area of the city was given over wholly to one color; people lived cheek by jowl as to their color loyalties in the arena, and a baker of the red might shout jolly obscenities to a fishmonger of the green, while a haberdasher of the yellow tried to sell his goods to a housewife of the blues. All would wear their favors as a matter of course, and gnash their teeth when their quarter was down, and crow their triumph when in the ascendant. The reds, as second in the table, were able to swagger with a fine panache over the blues and greens, and yell shrill mocking promises of quick retribution to the yellows.

The main thing that took my attention about the four main boulevards of Huringa was the lighting. Down each side of the roadway a long string of lights flared. I found out about these lights—and marveled anew. They were illuminated by gas, by a natural gas source in nearby hills, which had been tapped and piped into the city and used in flaring gas jets. The sight was wonderful and impressive to me. This merely served to confirm my feelings that Havilfar was further advanced than the other continents of this grouping of four.

We soon passed down the steps and so came to the waiting carriages, and the zorcas and totrixes and sleeths. These amazing gas jets flared brightly and lit up the scene in garish colors, the red of the favors around us, the brilliant harnesses, the gems and gold and silver, the waving feathers, the eye-catching brightness of fresh colors everywhere. The waiting zorcas stamped their hooves, the sleeths scraped their claws, slaves in their gaudy liveries opening carriage doors and soothing impatient animals and folding up steps and whipping up their totrixes or zorcas, everything melded into a bright scene of splendour—but I could not see the stars or the moons of Kregen above me in the night sky.

This was my chance to slip away. Strom Noran shouted some witty sally and cursed his slave hostler to hold the

Havil-forsaken sleeth still. He mounted, drawing up a very tight rein. The reptile reared on its two powerful hind legs, its claws biting into the ground, its silly forepaws flailing the air. Its small wicked head flicked a forked tongue and hissed demonically. Strom Noran stuck in his spurs and yelled and the sleeth went bounding off in that ungainly two-legged waddle they have, which can cover the ground at a fair turn of speed, for all that. The sleeth is an uncomfortable mount, and one I do not much care for, nothing being preferable to the zorca or vove. But these racing reptiles were all the rage in Havilfar, and the youngbloods risked their foolish necks in buying and riding the fiercest of them. To me, riding a dinosaurlike sleeth carried too many overtones of the Phokaym.

Now I was fairly out of the amphitheater and among the fashionable sporting crowd of Huringa and I noticed at once that almost no one was without a color favor. I chanced my arm and slipped between a gesticulating bunch of greens, hotly debating the very fight I had myself had this day, when the Rapa kaidur of the greens had fallen to my sword. They concealed me from Callimark and Aldy and the others. The last I saw was Dorval, very contemptuously mounting up on his zorca, and yelling at Callimark that he'd take him on his sleeth to the end of the boulevard, by Gaji's slit ears, for two hundred.

To which Callimark, foolish fellow, yelled: "You're on, Dorval! And I'll lick you—"

Sleeth and zorca sped off. I knew which one my money would be on. I let them go and cut away from the greens, who had come to no agreement why their great kaidur had failed against that kaidur of the reds, Drak the Sword, and so managed to slink off into an unlighted alleyway.

I confess I knew little if anything of Huringa, and·I learned precious little more that night.

Once out of the glare of the gas jets I could look up and ease my eyes and see once again the glory of the stars and She of the Veils riding clouds high above. Colored lights festooned the sky up there, moving in long smooth arcs from horizon to horizon, dropping down and rising up. These were the riding lights of vollers. I watched where a group came to ground and set off walking. I went with care. My thraxter was loose in its sheath; and although I saw plenty of people coming and going about their business, and passed from torch-lit areas to other places of pitch-blackness, I was not molested.

The flierdrome lay before me, blazing with lights, and the expenditure of oil must have been prodigious. Most of the lamps used a cheap mineral oil called rock oil, and not the more expensive, infinitely purer, and more beautiful samphron oil. I selected the voller I wanted. A four-place craft with a low rail, without a cabin and with fast lines, it would, I fancied, take me swiftly to Migla—or Valka.

I vaulted the low drome rail, raced for the flier, leaped in and thrust the ascent lever hard over. The flier zoomed up in a graceful arc, and from the ground and dwindling in the rush of my passage, I heard the shouts and angry calls of the slave attendants. Their woes were not mine and although I felt sorry for them, for they might well be punished, this was just another of the burdens of Kregen I must bear—for a time.

The night sky enfolded me. I set the course at west-southwest and cracked up to full speed. Huringa sped past below.

I was free!

And then—and then the black clouds boiled solidly before me and a mighty wind rushed upon my craft, spinning it end for end and the noise blasted into my ears, and I was falling ... falling ... falling into blackness. ...

## Chapter Eleven

# The neemus of
# Queen Fahia of Hyrklana

Sparks and stars and planets and meteors shot and crackled about me. The airboat fell from the sky as though smashed in the paw of a gigantic leem. Whirled headlong the voller sliced through treetops and foliage whipped about my ears. No control was possible. That black maelstrom stirred the sky into a caldron. Other vollers there were being hurled pell-mell. I saw two smash together and the small frantic figures of jerking passengers fall through the storm to the ground.

No need to ask by whose malign power this gale had been sent!

Once again, as had happened before, I was being warned off by the Star Lords. They did not wish me to travel to Migla and they were giving me no chance to find out if I might travel to Valka, away to the north across the equator. This was no ordinary storm. The blackness, the massive billowing of the clouds, angry, lightning-shot, and violence of the wind and rain, all were supernormal. I clung to the gyrating voller and I cursed the Star Lords. Oh, yes, I cursed them blue!

Another voller narrowly avoided crushing mine, for this craft that yawed away was a monster and I could see the deck covered with iron cages. Weight is of no consequence to a voller. In those cages, illuminated eerily by the flickering shards of lightning, wild beasts leaped and yowled and screeched. This was a flier bringing prize specimens for the arena.

Both vollers hit the ground at the same time. Mine went somersaulting over a low brick wall, smashing a thatched roof, ripping through a loloo yard, came shudderingly to rest against a low thorn-ivy hedge. I scrambled out. I had no wish once again to go breeches first through a thorn-ivy hedge.

The cages had burst on impact. Screams and yells, horrid in the uncertain light, created a bedlam. The aftercabin of the flier, a two-deck construction, had splintered to destruction, and costly silks and satins, mashcere and damask, floated and strewed the shattered house. Men and women were running in crazy circles. I saw Rhaclaws carrying torches and whips trying to round up some of the beasts—I saw a strigicaw tear the head off one and spit it out before racing for a second.

In that incredible scene of confusion with maddened wild beasts, of a ferocity known only to Kregen, terrifying humans, halflings, and apims alike, I stood for a moment. I knew I must help but knew, also, I was likely to get killed in affording that help.

Any hesitation was instantly banished as from the shattered wreckage of the cabin's upper deck the slim and half-naked form of a girl leaped and ran, screaming. Her hair blazed flame in the torchlight, by which I assumed she might hail from Loh. Now the thatch of the house was alight and in that curdling orange radiance I saw the low feline shape of a neemu racing after the slender white form of the girl.

The neemu had been injured, for it ran favoring its off front foot. Four legs have the neemus, round and smooth their heads, with squat triangular ears, and wide slit eyes of a lambent smoky-gold. All black are neemus, sleek and deadly, their fur highly prized, their ways amoral and feral. Their red jaws and sharp white teeth love nothing better than closing upon rosy living flesh. Vaguely pumalike, the neemu, vicious and treacherous and utterly deadly.

No thought was necessary.

I leaped forward, drawing my sword.

The girl cast me one terrified, appealing look, and collapsed, her foot twisting under her.

I stepped forward and the neemu did not hesitate.

It leaped.

That long sinuous black body packed with muscle sprang and in that rounded smooth head the lambent golden eyes glittered at me with deadly intent.

I slid the first lashing claw and because the beast was injured in its right paw was able to lean to my left and bring the thraxter around and down in a short and savagely chopping stroke at the neemu's neck. It screeched as it went past. It landed short of the girl, who cowered back, one hand to her mouth, her eyes enormous. Without giving the neemu a chance to recover—for that blow, mighty as it had been and bringing a gout of blood from the gash in the beast's neck, had not killed it—I jumped in again. This time the sword cut and thrust as it was built to do and the neemu shrank back, hissing and screeching, its glossy black fur dappled with blood, and so rolled over, slumped, and died. It did not die easily. Seven lives, neemus have, so goes the old superstition. I gave it seven thrusts, and then seven more, just to make sure.

The girl could not rise. She lay there, her gauzy scraps of clothing only partially covering her glowing body. She tried to speak, and I heard the whispered words "Hai Jikai!"

And then rough and ungentle hands seized me, and a giant Rapa cunningly cast chains about my limbs, and his fellows, Rhaclaws, Rapas, Fristles, and apims, manacled and fettered me.

"What are you about, you yetches!" I roared.

But they struck me across the face and then gagged me, so that I could not yell the curses that boiled and spluttered in my head. What nonsense was this, that I should thus be chained?

The answer to that bore down on me with all the old sense of injustice that festers in many parts of Kregen, as, indeed to our shame, it does on this Earth in the here and now. I was taken swiftly aboard another flier, for the storm inspired by the Star Lords had died as swiftly as it had begun, and with the passengers from the beast-carrying voller was carried with the utmost dispatch to the frowning fortress of Hakal, which dominates the city of Huringa in Hyrklana.

In certain essentials one fortress is much like another, although in Valka I have made certain changes that make of the Valkan castles the finest and most impregnable in all of Kregen, or so I fondly believe. Almost all Kregan castles are comfortable, of course, for comfort and Kregan nobility are tolerably well-acquainted. I was taken wrapped in my chains and bundled down into a cell, where sundry Rhaclaws picked me, a Rapa bit me (the Rapa beaks are notorious), and a Fristle flicked me across the face with his tail. Had my mouth not been gagged he, at least, would have regretted his conduct.

121

I kicked a number of them where it would materially impair their mating instincts; but in the end I was beaten down and chained up. They used a great deal of solid iron chain on me so that, finally, I was helpless.

After some time—time meant nothing among the nobility when dealing with their inferiors—I was hauled out and beaten again just to remind me. Then I was dragged helplessly up stone stairs and so through many back stairs and corridors into a low-ceiled room hung with many bright tapestries and furnished luxuriously with the wealth of empire, and flung down before Queen Fahia of Hyrklana.

I was hungry.

My chains chafed and my muscles were cramped and twisted. I had a headache and I was in the foulest of foul bad tempers.

The queen sat in a simple curule-styled chair, a zhantil pelt strewn carelessly upon it. A Fristle girl hovered with ready goblets of wine, another with tidbits on golden platters. A giant Brokelsh, dressed up in ridiculous finery, waved a feathered fan above her head, for it was full day and the suns pouring in through the open windows gave heat as well as light to the chamber. I took a quick squint—for my eyes were adjusted to the darkness of prison cells and not the glory of Zim and Genodras—to see whether or not the scarlet and golden Gdoinye or the white dove of the Savanti might not be looking in and having a damned good chuckle at my predicament.

"So this is the rast."

The queen's voice might once have been musical and low, but years of undisputed authority had coarsened it. She looked very much like her twin sister, the Princess Lilah; but there hung that coarseness about her, that reddening of artery and vein, that thickening of the flesh of her neck and chin, that cluster of lines between her eyebrows no amount of careful exercise and cosmetics could clear. Her hair had been plaited and dressed into a magnificent golden pile upon her head, ablaze with gems. She wore a long green gown and over that a bodice that seemed to be made from a blaze of jewels. Her feet were clad in satin slippers. She took a goblet of wine from the fifi and sipped reflectively, gazing at me over the rim. She was a beautiful woman, who was slowly losing the battle against too rich food and too much wine and too little exercise. She was

122

"So this is the rast."

aware of her beauty, and, probably, not completely able to grasp that she was losing that glory.

If I do not mention the lines of habitual cruelty that had sunk into her skin around her mouth and pinched her nose, I do so only out of pity for her. Zair knows, she had need of pity!

Now, when I was thrown at her feet, chained and gagged and helpless, she was at the height of her powers. She completely dominated all of Hyrklana, having pushed the kingdom's bounds out to every part of the island, and in the continual nagging misunderstandings with Hamal, the giant neighbor country in the northeast of Havilfar, having quite a few notable successes. Surrounded as she was by subservient pallans and courtiers, her merest whim was unbreakable law. She might live in a dream world, but where that world impinged on the greater world without, the dream world of the Queen of Hyrklana would always prevail.

Princess Lilah had said to me that she longed to return to her father's palace in Hyrklana. I was to learn that the old king still lived, in retirement, having abdicated in favor of his daughter Fahia. He had opposed this obsession with the Jikhorkdun, and Princess Lilah, also, had wanted no part of the arena scene. I remembered her horror at the idea of the Manhounds of Faol hunting people. The King's retirement had been engineered by his daughter Fahia. Fahia's husband, Rogan, the present king, was a mere cipher, a nonentity.

At the queen's side, reclining in a low couch wide enough for six, lay four beautiful girls. They were diaphanously clad and smothered with feathers and gems. One of them was the flame-haired girl I had rescued from the wounded neemu.

She looked at me now so piteously that I cursed my gag and bonds afresh, for I judged she blamed herself for my position, and I would have comforted her.

The gaunt figure of a pallan now moved forward. He wore a long robe of blue, girt with the symbols of his authority, and a face much like his must have promised hellfire to many an unbeliever before the fire consumed him utterly.

This was Pallan Ord Mahmud nal Yrmcelt. He was so addressed by the Deldar of the guard. My ears pricked.

The queen stared down at me as she sipped her wine. Then, in a gesture she might imagine to be regal but which was, in all truth, merely pretty, she flung the dregs in my face.

"Yetch! You destroyed my neemu!"

The flame-haired girl gasped.

It was quite unnecessary for the queen to spell out my crime. From the moment I had entered this luxurious chamber I had understood. For tied by silver chains, one on each side of that curule-chair, the feral black forms of two neemus were pulling toward me. They yawned to reveal their blood-red mouths and their sharp white fangs. She liked to tickle them now and then with a golden tickler a Fristle fifi had charge of, and when the queen commanded the girl would hand the golden feather-tipped rod across and the queen would stroke and tickle her pets and they would purr like enormous black cats. I knew how deadly they were. But these possessed themselves, partially trained, I had no doubt, willing to be fussed and petted by a human woman in return for a warm spot to sleep and much milk and meat.

The neemus regarded me with their baleful golden slit eyes, and yawned, and the queen tickled them and they purred.

"Take his gag off!"

The gag was roughly removed. I worked my aching jaws, but I did not speak. I stared up evilly at this gorgeous golden woman with her jewels and her feathers and her sleek black neemus and her slaves. I stared at that whole barbaric picture and I thought that perhaps I did not have long to live.

"You have not been put to the question yet, yetch, for you have been gagged, and so have had no opportunity to lie. I shall ask you questions. You would do well to tell the truth."

I waited. Now I had to think. The Dray Prescot of only a few seasons ago would have rolled in his chains toward this woman and caught her leg and so dragged her down and hoped her head might be chewed off by one of her pet neemus. The Dray Prescot who would have done that had been almighty lucky to have survived. The Dray Prescot who had come so far on Kregen had learned—a little, not much, as you shall hear.

"What is your name, cramph?"

This was the obvious question. To tell them I was a kaidur in their arena would mean I was markedly inferior, nothing better than a pampered slave, and so marked for destruction. To claim a spurious ancestry and say I was Varko of Hakkinostoling would be merely foolish. But, if I was a lord, a Kov—even a prince—I might stand some chance.

I said, "I am Dray Prescot, Pr—" and was immediately interrupted.

"You slaughtered one of my neemus, a prize, a hyrneemu I had paid for and had sent from a far distance. Your crime is a heinous one."

I knew she was playing with me, as her neemus might play with a woflo; but the test was yet to come.

So far I had concentrated all my attention on her and her immediate surroundings. There were others in the chamber, of course, high dignitaries and nobles, pallans of the realm. I ignored them. Dare I bring in the flame-haired girl? My eyes flickered toward her, and her pale face whitened more.

The queen fairly snarled at me.

"You look at my handmaiden Shirli! Perhaps you two have a criminal liaison? Perhaps you plot together against me?"

I shook my head, and those damned famous bells of Beng-Kishi clanged resonantly inside my skull. "Not so, Majestrix, not so. I have never seen the girl before the neemu would have killed her—"

"And if I believe you, does that give you the right to slaughter my glorious neemu so wantonly?"

"But the beast was about to devour the girl!"

"You yetch! Is that any reason to slay it? Of what value is a shishi compared with a glorious neemu, so black, so velvety, so smooth? You shall be slaughtered yourself, in a way that shall make you regret your criminal act! Oh, yes!"

I rolled over and struggled to stand up. I felt the indignity of my position. As I thus wriggled I saw a young man standing with the nobles and dignitaries, and he stared at me with so horrified a light in his eyes, so petrified a look of terror on his face, that he stood as one hypnotized.

I recognized him.

He was Mahmud nal Yrmcelt, the brilliant young man who had given me the kick that had freed me from the intolerable burden of the slate slab when first I had been pitched into this land of Hyrklana. And, more—his father was a chief pallan to the queen! And, more! He had been plotting treasons against his queen.

No wonder as he saw my eyes on him he trembled and that look of utter horror transfixed his handsome face!

I let my gaze travel across his face, pass him, and so stare at the others in that brilliant audience as I struggled to my feet. The guard Deldar moved in, his thraxter point pressing up against my side. I took a breath.

"I have committed no crime in any man's justice. I did not wish to slay the neemu; but the life of a girl is more precious in the sight of Opaz than even the life of so wonderful a wild beast as a neemu."

A frozen silence ensued.

The queen took more wine, and a slave wiped her forehead with a tissue-thin scrap of sensil. At last she spoke.

"Havil is the only true god."

She said this woodenly. I knew instantly that she did not believe this, that the worship of Havil was mere state policy, that she, herself, looked to other and probably darker deities for her inspiration.

"Yes," I said quickly, before they could get in. "Yes, Havil will relish the life of a girl over that of a neemu."

"Take him away—" the queen started to say, and I knew my blundering tongue had condemned me.

Mahmud nal Yrmcelt moved forward. Suddenly he was lively, light on his feet, smiling and smirking, bowing before the queen. "May I address the divine glory of your person, oh great queen?"

She looked down and she smiled, she smiled at this Mahmud nal Yrmcelt, did the puissant Queen of Hyrklana.

The moment was fraught with a great peril for us both.

"You may speak, Orlan, for you have always some jest, some merry jape to play. Proceed."

This Orlan Mahmud was sweating, and smiling and bowing, and was shaken clear down to his fashionable sandals.

"May it not prove a merry jest if this man faces his death in the arena, oh gracious queen?"

She put her hand to her chin. She pondered. Everyone waited on her words, for this was a weighty decision. Then she smiled on Orlan Mahmud nal Yrmcelt.

"You speak well, Orlan, and thus prove yourself a worthy son of a great father, who is my chief pallan. Truly, this yetch shall face his death in the arena!"

"Your Majestrix is too kind," babbled Orlan Mahmud. He bowed and backed away.

The queen shot him a sudden hard look.

If she wondered why this made her kind to him, she chose not to pursue the matter at the moment. I had read this Orlan Mahmud correctly. He had made his bargain with me.

"Don't tell the queen," he was in effect saying. "You are a doomed man; but this way you may save your life. There is at least a chance for a man who can lift a slate slab. . . ."

"And if he wins the contest, oh puissant lady?"

Queen Fahia chuckled and reached for a handful of palines on the golden dish handed to her by a Fristle fifi.

"I do not think that likely. He slew a neemu, very dear to me. Therefore by the green light of Havil it is only just he meet a test of greater import in the arena."

A long susurrating sigh rose from the audience.

They guessed.

So did I, too; but I wanted to hear this evil woman say it with those ripe cherry-red lips of hers.

"Dray Prescot, you said your name was. Well, Dray Prescot, you will be taken to the Jikhorkdun and stripped naked and given a sword and turned out to face a wild leem."

## Chapter Twelve

### Token for a queen from a dead Krozair

All the familiar sights and sounds and stinks of the arena rose about me again.

This was a special occasion, a gala arranged by the queen for her own special pleasure. The stands and terraces bulged with spectators, for all they had been let in free this day, and wine had been distributed, also, so that the canaille might cheer and yell for the queen. All the nobles' and dignitaries' boxes had been carefully decorated, and now they were filled, for not a soul there would offend Queen Fahia. She controlled not only the army, who were loyal to her out of consideration for the pay they received, and not only the Hyrklanian Air Service, for the same reasons, but also a large and formidable force of hired mercenaries, paid for out of treasury funds, but answerable to her alone. Rebellions did not last long in Hyrklana.

After my hair and beard clipping done by Tilly, my frisky little Fristle fifi, I had been easily recognizable to Orlan Mahmud nal Yrmcelt. I was not, by the same token, as easily recognized by anyone who knew me as Drak the Sword, kaidur of the Jikhorkdun. The irony of my situation was not lost on me. Because there were remnants of red favors on my clothes when I had been chained and flung before the queen, and because she was a somewhat vindictive little person, she saw to it that I was equipped for the Jikhorkdun by any other color than red. It happened she chose the green color—and I guessed that was no chance, for sacred to the greens was the emerald neemu.

A gruff old hyr-kaidur with a potbelly and graying hair and with his green favor stained with grease about his shoulder looked me over, behind the bars of the green

129

coys' entrance. He pulled his thick lower lip. He was apim, a man like me, and a comfortable sort, called Morok, and because he was a green, only a day ago I would have cheerfully killed him.

"Well, my lad," he said, pulling his lip. "You're in a right old leem's nest, and no mistake." And then he roared until the tears squeezed past his eyelids at his own jest.

Mind you—it made me feel like a good belly laugh, too.

This leem's nest was likely to be the last bed I lay upon, either here on Kregen or upon the Earth of my birth, four hundred light-years away.

When he had recovered himself a trifle, he spluttered out: "Can you use a thraxter, lad?"

"Aye."

He took me by the arm, looking swiftly about at the coys who had been shouted off from us, here up at the bars with the shine of the silver sand waiting beyond. "Hush, lad! We've had orders to give you a weapon you might perchance not savvy the use of. You slew the black neemu with a thraxter?"

"Aye."

He furtively looked around again, and wiped the back of his hand across his mouth. He was a green—but I had to pull myself out of this Jikhorkdun nonsense. He was a man, and he didn't much care for what he was being forced to do, sending a man up against a wild leem.

"Forget you said that, lad. I'll see you get a thraxter." Then he hawked and spat at a scuttling liki, and drowned it in the sand, its eight legs feebly writhing in a lake of spittle. "The leem will serve you like that, lad. Thraxter or stux or spear or anything."

"Perhaps."

"You're a cool one, by Kaidun! I'll say that." He looked at me and so did not see the tall gaunt form of the Pallan Mahmud walking from the milling coys toward us. "You'll get a thraxter, my lad, or my name ain't Morok the Mangler."

Pallan Mahmud spoke in that detached icy voice: "Your name may well be Morok the Mangled, kaidur, if you disobey the queen's express orders." He gestured behind him as Morok shrank back, his potbelly quivering, his face stricken. "The queen has given commands that this yetch, since he fancies the sword so much, is to be given a strange sword. One the like of which is unfamiliar to us.

130

She believes the thraxter will give him too much advantage, and what the queen believes is so, kaidur!"

"Indeed, yes, Notor Pallan, indeed yes!"

Two Rapas came forward at the pallan's bidding. I was looking at Morok the Mangler and thinking how strange are the ways of men. Had he known I had fought as kaidur for the reds he would have cursed me, and here he had almost run headlong into punishment on my behalf. So I took no notice of the Rapas.

"We had a slave who swore by outlandish gods and blasphemed Havil the Green," said Mahmud. He, like the queen, no doubt gave only lip service to the state religion. "He wished to fight for the reds, and so, naturally, he was given to the greens. He brought his own outlandish and uncouth weapon with him; but we took it from him as a curiosity, and the queen hung it in her trophy hall." Pallan Mahmud sniggered. "No man can really swing the sword, so monstrous is it. But, Dray Prescot, by the queen's express command you are to go up against the wild leem bearing this steel monstrosity."

So saying Mahmud gestured again to the two Rapas. Between them they carried the monstrous object forward, bowed, and presented it to Mahmud. He stepped back, pettishly waving them away. "Give it to this loudmouthed Morok the Mangled! Yetches, must I tell you everything!"

Mahmud flicked a lace handkerchief—a group of coys out there had just been butchered and the smell was warmish—and the kaidur Morok the Mangler, of the green, stepped forward to take this queen's gift of a sword from the two Rapas. He whistled his astonishment.

"Now, by Kaidun! You are doomed with this useless rubbish, Dray Prescot! It is a show sword, heavy and slow. . . ."

I stared.

I, Dray Prescot, stared at the weapon this kaidur held all uncomprehendingly. What did he know of its magical secrets?

A man had once died out there in the arena, at my feet, and had gasped a last word of greeting to his Krozair brothers of Zamu. And another man had come from the Eye of the World, and he had brought with him that which Morok now held, and these kleeshes had not allowed him to use it in the arena. Had he done so he would have become the greatest of hyr-kaidurs.

I had fancied the evil queen had designed to send me up

131

against a leem with a rapier; that would have been a jest much to her liking.

But she had surpassed herself.

They would not let me take the weapon yet, for fear I ran berserk before I was thrust out with the iron rakes into the arena. I glared hungrily upon that sword. I knew what manner of sword that was. It had come here, to the Jikhorkdun of Huringa, in the land of Hyrklana, in far Havilfar, all the way from the Eye of the World.

Could I believe that the Savanti—even, perhaps, the Star Lords—had intervened on my behalf?

That was the reading I thought then to put on this miracle.

Neither the Grodnims of the north shore nor the Zairians of the south shore of the inner sea go much afaring in the outer oceans as mercenaries. But a Krozair had once done so, for reasons I knew were not important, and had fought his way around the wide curve of the world, and so, at last, found himself taken up by the foul slave-masters seeking fodder for the Jikhorkdun. I saluted his memory.

There was only one other possible sword I could have preferred for the work in hand, and that was the Savanti sword.

But I was content with the beautiful blade that Morok the Mangler so contemptuously condemned, and tucked under his arm with a curse for the retreating backs of the Pallan Mahmud and his Rapa slaves.

I kept trying to look more clearly at the scabbard, for both scabbard and hilt, as well as blade, are marked.

This happening, I felt convinced, marked a new and important phase in my relations with those unseen forces that controlled my life.

Brazen trumpets blasted the hot air above our heads. A huge roar welled up from the packed seats. The time had come. I was naked. I held out my hand to Morok.

He looked sorrowful. "You're a dead man with this, Dray Prescot." He hefted the sword. "By Kaidun! What manner of imbecile made it so long? So hefty! And the length of the handle—the pommel flies about like a gregarian on a string."

Again the trumpets blasted their brazen notes into the heated air. The twin suns—and now if ever was the time to call them Zim and Genodras—flooded their mingled streaming light down in an opaz glory. The silver sand glittered. The roar continued, thousands of throats yelling for the spectacle to begin.

Morok the Mangler held out the sword to me.

"May the glass eye and the brass sword of Beng Thrax go with you, Dray Prescot. Aye, and his emerald lungs blow danger away from your path!"

A group of Rhaclaw kaidur-handlers came up, prodding, and so the time had at last come. I said, "My thanks, Morok. May Opaz guide you."

He concealed his shock. He held the scabbarded sword in both hands. "Havil the Green—" he began unconvincingly.

The Rhaclaws shouted, and the uproar from the crowd outside increased so that the very air shivered. I said to Morok, "I will not need the scabbard."

And so I, Dray Prescot, Krozair of Zy, once more took into my two fists a great Krozair longsword.

With this as weapon I would fight three leems. Or so I felt then, so elated, so buoyant, so cocksure—alas, all youthful follies—but ... but ... once more to grasp a great Krozair longsword!

Memories ghosted up—to be instantly suppressed—of the clean onward rush of a swifter, of the shock of ramming and the wild elation of boarding, of the glorious red of Sanurkazz smiting down the hated green of Magdag. And, in my fists—gripped in that cunning Krozair grip—a great longsword!

I marched out into the arena and the howl that went up at the sight of me dwarfed anything before. The crowd had been inflamed. The queen had ordered this rogue slaughtered for their pleasure, and a man against a leem was a rare and wonderful sight. And, too, brother, the seats were free!

I had long experience as kaidur in knowing from which different pens the wild beasts would be let out. Not that I had fought a beast for some time, for kaidurs were reserved for more skillful combat one against another. So I walked slowly out, and I must have presented a lonely figure, a lone spectacle, a single man dwarfed to insignificance in that mighty amphitheater and the vast sanded arena below.

The animal roar from the crowd could be erased from my consciousness except as it might signal the leem's release behind my back. I could feel the sand under my feet—dear God!—I can feel it now! The warmth of the suns pressed on my back. I held the longsword in my left hand, under the pommel, loosely, the blade slanted up over my left shoulder. How the crowd enjoyed the sight of that monstrous blade! How incongruous it seemed to them. They were accustomed to the cut-and-thrust thraxter, with its medium-length straight blade. The Krozair longsword dwarfed the thraxter at every point. Truly, this longsword was no weapon for a man unskilled in its use. A kaidur might seek to use it, and no doubt would acquit himself well; but for a great Jikai one must indeed be a Krozair!

The hideous shrieks from the crowd reached incredible proportions—and then fell eerily silent, and so I knew the leem had been released. I turned slowly to face the pen, for the clever managers of the Jikhorkdun had waited until my back was turned to release the leem. Maybe they thought they were doing me a favor, and that it would be all over before I had a chance to turn. If that, then they risked Queen Fahia's regal displeasure.

There had been time, in that short interval, to look at the sword. It was a quality blade. Neatly incised, it bore a name—a name I will not reveal to you—followed by the letters KRZY. So I knew I had the best brand possible in my fists.

The chance I had accepted was that the queen might play a further jest on me and release a volleem, one of the flying monsters we had met on our journey to Migla, or some other of the specialized forms of leem. But the beast that slunk toward me over the silver sand, belly low, tail flicking, his clawed paws going up and down in a regular stalking rhythm, very menacingly, was the normal variety of leem I knew from my days with my clansmen guarding our herds of chunkrah on the great plains of Segesthes.

A leem is a feral beast, eight-legged, furry, feline and vicious, with a wedge-shaped head armed with fangs that can strike through oak. It is weasel-shaped but leopard-sized. Its paws can smash a man's head.

This one was a fine vicious specimen, with ocher-colored fur, and black paws, and a black tuft to his tail, which is unusual. He had been saved against a great occasion, and the crowd knew Queen Fahia would never release him against someone she did not want ripped into the tiniest of bloody scraps.

I do not believe myself to be an overly superstitious man. I know what I know about the dark forces that

134

may—or may not—have their being beyond the walls of our senses. But when, with that damned leem stalking me across the sand, I saw a patch of blood not properly raked and saw the unevenness of the sand there, I paused. The slaves charged with sprinkling and raking and clearing away the corpses and the abandoned equipment had been in just as much a rush to finish as the crowd to begin. And the arena was a large arena. I kicked the rough sand. The first kick revealed the hilt of a thraxter, broken off. I frowned. This would be no place to make a stand when I would need all my agility. I kicked again. A scrap of red cloth showed.

Again—was it the Savanti—was it the Star Lords?

Who can say?

I bent and jerked the red cloth free. Someone of the reds had died here. I stuck the longsword point first into the sand and wrapped the breechclout about me, tucking the end between my legs and pulling it up and tucking that in, and this time I made a thorough job of it, thinking of my past ignominy.

The crowd started yelling again as I did this, and a few rotten gregarians came hurtling down. I took the longsword out of the sand and this time I held it in the Krozair grip. My right hand gripped firmly but most subtly close up to the guard, my left fist beneath the pommel. That way, with about two handspaces between my fists, the tremendous speed of leverage that makes the Krozair longsword so deadly was fully available. As to the power—I knew this leem would feel that.

The leem was hungry.

Well, that made two of us.

He opened his jaws in that wedge-shaped head, showing his fangs. There were shrieks from the terraces. That sight alone was enough to make a coy faint.

He paced slowly toward me, readying himself for the spring, no doubt already imagining himself settling down with me between his front paws to satisfy his appetite.

Leems are able to spring for enormous distances.

I moved away, making the crowd screech. I wished to clear that treacherous unraked area of sand. If the crowd did not wonder why I was not running like a crazed loon around the arena I put that down to the fraught feelings of everyone there. They all knew this was a confrontation.

I heard the odd single comment, spurting through the crowd's noise. The leem advanced. I set myself. The sword went up over my right shoulder. The crowd slowly fell silent. The suns shone, there was no wind down here in the arena, I was sweating a little, and the leem stalked forward. His head was low, his eyes upturned to me, and his jaws opened as his tail flicked from side to side. One after the other with menacing precision he put those eight great claw-armed pads down, the talons extended and gleaming brilliantly.

The leem sprang.

So fast it all was. So fast and deadly.

He soared into the air with his four front paws extended, his rear paws trailing, and his tail rigid. So fast . . . I went for a knee-bending roll one way and then came back the other and as he went past cut the great sword down. I put tremendous effort into that blow, an effort more of aim and precision than of mere muscular strength, knowing the Krozair longsword would do the work if it was handled correctly.

I am a Krozair of Zy, and in all humility I may say that, indeed, I do know how to handle a Krozair longsword.

The brand sheared through the leem's front foreleg. He went on and rolled in a great swashing of ocher fur, yowling, splattering blood from the stump; but wrenching himself around and standing on his remaining seven legs. Blood pumped thickly from the stump. I regarded him gravely. I decided not to pick up the severed leg and hurl it at him. He was a beast, and for all that we detested leems on the great plains of Segesthes that would have been an indignity to him, for a leem, like any other animal, man or beast, must follow his nature.

Also, the blood might have made my hands slippery.

He rushed again, and he sprang with as much sheer feral verve as before, having four back legs from which to make his spring. I removed the other front foreleg.

This time he came around more slowly. He was not weakened by loss of blood yet; that would take, in a leem, a little time. They are not easy to kill. When he charged me this time, I fancied, he would act differently, and not just because he had lost two legs.

He came in again. This time I leaped for him, got under him as he passed above me, and, ducking, I severed his rear hindleg. He went on, rolling, and this time he came back so fast, springing from his uninjured side, that a claw raked down my side and my blood dropped to mingle with his on that bloodstained silver sand.

But if he was taking the fight to me, I took it to him. He sat back, as a cat does, for an instant. Then he swiped at me with his second foreleg. I did not strike back but ran sideways, turned and feinted to hit him from that side. He pivoted and I went the other way—fast, fast!—and got six inches of steel between his ribs. That was not enough to reach his heart, of course, his main heart, and I had to skip back most circumspectly. I had missed my aim, but I did not curse. This was a game of life and death we played, this leem and I beneath the Suns of Scorpio in the arena of Huringa. He would not waste time spitting at me.

He did hunch his back, though, and I saw the way his stumps bled, and I knew the thing was really over; but before that he could squash my head with a single blow. I leaped again and swung and gashed a great slice across his shoulder. He tried to take me in his mouth and I drove the Krozair longsword at him, and again I missed and merely succeeded in slicing alongside his nose. The blade was sharp. Had it been blunt, as was the blade with which I fought the shorgortz, I believe I would not have been as quick as I was; I do not think the leem would have got me, for the blunted longsword is a great bone-smasher.

The crowd had been silent. Now they began cheering again. I banished the noise; but I did notice the shouts and calls came when I attacked the leem. So, being a show-off in some things, I made a great point of attacking the leem, of charging him, and of smiting and hacking. He lost another leg—and now he did not want to know anything at all more about this man-monster with the brightly shining metal tongue who so tormented him.

He backed off, hissing.

I do not like leems, as I told you, for their ways and damage they have done me. But I could feel it in my heart to feel sorrow for this great beast. He was done for, and I think he knew it. Blood fouled his ocher fur. His eyes did not glare with so much bestial ferocity. He hissed and he slunk away, his ears low, his tail dragging.

I had an idea.

The leem was hobbling—for him—on four legs, but he could still run. I herded him. I wove a net of steel about him and drove him back and back, chivying him from the side, making him go where I wanted. His muzzle was a mask of blood. He slunk back, hissing, and tried to leap aside, and I thrust into that flank and so forced him back. When he was where I wanted him to be, and he attacked again, I leaped and sliced the great sword and so took off his fifth leg. Now he would limp in very truth. He spat now, and hissed, and then he began to shriek. I circled him. He tried still to get at me.

When the moment came I sprang.

I landed with both feet on his shoulders—those beautifully articulated shoulders that swing two pairs of legs—and got my left arm around his head and under his throat, and so passed the sword downward and through his heart—both the main heart and then, unnecessarily, the subsidiary heart. I leaped clear, and I leaped clear backward, deliberately. In death he writhed and slashed and screamed and foamed and bled—but he died.

Anyone or any beast tends to die if a Krozair longsword passes through the heart.

I cut off his tail. I held it at my right hand, by that tuft, and I sloped the bloody longsword over my shoulder.

The place I had herded the leem to was exact. I looked up, and there, sitting regally in her royal box, directly over my head, Queen Fahia looked down, her golden hair and white face unmistakable in that colorful brilliance surrounding her.

Absolute silence.

"Here, queen!" I roared. "A token from a Krozair!"

And I hurled the bloody leem tail full in her face.

# Chapter Thirteen

# "Drak the Sword! Kaidur! Kaidur!"

Defiant, theatrical, ridiculous, that gesture.

As soon as I hurled the bloody leem tail I leaped nimbly away and to the side. Eight stuxes and half a dozen crossbow bolts pierced into the sand where I had been standing. If this was the way I, Dray Prescot, Krozair of Zy, was to die, then I would make of it a great Jikai, and die well, by Zair!

I started for the tall wall festooned with silks and carpets and flowers supporting the royal box. I held that marvelous Krozair longsword before me, double-handed, as I had been trained and as I knew how, and as I went forward so I flicked and batted away flying stuxes and crossbow quarrels. The whole crowd remained absolutely silent. That silence hung eerily over the enormous amphitheater. Every eye, I knew, was fixed in a hypnotic gaze upon that macabre scene, a half-naked man clad in a brave red breechclout, advancing with a monstrous brand in his fists, forging through a flying hail of death. I picked the way I would climb up where no man believed a kaidur could climb. I seized on the flying stuxes and bolts and swatted them away with the wrist flickings that are the joy of a Krozair.

Queen Fahia looked down and saw my face.

She flinched back.

I think she recognized that I would reach her.

She stood up.

Tall and regal, her pile of golden hair ablaze with gems, she lifted her white arms upward, and spoke harsh words that instantly halted the flickering streams of bolts and stuxes.

She lowered her arms and placed her hands on her

139

breast, crossed, and she looked into my eyes and I stopped and waited for her to speak.

"You say your name is Dray Prescot. You cry upon unfamiliar spirits. What token is it that smears blood upon a queen's face." And, indeed, her pale face showed daubs of leem blood, spots splattered across her gown and hair. She stared at me with wide and brilliant eyes, willing me, I knew, to submit to her beauty and authority.

I threw my head back, challenging. "What queen is it that sends a man to his death in the paws of a leem?"

"You merited that death."

"You merit a death no different."

Some hot-tempered young mercenary of her guard could not contain himself longer at this and he let loose. I flicked the bolt away and stared evilly at this Queen Fahia.

But she was a queen, long used to absolute authority.

"You are very clever with that monstrous steel brand. What if I order two of my guardsmen to loose together?"

"Order them."

I think she had now reached a conclusion I had already come to—and the crowd, in the way of crowds who sense these things, already guessed. She did not wish to have me killed until she had satisfied her feminine curiosity and slaked her pique. But the challenge I had issued was direct. She nodded curtly to her guard Chuktar. He was a Chulik. I had seen very few Chuliks so far in Havilfar. I guessed he was a most expensive paktun, hired to train and command her private bodyguard.

Two crossbowmen lifted their weapons and, at the Chuktar's barked command, let fly.

At the moment of this word *"Loose!"* I took three neat little side steps. The bolts whistled through thin air.

Every throat in that vast amphitheater roared out—a great volume of raucous noise—for they were laughing!

Only Queen Fahia and those about her did not share the jest.

Fahia spoke again, swiftly, to the Chulik Chuktar. He nodded and sent a file of his men running down the concealed stairs that would enable them to pass onto the sand of the arena through doors solidly bolted only on the inside. I braced myself.

"You will not be harmed, Dray Prescot. I wish to talk with you, before I decide what is to become of you."

I knew that part of it. I considered what was best to do.

The dead leem lay bleeding in the sun. I walked across to it and looked down. The flies were already gathering and I swatted the sword about, aware that this was not a lowly task for that marvelous brand. The leem was wearing a silver collar. During the fight I had not thought about it, for the Krozair steel would shear through silver as though flesh and bone. Now I bent and unlocked the silver collar, lifted it up so that it glittered in the mingled rays of the suns.

The queen's guardsmen appeared from the hidden entrances onto the arena, other guards always alert and vigilant there.

And then—I suppose Naghan the Gnat started it, for he was a quick-witted rogue, and cunning, and yet a staunch armorer-kaidur—from the red benches a great storm of cheering rose. The kaidurs there, the apprentices, even the coys, were jumping up and down and yelling and shouting and, almost at once, the whole red corner of the amphitheater began to erupt in a bedlam of victory shouts.

"Drak the Sword! Kaidur! Kaidur! The red for the ruby drang! Drak the Sword!"

So they had at last recognized me. I felt a fitting further gesture might be in order, for I much disliked the queen's new silky approach. I walked slowly over to the red corner and I lifted the silver collar taken from the dead leem and I hurled it high. It spun and glittered in the sun as it fell among the trophies of the reds, proudly displayed in their sacred prianum under the red and gold awning.

Absolute silence from blue and yellow and green.

Rapture unbounded from red!

Then the two files of mercenary guards closed up and I went with them, out of the arena with its blood-soaked silver sand and down the long secret tunnels and up the secret stairs into the regal presence of Queen Fahia of Hyrklana.

They made me wait, all blood-splashed and sweaty as I was. Wishing to reinforce my advantage and to consolidate what little hope I might have, I had given up the sword. A Rapa had placed his curved dagger at my ear at the time. I could have fought the lot of them, and slain them, and so raced from the secret passageways. But life thereafter in the Jikhorkdun would have been impossible. And I did not forget the great storm that had first thrown me into contact with this catlike Queen Fahia and her black neemu pets.

More and more I was understanding that it was well-nigh impossible to anticipate the wishes of the Star Lords. They had been patient with the escape I had made with Princess Lilah, and they had—even then—been storing up that information against a later day. I wondered about the other people I had rescued on Kregen at different times and places, and wondered how they were destined to fit into the pattern of the future.

All the time I waited I guessed Fahia would be taking the baths of the nine, no doubt in ponsho-milk, relaxing and preparing for an interview she would be absolutely without doubt must go her way. She would be perfuming herself, and donning marvelous clothes of fabulous value, adorning herself with gems and feathers and silks and furs, her face painted and powdered and perfumed, her finger-nails lacquered green, her eyes heavy with kohl, her lips rich and moistly red. And her hair—hair of that brilliant gold would be coiled and coiffed to display all its luster and brilliance, and sprinkled with gems so as to bring out with great artifice every last beauty.

When, at last, the Chulik Chuktar with a bodyguard came for me and I was ushered into her presence I felt cheated.

She knew her own power, did Queen Fahia.

She sat in that curule chair with its zhantil-pelt coverings, and the barbaric furs and jewels and feathers and silks were all there, each adding its contribution to the gorgeous spectacle filled with light and color. She herself sat there in a classically simple red gown, slit to the thigh on both sides, girdled by a golden belt. Her golden hair, her face, retained still the splotches and stains of the dead leem's blood.

The black neemus yawned and opened their lambent golden eyes, and stretched, tinkling their silver chains. The slave shishis huddled in their transparent silks. There were no councillors or pallans present, but Orlan Mahmud was there, and a few other young men I did not recognize. Women also were there, and at least two Fristle women of exceptional beauty and power in their looks, not slaves but free halflings at the queen's court.

The Chulik positioned his crossbowmen in a single line to the right and left of the curule chair, facing me. I noticed the way the courtiers moved out of the area that could be turned into a sieve of death.

"You told me a lie, Drak the Sword." Those were her first words.

I did not reply.

Her color was still pale, still wan; she had had a nasty fright. I knew the way the crowd's fickle behavior would be read by the queen, how she must seek to placate them as she detested them, despite her power.

"You are a kaidur, and now, after the exploit today, a hyr-kaidur. Your name is Drak the Sword. What, then, this nonsense about a fanciful uncouth name like Dray Prescot?"

"A man may have a name before he gains a name in the Jikhorkdun."

Her eyes regarded me. "Aye, that is true. And my Jikordun divides the leems from the ponshos."

She said *Jikhorkdun* as *Jikordun,* as many people did, slurring the word for ease of pronunciation. Few kaidurs spoke it that way.

"Had I known you were a kaidur, Drak the Sword, perhaps I would not have been so swift in my just vengeance."

There was a very great deal to be read into that statement.

I decided to play the most obvious reading, the one most likely to reflect the state of the game. I said, "I believe I did not express my very real sorrow at the destruction of the neemu." I was deliberately refraining from calling her queen or majestrix or any other of the many terms for referring to royalty I spare you. "I feel I am able to make restitution."

"Ah!" she said, and she sat forward, and again her chin settled onto her upturned fist. Her eyes regarded me now with a look reminiscent of the look that leem had first given me. "Yes, Drak, I think you may!"

Again pushing what I fancied the Star Lords, in their usual obscurantist way, were urging me to, I said, "You have but to command."

"I know that!" Her chin went up, off her fist, and her eyes blazed at me. "My commands are obeyed. But before that, Drak, I would talk of your great victory, for the leem was a mighty and powerful beast, and notable for its kills."

So we spoke for a space, of this and that, and presently she motioned for me to come and sit on a stool brought forward by a flunky—a little Och in embroidered livery—and placed at her feet. I sat down and told her a pack of

143

lies, about swinging the sword as one would an ax, and of how I rather fancied I would use it again, Havil willing, in the Jikhorkdun. She nodded and sucked in her breath, her bosom rising and falling, her eyes bright and leechlike upon me as she heard talk of other combats, some she had seen and some not. Her passionate interest in the arena was not faked. Statecraft, love, food, money—all were of secondary interest to her beside this consuming passion for the Jikhorkdun.

Knowing this, thinking I knew what the Star Lords were about, I forced down my desires to smash them all up and get out of here and aboard a voller and make for Valka—for I knew another great supernatural gale would brutally beat me back.

This game here must be played out first.

As a queen and a despot she had her pick of the kaidurs. Her chamberlaids would bring them to her chambers at night, and she would use them as she saw fit, and so send them back to fight for her in the arena. I already knew that apart from the four color corners, there existed a small and select band of kaidurs devoted to the queen—Queen's Kaidurs—and on special occasions these would fight wagered combats of phenomenal value. Usually they won, and would dispose of the opponent fighting them, no matter what color he happened to be. Much later, long and long, I discovered just why the Queen's Kaidurs almost invariably won.

She did not make me an offer to become a Queen's Kaidur. She had said, though, "You are a hyr-kaidur now, Drak. And as a great kaidur you may wander the streets of Huringa. Would you seek to escape? I remember the flier. . . ."

Here was where I took two korfs with one shaft, as Seg would say.

"No idea of escape enters my head. There was a girl—I have completely forgotten the shishi, now, since—since—" And, artfully and contemptuously, I hesitated, and looked at her, and looked away. "No, I would on no account seek to escape from Huringa which is ruled by Queen Fahia."

The performance sickened me. But if the Star Lords wished me to remain here, and I was to do so with my head still affixed between my shoulders, the pace must be forced a little. All that natural charisma I have told you of was working for me now, keeping me alive, as I know; I had to give nature some assistance, some better chance.

"I believe you, Drak the Sword."

This first interview—first in our altered circumstances—drew to its close. But she was a sharp lady, and a queen, and so as I was retiring, she said, her voice roughened and back to its habitual coarseness from the more mellow tones in which we had conversed: "And, Drak the Sword! You swore to make restitution for the slain neemu!"

"Aye. Point out the way—"

"Sufficient that you remember. Now go. I shall send for you again."

Amid much scraping and inclining—she insisted on the full incline in matters of state—we went out. I guessed I was expected to report back to the red barracks where no doubt Nath the Arm and Naghan the Gnat would greet me kindly enough, even if Cleitar Adria might glower with jealousy.

I found myself walking along the corridors with the marble wall-facings and Pandahem jars of flowers and Lohvian mirrors from Chalniorn in company with Orlan Mahmud nal Yrmcelt and his friend, a commanding-looking apim with a somewhat pudgy face and plump body, sumptuously dressed, who I gathered was Rorton Gyss, Trylon of Kritdrin. Orlan Mahmud had been overeager to push up to my side, nudging other people out of the way, for a hyr-kaidur is assured of constant attention from admirers and well-wishers. I knew what was troubling him.

"Simmer down, Orlan," said the Trylon of Kritdrin. "The hyr-kaidur is a man, by Havil! He knows the value of a closed mouth."

Orlan Mahmud shot me a glance. "My father," he said, all his liveliness gone. "I still fear him."

"That, my boy, is why I never married. I like women, Havil knows, but I prefer to cast my bread upon private waters." And Rorton Gyss chuckled. A genial, pleasant thoroughly civilized Horter, this Rorton Gyss, and, as I was to find, with a mind of his own and a will of alloy-steel.

They took me down from that high fortress of Hakal, frowning over the city of Huringa, and by more open ways this time we crossed to the Jikhorkdun. Here we stopped by a tavern into which, by virtue of my new status, I was now allowed. Many taverns and inns had been built into and alongside the Jikhorkdun and its surrounding warrens but inevitably never enough for all the public. Only nobles and high Horters might venture into the amphitheater tavern. One seldom ever heard anyone addressed as plain Horter; it was all Kyr and Kov and Tyr and Rango and Strom. We sat at a plain sturm-wood table and an apim girl served us light yellow wine from Central Hyrklana—reasonable stuff, light and refreshing and ideal for the heat of the day. If a deal was to be proposed, Mahmud and Gyss were going about it in a civilized manner.

The deal was simple.

I kept my mouth shut about Orlan Mahmud's involvement with those people plotting the queen's downfall, or I had my throat slit by certain paktuns whose names needn't be mentioned among Horters.

"You would take my word?"

"Of course. You may be a kaidur, but we can tell you are also a Horter."

I sipped my wine and inwardly I laughed at them. Fools! I was no gentleman—I never had been, save by a king's commission to walk the quarterdeck of a King's Ship, and I never would be. But, for all that, if I gave them my word I would keep it. Also, and I did not discount this aspect, they knew that it would take more than one paktun of very great skill indeed to deal with me, and further, that the queen would be most wroth and would relentlessly pursue an inquiry.

"Perhaps," I said. "You do not ask yourself what I was doing there, at the time the great slate slab fell."

This had occurred to them. It was not a weapon they might use against me except after I had denounced them, as they knew.

"You, too, are against"—Orlan's gaze flicked around the tavern and back—"the queen?"

He whispered that, a conspirator to the life.

"It might very well be," I said. And added, "Or, it might not. For I think the queen will smile on me now."

"Aye!" Gyss drank his wine at a single gulp and called for more. "And we know where the queen's smile leads! A garrote, and a stone lashed to the legs, and a hole in the River of Leaping Fish."

Then someone recognized me and a crowd gathered and I had to rise and smile at them—most painful—and so make my escape in a shower of back-claps and handshakes and adulatory speeches. We walked quickly along the alleyways threading the warrens of the Jikhorkdun, and my state attracted so much attention that in the end I had to bid Orlan Mahmud and this Rorton Gyss farewell and run for the red barracks.

"We will see you tomorrow, Drak the Sword!" called Rorton Gyss. This Trylon of Kritdrin had impressed me. He seemed a man who knew his own mind, and went for the truth, no matter what or who stood in his way.

He was a supporter of the yellow; that was unfortunate; but as I have said, color supporters might mingle freely with only the occasional fight, for Mahmud was of the red. And, if Gyss was of the yellow it would mean he could bring a whole new dimension of support to the cause he espoused with Mahmud.

Nath the Arm greeted me with a great bellow.

"By Kaidun! Drak the Sword—you are a hyr-kaidur now! It was superbly done, Kaidur to the life! Just remember: easy come, easy go. There are many coys pushing up, and the glass eye and brass sword of Beng Thrax may smile on them also!"

Naghan the Gnat jumped up and down in his excitement, and all the red barracks waxed warm over the triumph. The silver collar of the leem was a great trophy. I thought of the leem's tail—and I did not smile.

I had not missed the shifty liquid eyes of the little fellow who had followed me, keeping as he thought out of sight, his plain brown tunic and kilt worn without color favor. A spy, he was, spying on me ... following me through the Jikhorkdun to the red barracks of Nath the Arm. He could not follow me inside, and on that I cursed him and forgot him. ...

# Chapter Fourteen

## The life of a hyr-kaidur in the Jikhorkdun

My life in Huringa proceeded much as any other kaidur's at this time, for I was waiting for the signal to which I might respond. If the queen was to be overthrown, poor soul, for all her evil, then the plan must be good and absolutely watertight. She controlled everything personally, with pallans to convey her orders and, sometimes, to venture on advice. I palled up with Mahmud and Gyss, and was sent into the arena from time to time, usually to rapturous applause, and otherwise lounged around fretting over this damned interdict of the Star Lords, and drinking and having what fun was offered. Here I brushed up on my knowledge of Havilfar, as you shall hear when overt knowledge is essential. A parcel of Chulik slaves were brought in.

We all went down to the bagnios to see them.

Now Chuliks are not often kept as slaves. Their chief value lies in their fanatical obedience to orders and their absolute loyalty while they are being paid. They are superb fighters. I had met a Chulik render captain; that had been unusual.

Chuliks are an extremely fierce manlike race of people with oily yellow skin, the head shaved so as to leave a long pigtail, two three-inch-long tusks thrusting upwards from the corners of the cruel mouth, and round black eyes. On the Chulik islands stringing off the coast of southeastern Segesthes the training of the males from birth is designed to produce high-quality mercenary soldiers, and they generally command higher fees than other races. There are large colonies of Chuliks in other islands and continents, of course, as I had found in the Eye of the World and in the Hostile Territories, and these people, like the other races about them, know nothing of the outside world. Chuliks may share some of the normal attributes of mankind, like two legs and two arms and two eyes; but they have little of the attribute of humanity.

So it was that the idea of Chulik coys intrigued us all.

"Well, Drak, and how do you fancy their chances?"

"By Kaidun, Balass," I said. "They are a mean bunch."

Balass laughed. Balass liked laughing. He was a black-skinned man from Xuntal, with fierce predatory hawklike features, and brilliant eyes, and he was a fine fighter, a kaidur. I had found in him a chord of friendship that I was loath to touch, for fear he would be dragged across the silver sand smearing his lifeblood, hauled out by the cruel iron hooks. He was named Balass the Hawk. Balass, as you know, is an ebony wood, often used for purposes of correction and chastisement.

"A cage voller flew in today with many volleems," said Balass the Hawk. His bright eyes showed all the mischief and merriment the news meant.

"Oho!" I said. "Then it behooves us to see this, kaidur. Indeed, yes, Balass the Hawk, this must not be missed."

"Beng Thrax's silver kneecaps must support us all." Balass chuckled. We both knew what these Chulik coys would face, pitted against volleem.

Volleem, the flying form of the leem, is a nasty brute at the best of times, and we wondered what the Jikhorkdun managers would think up to make the spectacle more interesting.

You see—I have reported this conversation as I remember it—how bound up I was becoming with this whole evil business of the arena. And yet, it was not wholly evil. In straight combats between men of equal skills and armed in the same fashion, many virtues for a warlike nation must accrue, especially when that nation is faced with ferocious depredations by vermin like the Leem-Lovers from the southern oceans.

Each of the four colors received their quota of Chulik coys and the managers designed a different test in each case.

The greens were caged, a Chulik and a volleem together, and left to fight it out with spears.

The blues were herded in altogether, with a variety of weapons, into a vast cage erected in the center of the arena and all their quota of volleems released upon them at once.

The yellows, being in the ascendant, were kept in reserve.

The reds were given an assignment that brought howls from the red benches where the kaidurs lolled on their ponsho fleeces and shrieks from the red terraces soaring up in the amphiteater.

Each red coy had a strong steel chain attached to his left ankle, and the chain passed to a ring riveted around the front rear leg of a volleem. The thraxters the Chuliks were issued would not cut the steel chain, light as it was.

The resultant spectacle raised a pandemonium of noise and screams and yells.

Silver sand puffed. Bright blood flew. The battering of the volleems' wings, the shrieks as men and beasts were torn and slashed, all blended into a bedlam of horror and revulsion—and yet men and women of many races sat in the terraces and enjoyed it as a spectacle!

And all the time the citizens of Huringa thus disported themselves their slaves labored to manufacture the produce and grow the food that kept the city and the state great.

I felt the Star Lords had set a purpose to my hands, and I itched to prosecute it with more zeal than the careful machinations of Rorton Gyss and Orlan Mahmud and their friends would allow.

The volleems massacred the Chulik coys. All their weapons-skill could not overcome the tremendous odds. Only one Chulik survived, badly lacerated and injured. He was a red coy, and when he was carried in, dripping blood, we all rose to him, Chulik though he was.

His name was Kumte Harg.

The volleems would be cared for, rested, fed, and then when they were back to full strength again, would be starved ready for the next bloody spectacle.

The only subject of conversation from then on was just who would be sent out to face them, and with what.

I fancied that Drak the Sword would find his fool self mixed up in that confrontation somehow.

For a successful kaidur whose ambitions lifted no higher than the plaudits of the crowd, the rewards of victories, the acclamation of his comrades and peers, this life I was now leading could scarcely be matched. I had continually to fight against its seductive sway. The real tests came in two forms: in the first that I would forget who and what I was and revel in the better aspects of the Jikhorkdun, overlooking or excusing the wilder and more bloody aspects; in the second that I would be sent out against an opponent better than I.

Ascent up the scale of success was relatively rapid. An unknown coy one day would be the apprentice of the next few sennights, and then with each successive accolade would climb the ladder until he made kaidur. Some men managed this very rapidly, others at a more sedate pace. For them all, the descent would be swift.

So it was that I rigidly kept myself apart from the other kaidurs, even Balass, to my sorrow, for he was a fine man, and trod the lonely path of the true hyr-kaidur.

During this period I was well aware that I was, as it were, serving an apprenticeship of a different sort and to two different masters—rather, to a clique of masters and to a mistress.

The would-be rebels contacted me from time to time, and always it was big talk of what they would do, and how, and never when. The queen sent for me, particularly after a great Kaidur, and we would talk. Always, these audiences I had with her were in the chamber, with her sitting regally on the curule chair. Her neemus and her shishis flanked her, fifis fluttered to and fro with wine and palines, and the giant Brokelsh waved the gorgeous feathered fan.

The cunning managers of the Jikhorkdun ensured my fights were carried out with weapons familiar to them. Each time I saw the queen my question was always the same.

"And when are you going to put that great sword back into my hands?"

She would give a little frown, and, out of custom, I would add: "Queen?"

She would laugh lightly, an evil little tinkle.

"When the time comes again for a great Kaidur, Drak."

So I would not press the matter.

She said, once, I remember: "It says in the *Hyr-Derengil-Notash* that all things are as they seem to all men." This famous book, the *Hyr-Derengil-Notash* (the title means, very roughly, the high palace of pleasure and wisdom), is often resorted to by philosophers. It had been compiled by a Wizard of Loh some two thousand five hundred seasons or so ago, and copies existed in various forms, each with its bibliography and separate notations, and you may be very sure the Kregan academics argued long and earnestly over their wine as to the analysis and interpretations to be placed on each separate word and phrase. She looked at me with those bright blue eyes of hers, so like her sister's, speculative upon my ugly face. "It says, Drak the Sword, that where there is evil there must be good. And where there is good there must be evil."

I nodded. "The interpretation is still debated, Queen."

"My interpretation satisfies me. Evil must of necessity exist. The *Hyr-Lif* says so explicity."

One of her neemus yawned. His fangs were very bright and sharp. He closed his eyes, yawning.

"Yet does not the book say also something of the relative amounts of good and evil? Does it not say that an ounce of evil is enough for a ton of good?"

"It does, Drak my smooth-tongued kaidur. And, also, as you know well, the *Hyr-Lif* says that an ounce of good is enough for a ton of evil."

"The *Hyr-Derengil-Notash* means all things to all men. It is read as the heart commands."

She nodded, for the statement was so prosaic, so universal, no answer was needed. Kregans often refer to the heart as the seat of emotion and knowledge, although the doctors, so skilled with their acupuncture needles, are well aware that it is the brain that controls the body. She waved for wine and a neat little fifi with sleek black fur glided across, her silver vestments and diaphanous robes billowing, her ankle bells chiming softly. I still had not formed a final opinion on ankle bells.

The wine was good, light, for it was daylight, yet pungent and redolent of the sunny north.

I drank with pleasure. I should say that I still did not know the crude red wine the kaidurs quaffed before combat, Beng Thrax's spit, was drugged with the sermine flower.

Truly, as I sat there with the Queen of Hyrklana sipping fine wine, munching palines and miscils, waited on by scantily clad jewel-entwined slave girls of surpassing beauty, I was a part of the Jikhorkdun that many and many a coy would give his ears for. The life, for all its horrors and bestiality, could claim a man utterly.

Of course, many women were available to the kaidurs, for if a great lady could flaunt a hyr-kaidur as her latest conquest she would score a notable coup over her fashionable rivals. Huge sums were paid by some of these ladies of Huringa for the favors of a kaidur. I gave none. Pressures were brought to bear, and I hurled them back, concealing my contempt, pleading other excuses. The queen, I know, was apprised of this and approved. For she, Queen Fahia, assumed I was deeply enamored of her. I appreciated the dangers of this course, and was somewhat apprehensive in a distant way for what might follow. But I felt it imperative that my freedom of maneuver should not be impaired.

As an example I attended a secret meeting of the Horters and a few nobles in a house at the end of an unlighted back alley. It was all talk and speeches and wild declamations and, a thing that made me perk up a little, a counting of weapons and men available. They were small enough, to be sure. We left unmolested, and sang as we wended our way through the streets, Rapa and Fristle slaves lighting our way with flaring torches. The armed guards of the queen, prowling the streets on the lookout for any mischief they might knock on the head, let us go, for we were merely a gang of drunks. But for me, as a hyr-kaidur, these excursions were fraught with a peril quite foreign to the Horters.

At subsequent meetings I tried to insist on a more practical approach and in this Rorton Gyss backed me up.

"We need to think more forcefully," Gyss said. He spoke in his own downright way, direct and yet charming. "We must so organize the people who share our views that the government is attacked simultaneously on all sides. We must do this thing, for this evil queen is leaching the lifeblood of the country away. I came over the road from Shander's End today, and the surface is not fit for troops to march, and the money for its upkeep was spent in Chem buying boloths for the arena. Is this the way to run a country?"

I tell you, you who listen to these tapes spinning through the recorder, I, Drak the Sword, kaidur, took more interest in that part of his speech wherein he mentioned that boloths had been purchased for the Jikhorkdun. I confess it. I sat up. The boloth can be best described by imagining four elephants affixed in such a way that there are eight tusks facing forward, eight legs a side down the body, and a tendrilous mass of whipping tails at the other end. Its hide is hard and gray like a rhinoceros along the back, a brilliant leaf-green along the sides, and yellow beneath. It is slow. But it can still gather

153

enough speed from its sixteen legs to build pace sufficient for a few hundred yards to outrun a totrix. After that it must pause for some time to allow its three hearts to pump fresh oxygenated blood around that ponderous body.

As an afterthought—it has an underslung jaw that can gobble a strigicaw, all spitting and snarling, at a gulp.

When I got back Nath the Arm was frantic. "The queen has sent for you, Drak, by Kaidun! You must go to her at once! By Havil the Green," he said, lapsing into unfamiliar theistic regions for him, "hurry, lad, hurry! Or all our heads will roll!"

"I will wash and dress myself in fresh clothes," I said. "Nath, if any heads are removed they will all be mine."

As I prepared—for this summons from the queen came at an inconvenient time—I pondered what Orlan Mahmud had reported at the meeting. He claimed to have set ablaze two of the state manufactories for vollers. He said his men had burned not only fifty fliers, but the sheds and yards also. When I was ready I took up my thraxter and, with a last flick of her tail from Tilly, with Oby opening the door for me, I went up to see what Queen Fahia wanted of me.

# Chapter Fifteen

## Of Rorton Gyss, Balass the Hawk, and wine

This time Queen Fahia received me in a low-ceiled inti-mate chamber high in the Chemzite Tower of her fortress of Hakal.

She reclined on a low couch strewn with zhantil pelts and furs, silks and sensils, propped on one white elbow. She knew she looked incredibly seductive, for the tall and unflickering candlelight gleamed in mellow warmth from her skin and hair and that soft haze concealed the lines of arrogant power stamped on her face. She wore semi-transparent billowing trousers, and a translucent jacket artfully half open, and their silk blazed a brilliant scarlet into the scented bower.

I was ushered in, my thraxter taken from me, and fifis already giggling to themselves showed me to a low stool beside the couch. Nearby stood a hurm-wood table loaded with golden goblets and glass bottles, the dust removed only from the labels, with many glass and porcelain dishes loaded with fruits and a golden dish upon which miscils lay ready to crumble into instant deliciousness upon the tongue.

"Drak the Sword! I have been waiting for you and for-tunate you are that I had affairs of state to occupy me."

If this pantomime was to begin at all, I would start by laying down the ground rules myself. She was clearly bent upon complete conquest. I had evaded her, as I knew, be-fore; this time the test had to be faced.

"Pour me wine, Drak." She gestured vaguely at the ta-ble, and so, determined to please myself, I chose a bottle whose shape and color I recognized. The date on the label

155

referred to the Vallian calendar, and it was, I saw, a damn long time ago this wine had been prepared. I poured carefully, and handed her the glass. She looked over the rim at me.

"Vela's Tears, Drak?"

"Aye, Queen. It is a wine of Valka. You have heard of Valka?"

"Friends of the cramphs of Hamal." An old sore had been itched here. She was the queen, concerned for her country, for this moment her role as a seductive voluptuary momentarily forgotten. "The Emperor of Hamal supplies Vallia with vollers and the rasts of Vallia do not venture so far south as here to Hyrklana. Our vollers are as fine as those of Hamal. But the empire blocks our commerce."

As you may imagine, I drank this up with as much pleasure as I sipped that superb wine, Vela's Tears from my own Valka.

The strong red wine suited my fancy. Usually I frowned on this drinking of unmixed wine, for that is a fool's trade; but I fancied I needed the assistance the alcohol would give me in dealing with this wanton woman, for if she became a trifle fuddled I could then slip away and leave her to sleep it off. So I drank sparingly, and replenished her glass.

"Two of my manufactories were burned, Drak. Many fine vollers are ashes; but they may be rebuilt. But the yards and sheds are gone, and the tools—when I lay my hands on the yetches responsible I will deal with them!" She was panting, and the color flooded her cheeks. Candlelight flamed in her hair and glittered from her jewels. She held out a hand to me.

"I need a strong man, Drak. A man to make me forget my cares and worries." She was smiling now, her moist red mouth open and inviting. "A hyr-kaidur, Drak! One who knows what a sword is for."

Into that appealing hand I placed a fresh glass. This time the wine I had poured for her was a brilliant green concoction from eastern Loh, crushed from the fruit of the pimpim tree, thick and cloying on the tongue, overly sweet—and strong!

She continued to look at me as she drank. I merely touched the tip of my tongue to the pungent liquid.

"You speak of swords. When am I to receive that great sword—?"

She drank, and swallowed, and interrupted me. "You saw Hork the Dorvengur?"

"I did. He was brave, but a fool."

Hork the Dorvengur had been a hyr-kaidur of the green. He felt a personal slight that I had performed a great Kaidur with this strange sword and with a leem and had sought to do likewise. The leem had ripped him to shreds.

"If I give you the sword, it may be to face a foe far worse than a leem."

"There are many more dangerous foes than leems, although few as vicious, and, even, if your treasury can afford it, you might buy larger and stronger cats. There are risslacas. There are the boloths you have just bought, and the volleems which destroyed the Chulik coys. And there are many many more hideous horrors in this world of Kregen you might buy and send against me in the arena. But, I think—"

Again she interrupted. "You think that with that monstrous sword you would stand a chance?"

"Better than with a djangir, at all events."

She laughed. "I love to see the bosks running with their heads down, their long horns outstretched; it is a great Kaidur against the shortsword."

With some amusement I noticed that of all subjects we had got on to, the one consuming her passions was the one most calculated to make her forget why she had invited me up here. We talked Jikhorkdun for some time, and she drank steadily as I pressed her. Her knowledge of the arena was prodigious. She had the great feats of the past off by rote, dates and times and states of play, and all the records of the color champions for many seasons past. She knew so many names of hyr-kaidurs that she made me feel very small beer indeed—which was a most useful ploy, as I discovered.

By careful and callous manipulation of Jikhorkdun talk and of wine I jollied her along as the night wore on. She was in reality a cruel and evil woman; but she was also aging and losing her beauty, and a trifle drunk and maudlin, and, I judged, more lonely than any person should be condemned to be. After a time she slobbered after me; but I laughed—I did!—and gave her more wine, and started on about how she had never allowed neemus into the arena, and so diverted her attention to areas in which she felt far more passion.

157

"Never, Drak-ak the Sword! Neemus are a part of me! They are so sleek and slender and all the female secret things a man will never understand." A tear cut its way through the powder on her cheeks. Her flush was now wine-red, startling against the cosmetics.

I might never understand women's wiles and secrets, but this case was too plain. She was the twin sister of Princess Lilah. Lilah although cold and aloof had been slender and beautiful and young. This Queen Fahia, the same age, was growing fat, her face was lined, her bones and sinews, as I guessed, feeling creaking and old. Yes, evil as she was, one could find a pity in one's heart that was not put there through mere duty and form to any of the better creeds of Earth or of Kregen.

She hiccuped again, and knocked a goblet over, and laughed shrilly, and Oxkalin the Blind Spirit guided me as I said: "I fight tomorrow, Fahia. You are exceedingly lovely, but the husband your king . . . I must leave you." I deliberately did not phrase that in the usual way in requesting permission to leave. I stood up. I had guessed that for at least the opening sessions of the night's business she had had eyes spying on us. A golden bell stood on a lenken stand. If she struck that, once, probably, armed men would pour in. I wondered if she struck it twice the eyes would withdraw.

"You fight tomorrow, Drak the Sword? Then I will cancel the combat—cancel combat—fight tomorrow. . . ."

With her mouth open and her eyes slowly closing, she sank back on the couch, breathing in rapid shallow breaths that slowed and drew out to a deeper rhythm. I lifted her naked feet up into a comfortable position on the couch. I looked about at the table with the wreckage of the night's drinking. I popped a handful of palines into my mouth and saw the second bottle of Vela's Tears, untouched. About to pick it up, I paused.

Those eyes . . .

I picked up the bottle. I held it in my left hand, even in that moment relishing the feel of something that had been born in my Valka, and I picked up in my right hand the small mahogany-handled gold-headed hammer and I struck the golden bell.

The chamber filled with armed men.

Their Hikdar stared about, at the sleeping queen, at the golden hammer in my hand, the golden bell still quivering.

He commanded a detail of armed and armored men and halflings, and he stared at me like a loon.

I held up the bottle of wine.

"Have you a clean glass, Hikdar?" I said. "The queen and I have used up all that were here."

Queen Fahia gave a little snore just then, and mumbled her lips about, and dribbled a trifle.

The Hikdar's chest swelled. His eyes threatened to pop like overripe squishes. He could barely turn his neck in the iron collar of his corselet for its swelling.

"Deldar Ropan! A glass for the kaidur! And jump!"

Dear Zair! How I plagued those guardsmen!

That was the first time we had a cozy tête-à-tête, Queen Fahia and I.

She would give me no sensible answer about the Krozair longsword. Other kaidurs made the gallant attempt to use it in the arena and most were slain, although a fighter from the blues, surprisingly, bested his opponent, a strigicaw, and so scored a notable triumph for the sapphire graint. The queen insisted that the longsword be returned immediately after every bout. It hung among a splendid display of arms in her trophy chamber, magnificently decorated and appointed, in a great hall of the high fortress of Hakal.

Balass the Hawk was only too pleased to give me the benefit of his assistance and contacts when I made a certain request of him. Shortly thereafter, in exchange for a boskskin bag containing quite enough golden deldys, I received a small dark purple glass vial of a curious shape, heavily stoppered.

"One drop, Drak," said Balass, chuckling. "Guaranteed to knock over a dermiflon."

That blue-skinned, ten-legged, idiot-headed monster grew so fat and ungainly that it could barely waddle and only its sinuous and massively barbed and spiked tail saved it from extinction at the claws and fangs of strigicaw or chavonth. To say anything would knock over a dermiflon was guarantee enough.

So, armed with my secret purple vial with its drop-by-drop dermiflon guarantee, I could face those intimate little drinking nights with Queen Fahia with greater equanimity. She did say, and more than once, that my company was very soothing to her in her great worries and problems, for she always slept well after I had visited her.

Poor soul!

But she could wield as much power as an absolute despot ever can over his or her subjects, and my head was still a-rattling between my shoulders.

I often wondered what the results for the island of Hyrklana would have been had the fifteen-minute interval that separated Fahia's and Lilah's entrances onto the stage of Kregen witnessed a reversal, so that Lilah had been the elder.

You will forgive me, I know, in my cynicism, if I suggested to myself that Queen Lilah would have been little different from what Queen Fahia in reality was. If the Star Lords truly had commanded me to a work here, I must also be aware that the realities of the situation, in political terms, could never obscure the greater human realities.

Only those people who have had to sign another person's death warrant can truly know the realities, the miseries, the agonies, of power.*

". . . once and for all that evil queen! Drak—it must be you who slays her! You are the chosen one!"

"But, Orlan—to kill a woman, like that—I care nothing that she is a queen—"

"It is a deed done for all Hyrklana!"

"But I am not of Hyrklana."

At this Rorton Gyss lowered his wine glass and stared at me. Always charming and courteous, the Trylon of Kritdrin now spoke in a smooth sensible way that admitted of no argument.

"You may not be of Hyrklana originally, Drak the Sword. But you are a hyr-kaidur, of the Jikhorkdun in Huringa, and that does make you indisputedly of Hyrklana. Whether you will it or not, my friend, it is so."

"Maybe. But there are armed guards she can summon instantly."

---

* At this point occurs another of these annoying breaks in the Tapes from Rio de Janeiro. Prescot has just begun a fresh cassette. There is a sound of a door opening in the background. Then a voice calls in Portuguese: "Dray, my friend. The cars are waiting. Leave those infernal recordings of yours!" And, distantly, there is the sound of a girl laughing. Then follows merely a muddle of noises, and the tape itself is badly creased within the cassett. This has been straightened; but quite clearly Prescot picks up the story after a gap of some time in his sojourn in Huringa in Hyrklana. What is missing we, of course, do not know. However, I think the gladiatorial life was by this time palling on him, and the disappearance of Nath the Arm from the story also offers substance to that theory.    A.B.A.

"We know. But, Drak"—Orlan looked with a sickly smile at me, at which I pondered how much he really cared for the queen—"you are a kaidur. When you caress her, and bend over her, your arms about her, kissing her. Then you may place your hands upon her neck, so, and twist, so, and she will go quietly, and you may lay her, so, upon the couch."

And Orlan Mahmud placed upon the table the two halves of the ripe fruit he had twisted apart.

We all looked at the two halves of that rich fruit as its juices seeped onto the sturm-wood. It was a shonage fruit, I remember, larger than a grapefruit, as red as a tomato, crammed with rich flesh and sweet juices. No one spoke.

The little secret meeting room hidden in the rear of a hovel in a dingy portion of Huringa had never seemed more remote, clandestine, and filled with dark menace. I could do to Queen Fahia what Orlan Mahmud had done to the shonage; and I could do it silently and shielding the deed with my body from the alert gaze of the watchers outside the queen's chamber. I could.

I doubted if I would.

I said to Orlan Mahmud nal Yrmcelt: "You know the queen's chamber in the Chemzite Tower. You have perhaps been there yourself?"

His young face flushed and that sickly smile returned to his features. "I have. Once."

Before I could push any further the Trylon of Kritdrin interposed, smiling, charming, forceful. He had seen how it stood with me, I think, for he was a shrewd man. "Let us leave this portion of the plan for now, comrades. We will return to it when we are sure the quarters will rise."

On that the treasonable business of the meeting could be concluded and we could get down to aspects more agreeable to me, the drinking and singing. If I give the impression that I drank a lot or was some kind of drunkard, this is not so. Water of most of Kregen is drinkable except where fouled by men, and the varieties of fruit juices are immense and wonderful. Also, I always prefer Kregan tea. The cover, that we were a drinking club, had to be maintained. So, singing, rolling along, our arms across one another's shoulders, we staggered happily back into the street and so wended our merry way toward the south boulevard which led to the Jikhorkdun. Before we reached it, in an alley where a torch threw lurid gleams across the stones of the walls, and with Orlan hanging on to me and roaring out about "Tyr Korgan and the Mermaid," Rorton Gyss leaned across and whispered fiercely in my ear.

"We are followed, Drak! A thin little rast in brown."

Trust Gyss to have his eyes and ears open in this wicked world.

I looked back. It was the same man. I had forgotten him; now I remembered. He wore a djangir, and he looked mean, and he hovered at a corner where the stones had been grooved by the centuries of wear from the iron-rimmed wheels of passing quoffa carts. Hyrklana is rich in iron.

He hung back there, waiting for us to pass beyond the torch before following. Orlan stopped singing, just where Tyr Korgan takes his third great breath of air and dives to inspect the Mermaid in wonder. He was not so far gone as to call on Opaz as he halted, all wine-flushed.

"What is it, in Havil's name?"

"Hush, Orlan!"

Some genuinely staggering, some shamming, the conspirators turned to look back. The spy realized he had been discovered. He took to his heels at once. With a wild whooping the whole bunch pelted after him.

Only Gyss and I remained standing beneath the torch.

"Onkers!" said Gyss.

I knew what he meant. "I doubt he is a queen's man, for she would have already struck." I told him of seeing this man on the day I had become a hyr-kaidur. He frowned. "It is inconvenient. We must tread cautiously, leave for the country for a time. The day of wrath is postponed." He added, without rhetoric or bombast, false to his nature as they would have been: "But it will come, Drak the Sword. The day of judgment will come."

So we left the conspirators, like would-be leems, to go chasing after the spy as leems chase a running ponsho. We calmly walked back and I said to this quiet, contained man, "I think so too, Rorton Gyss. Remberee, Trylon of Kritdrin."

"Remberee, Drak the Sword. Remberee."

That night Queen Fahia summoned me to her perfumed bower in the Chemzite Tower of the high fortress of Hakal frowning down from its rocks over the Jikhorkdun. Armed with the purple vial of curious shape, dressed finely, I went. As usual the guards took my thraxter. Strangely, secure in the protection of the purple vial, I welcomed these philosophical discussions touching the arena.

The queen would talk of the high excitement and the peril and the blood of the Jikhorkdun with a panting eagerness, her full moist lips shining, the lower lip locked by her teeth as she listened to tales of a great Kaidur. This absorption with the scintillating evil surface of the Jikhorkdun did not prevent her deep obsession with its inner philosophies, and we explored areas both of analysis and synthesis, of ideas and theories, that showed she understood far more than her voluptuous figure and jeweled body might give one to think, assuming she had no brain at all. She put great store by the *Hyr-Derengil-Notash*, that *Hyr-Lif*. Only the greatest books of Kregen are dignified by the description "lif," and only the greatest of these may expect to be honored by the "Hyr." Her amorous advances would be reserved for a later time, when she had molded me, as she would think, into the kind of kaidur suitable to her high-flown fancies.

Once she was in a black temper. "I have had word out of the chief place of Hamal, that vile city of Ruathytu. They seek with their left hand to throttle realms to their south and with their right hand they prevent men from Zenicce and Vallia reaching us to buy our vollers. By Havil the Green—one day . . ."

Then she laughed, a little shrilly, wildly even. "The yetches of Hamal are like Djangs with four arms, for they clutch to the west over their mountains, and to the north across the sea."

I admit to a strange thump of the heart when she said that name—Djang.

So, on this night, with her prowling black neemus taken on their silver leashes by their attendants and with many kisses and cooings from her, Fahia received me. Interestingly, instead of the usual red she wore in honor of the ruby drang, she wore a shimmering white gown, and from the costliness of the silks and sensils I guessed it had been the work of many slave-girls' needles. Cunningly slit at thigh and belly, it clung to her, and slid and susurrated when she moved. Diamonds cascaded about her. Her hair of that brilliant corn-gold had been let down, and, without a single gem, swirled about her figure. In the rosy candlelight she did, indeed, I admit, look most alluring and desirable.

Her moist red lips parted in a smile.

This was the woman the conspirators wished me to murder. However much she deserved the fate, could I take that white neck, with its hint of pudgy fatness, into my fists and so twist and stare down upon her without compassion as she died?

Hardly.

Her Fristle fifis fussed about her, and a couple of new apim girls, glorious in their fresh beauty, brought in her toilet necessaries. One carried the golden bowl and a towel, the other a pitcher of scented water and a fluffy, soft, pampering towel. The queen retired behind a small screen of interwoven papishin leaves. The two apims, slaves, wearing clean white loincloths, would not look at me. They trembled with fear as they ministered to the queen.

Almost, then, I did as I had been requested.

The single drop from the purple vial of curious shape did its work, and I was able to drink moderately and watch as Queen Fahia slipped into a sound sleep. I made her comfortable and then went out. The Hikdar of the guard knew me by now. We exchanged a few words; but he remained resentful of that first prank I had played on him. I went back to the Jikhorkdun.

The next day I heard the report that a man had been found dead in a back alley of the city. His brown clothes had been cut to ribbons, and his body slashed in a score of places. So my fine drunken conspirator friends had caught their ponsho.

All the same, most of them found reasons to leave the city and go to their estates in the country of Hyrklana. For a space, then, the queen was to keep her life and my life at the Jikhorkdun would continue. Were the Star Lords, I wondered, really at work here? To test that I went out the very next night, stole a voller, and was battered and beaten back by a gale whose savagery sprang from supernormal forces.

I raged.

By Zair! I was trapped in this round of Kaidur, and I had begun to detest it urgently.

It has come to me as I tell you my story that you must conceive of me as a dour, brooding, humorless sort of apim, whose face hurts if he smiles, who does himself a serious mischief if he dares to laugh. I admit to a starkness of character, a feeling of doom that will not leave this side of the grave; but I do laugh, wildly and with great mirth, when a situation appeals to me in its incongruity, and I can smile most tenderly when my Delia is with me, and my twins, Drak and Lela, chuckle and laugh and grip my fingers with their tiny chubby hands. By Zair! But I talk now as I thought in those dark and scarlet days of the Jikhorkdun in Hyrklana. Babies grow up, as you shall hear, and their problems sometimes made my own seem mere pimples upon a boloth, trifles I scarce need mention beside the enormities of terror they were to face.

So I fought in the arena, and won—for defeat would end in death and the Kaidur would be over for me then—and I took a second purple vial from Balass the Hawk in exchange for a boskskin bag of golden deldys, and Naghan the Gnat was set to attend personally to my armor, at which I was much pleased, and Tilly plagued me with her long, supple golden tail, and Oby practiced swishing a thraxter about, and the long days passed. The twin Suns of Scorpio went on their eternal swinging paths about Kregen and the seven moons cast down their fuzzy pink light, and the air grew sweet with the scent of flowers, and the wealth in my marble chambers grew and swelled until in mere material terms I was a paladin of kaidurs. The queen, I knew, was kept happy by other kaidurs, and she had fallen into the habit of talking with me, seeing me when the circle of her life prevented other pursuits, and in these conversations I think we both realized our lives were restricted and circumscribed. Princess Lilah did not return to the kingdom. I never saw the king, Rogan. The hyr-kaidur Chorbaj the Stux was slain by Cleitar Adria. And on that night the queen summoned me. It was unusual for the pattern of living that had been established, and I was surprised. I dressed carefully and went to see her in the exotic chamber in the high fortress of Hakal.

"Chorbaj has got himself killed," she said, flinging herself down on her couch. She wore a brilliant green sarong-like garment, almost a shush-chiff, which was encrusted with gems, and yet her white body glowed through cunning interstices in the sensil. I remained alert, my hand gripping that purple vial of curious shape.

"It was a great fight, Queen," I said.

"Aye! A hyr-kaidur to the life. You reds crowed today, when the iron hooks dragged the bleeding corpse of Chorbaj the Stux from the arena."

"The greens were not pleased, I'll allow that."

"I had thought to send for Cleitar Adria, but he took a cut in his victory."

"I am here."

"Yes, Drak the Sword. You are here. And tonight we do not simply talk and you do not lull me to sleep with your fine stories, like Sosie and the Kov of Verukiadrin!"

*Sosie and the Kov of Verukiadrin* is an incredibly similar story cycle to our Earthly *Thousand and One Nights*, and Sosie and Scheherazade are twin sisters separated by four hundred light-years.

"You were expecting Chorbaj the Stux," I said. "He was a great kaidur. The Jikhorkdun is the poorer for his loss."

"You, a red, can say that? A kaidur's life is short and violent, and he must take what pleasure and profit he can."

I did not reply.

She gestured for wine.

I went to the table, and as was my custom I poured her a mild wine to begin with, so that when I slipped into her glass the single drop that would knock over a dermiflon I could drown any trace by a wine stronger and more pungent. She rang her little silver bell for her attendants, and her fifis scuttled in, giggling, flicking their tails about, and a couple of apim girls came in, one with the great golden bowl covered with an embroidered damask, the other with the pitcher and the fluffy towel. Queen Fahia stood up and walked to the screen.

"Hurry, you useless yetches!" she snapped at the girls, and one of them gasped in terror, and ran with the pitcher of warmed and scented water. The other stood stock still, and Queen Fahia reached for her whip, with the silken bows and tassels and the exceedingly ugly and painful lashes.

"Must I slash you, cramph!"

I looked at this new girl, turning in curiosity, and so saw her, and dropped the wine glass and the purple vial and stared and stared. . . .

Delia, my Delia, in a slave breechclout, stood there, her eyes enormous and fixed on me with a look of utter disbelief.

# *Chapter Sixteen*

## Delia shows me around the high fortress of Hakal

Nothing could have halted my instinctive reaction then. No thought of security or of peril, no other thought in all of Kregen obsessed me. I am a man obsessed with only one idea in the whole of my life. I am obsessed with my Mountains.

I simply rushed toward her and knocked the golden bowl spinning from her hands and so took her into my arms. I clasped her to me, and she clasped me, and we stood there, unable to speak, hardly breathing, locked together.

Delia! How she had come here I could only guess. I held her dear form in my arms and I felt the quick beat of her heart against me and the warmth and softness of her figure pressed against me, and all of Kregen might have gone hang.

Over and over again I have cursed myself for a blind selfish fool. An onker! A get onker, as the Star Lords dubbed me. Oh, how incredibly idiotic I can be, at times, I, Dray Prescot with all the fancy names and titles and honors! Oh, the most fitting title I can ever earn is idiot onker, fool of fools!

Rough hands seized me and dragged us apart even as the soft malicious chiming of Queen Fahia's golden bell rang in my ears. Armed men dragged us apart. I allowed myself to be pulled from my Delia for a heartbeat only.

Fahia was shrieking: "So this is the wench! This is the shishi! Rest assured, Drak the Sword, you will never see her again!"

I finished up my delayed business with the guard Deldar by kicking him where I once kicked Prince Cydones

Esztercari. The fool had drawn his thraxter so that I was able to take it away and instantly parry a blow from a man who came in most brutally and so thrust him through the eye. They wore corselets after the fashion of Hyrklana; but they had left their shields in the guardroom for this kind of guard duty, for which they were sorry in due time.

In a frenzied flurry of action I chopped down two Rapas and two apims and went for the men grasping Delia. She struggled. She was no waxen effigy of a girl who would shrink and scream in a situation like this. I knew my Delia of old. Had we not, together, disposed of black-clad assassins on our wedding night?

Fahia was screaming on: "Seize him, you onkers! Chain him up with iron chains! Seize the rast! You fools, you cowards!" She was right to call them fools, for any man who lays a hand in animosity on Delia of Delphond is a fool, for he is a dead man. She was wrong to dub them cowards. They fought bravely. They tried to get at me and I simply leaped on them like a leem and slew them and their blood splattered horrendously into that perfumed, decadent chamber. The fifis had run screaming, their tails curled up past their shoulders in fear. The other apim girl stood, still carefully balancing her pitcher, and her mouth opened in one long scream of terror.

Delia broke free, I sliced her other guard, and she scooped his dagger. It was a Hyrklanan blade, ornate and heavily curved. It went in curving, as it was meant to do. Delia looked up at me and the glory of her face and figure, the brightness of her brown eyes and that gorgeous hair with its outrageous tints of auburn, spurred me as nothing else in two worlds can.

"Oh, *Dray* . . ."

"Out of here, Delia, my heart. This is fit country for leem, little else."

Fahia was raving.

"You will be cut down! You are condemned! I shall see to it you die a death so exquisite—"

I turned.

I was less than gallant.

"Cease your babble, fat woman! Know you not this is the Princess Majestrix of Vallia! That her father is the puissant Emperor of all Vallia? Beware lest an avenging army lays your land in waste and utterly razes your city of Huringa."

"You lie! You lie, by Lem, you lie! You are a kaidur and she is a slave shishi! You will die, by Lem, you will die!"

I left her there screaming and screeching and I felt sick at heart at her words.

*By Lem!*

So the evil cult of Lem the Silver Leem had in truth penetrated into the highest ranks of Hyrklana, and I shuddered to think what doom must fall upon this land.

Outside in the corridor we ran through the ways I knew, and Delia ran fleetly at my side, for I had no need to drag her along with me, as I had dragged Princess Lilah, and Tulema the dancing girl from a dopa den, and those two silly girls, Saenda and Quaesa.

Guards tried to stop us, of course, mercenaries of various races. With the protection of Delia as my reason for living they had no chance. No blood-lust obsessed me; as I have told you, fighting and killing are abhorrent to me except where they are inevitable, and Zair himself does not point a different path.

Fleetly we ran down the long curving marble staircase. Its walls were covered in carved representations of many of the marvelous legends and stories of Kregen, and we ran hurtling past hero and demon, god and devil, monstrous beast and beautiful woman, swirling pictures of love and combat, of sack and creation. A file of apim guards ran out below and I did not check but leaped the last fifteen stairs and so smashed among them and in the quick and bitter flashing of swords cut them down. A shriek rang out at the head of the staircase.

Delia and I looked up.

Queen Fahia had dragged herself to the marble balustrade and leaned there, panting, glaring down at us with mad eyes.

"You cannot escape from Huringa! Every hand will be against you!"

A Rhaclaw's immense head appeared beside her and he lifted a stux and hurled. I did not swat the stux away. I seized it out of the air, and reversed it, and so hurled it back.

"Any man who dares touch Delia, Princess Majestrix of Vallia, dies! Remember that!"

Fahia ducked and the stux took the Rhaclaw in his bloated head so that it burst and showered the queen with blood and brains. We left her to her shrieks and threats and ran on.

A terrified apim slave girl crouched away from us as we rounded the next corner. Ahead lay a long passage studded with many doors, and then we might go on to the outer ways and so the street, or down and through the secret passages to the Jikhorkdun.

The apim girl was slave to a pallan's wife, a noble lady who stared down her nose at us, at a savage-faced maniac with a bloody sword in his hand, and a stunningly beautiful girl clad only in the white slave breechclout of the queen's household. Ordinary slaves wore the slave gray.

"What tomfoolery is this?" the noble lady began. I had seen her fawning on the queen. "You will be severely punished."

She wore a fine deep-crimson robe, with a smart furred cape over that, with many jewels, and her sandals gleamed with gems. I took the robe in my left fist and twisted the noble lady about and so held her as Delia, with me at once, flicked her long slender fingers down the latchings. The robe fell free. The noble lady was screaming and struggling.

"Guards! Guards! Slay me these slaves, *instantly!*"

Her command would have been obeyed, instantly. Only two guards arrived on the scene, for the others hereabouts were dead, and these two joined muster with them shortly.

Delia donned the crimson robe. The noble lady wore a white sensil chemise.

"No time for the chemise, my heart—"

"The dress stinks!" said Delia. In truth, the noble lady's taste in perfume was overly strong for our nostrils.

Dressed decently in the crimson robe with the furred cape flung across her shoulders and with those jeweled slippers on her feet, my Delia could proudly face the city of Huringa.

We ran on.

No coldly calculating thoughts of victory or defeat entered my mind. I knew we had to get out of here. If we did not, it would be the arena for us. I had no need to be told what the stakes and the bosks would do. Queen Fahia would delight in putting us both to the supreme test. We sped past the hard and cold marble, and every now and then a mercenary guard sought to dispute our passage.

Delia gasped out words as we ran and I did not stop

her, for she trusted in me and I was fascinated by what she had to say.

"Only four days ago, beloved, the battle. The Battle of the Crimson Missals! When you disappeared in the thunderstorm I heard you say you would not go to Hyrklana. And so—and so—"

"I will tell you, Delia, my heart." At this point I stopped talking and crossed thraxters with a Rhaclaw who bore a shield. He wanted to fight in the proper, ordinary, decent way of two men fighting each other. There was no time for that. I ran at him leaping in the air so that he lifted himself for my attack, and then I let myself drop to that polished marble floor and, feet first sliding on my bottom, I skidded toward him. My feet shot between his legs, I passed under the bottom rim of the shield. Flat on my back I whistled under the shield and so thrust upward with the thraxter most hurtfully, gutting him. After that we had a shield to lift on my own left arm.

"I did not wish to come to Hyrklana. But—but I did. . . ."

"And I followed. Seg and Inch, we took our airboats and we came to Hyrklana. But, as usual, the airboat broke down and I was taken by Rhaclaws. This mad Queen Fahia saw me and bought me—"

"Aye She has first choice of all the most beautiful young girls, by Vox!"

"And so I was instructed to become the chambermaid to the queen."

"That chambermaiding did not last long, thank Zair."

"I fancy the queen is mighty angry—look out, my heart!"

I had seen the crossbowman.

He leered at me over the bolt of his weapon and I saw his shoulder bunch to pull the trigger—poor practice, that, I remember thinking as I hurled the thraxter. He died with the steel through his mouth and spearing up into his brain. I put a foot on his head and hauled the thraxter free. Still with the shield shoved up on my left arm I stuck the thraxter, all bloody and smeared with brains as it was, into my mouth, puckering my lips in the old way to avoid cutting them, and snatched up the crossbow. I whirled. A Hikdar was running toward us waving his sword as though he acted in a play. The bolt took him through an eye. I threw the crossbow down and with Delia at my side sprinted on for the far doors. They were

171

lenken and bound with gold. The uproar behind us boiled up. I could not go on swiftly enough and so out into the street. So it must be the dark and secret ways that led to the Jikhorkdun for us.

Staring down past the half-folded doors that led first of all into a narrow passageway and then a steep and slippery flight of stairs I heard a grunting gasp and a meaty chop and a mangled scream of agony behind me. I whirled. A Rapa staggered back with his beak hanging and dripping blood. Delia didn't bother to slice him again but pointed past my shoulder, so I turned back. Armed guards with weapons bright in the lamplight boiled up that stair and crowded out past the half-folded door. The Jikhorkdun was not for us. The massive gold-bound lenken door would not be opened without a fight, and even so wonderful a girl as Delia could not open it single-handed as I held off the guards. I cocked an evil eye upward.

A small arched stone entrance was barred by a sturmwood door. I ran at it, and kicked it in so that the lock ripped away and the wood gleamed freshly splintered. Delia bundled in before me and I hung my shield over my back, and felt the glancing shock of bolts ricocheting from the bronze-bound wooden surface.

"Up, Delia, my heart!"

"Follow close, close. . . ."

The door was a ruin and so valueless. The first one through was a Rapa and he went shrieking back into his comrades, beakless. The next was a Brokelsh, and he somersaulted back with half his face sheared away. The third was a Gon, and his cleanly shaved scalp abruptly gaped all bloody through the wreck of his helmet. The fourth did not appear. Instead a stux flashed through, and then another. These I caught and returned, and heard two shrieks.

Delia called from above.

"Doors, Dray—all bolted save one—" And then I heard a beginning scream from Delia of the Blue Mountains abruptly chopped off.

I went up those stairs like a devil.

A horrid screeching spitting, a diabolical hissing echoed down the stone staircase. Frantic, I roared up the stone treads and came out onto a landing with the bolted doors and one door open. In the doorway crouched the black form of a neemu, its wicked eyes smouldering gold, its sleek black fur electric in the gloom, its mouth gaping,

"She faced a savage neemu with only a curved ornate dagger."

and the white fangs bared. On one knee the slender form of Delia waited, the dagger held before her—and I saw the fresh blood on that dagger, the blood-matted fur on the neemu's throat, the claw marks ripped down the crimson robe, and the torn tufts of the furred cape. Delia had screamed—and had cut the scream off deliberately so as not to alarm me further as she faced a savage neemu with only a curved ornate dagger!

I hurdled Delia and, shield-first, crashed headlong into the great black cat and so, with four precise thrusts, finished it.

"Are you badly hurt, Delia—Delia . . . ?"

"No—I surprised it—but it was—it was—"

"Through here."

I helped her rise. She gave me her smile, and then we were running into the long chamber beyond the open door with the ominous clashing of mailed men following us. Along the tessellated floor of the chamber we ran and then through a gallery lined with obscene idols of jade and alabaster and ivory, and so to a door, tall and narrow, hung about with emerald wreaths, hundreds of brilliant emeralds cunningly worked by a master artist into representations of triumphal wreaths. The door was of balass and it moved smoothly and silently as I pushed it open. We passed through into a great space of shadow and mystery. I closed the door behind us and lowered the counterpoised beam of lenk into its steel slots. A full-scale battering ram would be needed to smash down that high door.

We surveyed this place wherein we had fled, and saw that it was a shrine raised within the fortress of Hakal to the highest state spirit, the national god, of Hyrklana, for all that other cults and beliefs were undermining the strength of the old religion.

Samphron-oil lamps glowed a mellow gleam upon the shrine within that vast chamber, picking out the fantastic wealth of decoration, the abandon of riches, the exotic outpouring of art and skill. Central within the shrine and lofting higher than fifty feet rose the idol. The image was of a morphology serene and bland, with a bewildering wagonwheel of eight arms, each hand rigidly fixed in a ritualistic pose of power. The face might have been apim, with Chulik tusks, Womox horns, Rapa beak, Fristle whiskers. It combined many racial characteristics, and yet was of itself.

"Havil the Green!" whispered Delia.

174

"Had we the time, my love, I'd welcome the chance to prize a few of those emeralds free and tuck them into a lesten-hide bag." I laughed. "Korf Aighos should be here now!"

"Aye, Dray, if only he were!" She controlled herself, lifting her spirits. "And Seg and Inch and Turko the Shield!"

She went to move on and I placed my left hand, all bloody as it was, upon her shoulder.

"Do not move, my heart!"

She saw the four neemus, then, their heads low, their tails moving slowly from side to side, as they slunk out like four demoniac black shadows, creeping forward on their bellies.

Queen Fahia had released her pets to cleanse her palace of a man and a woman who had despised her before her people and thrown a stux at her, and defamed her.

I cocked an eye up at the statue.

With a sinewy thrust I lifted Delia so that she stood upon the idol's left foot. The leg had been encased in a greave of chased gold and emeralds, and at my urgent gesture Delia began to climb up the projections, as she would a ladder, so that soon she was some ten feet above my head. Then I slid the shield down before me and took a fresh grip upon the thraxter and faced the neemus.

They spat at me. Their lips writhed back and their fangs gleamed in the mellow samphron glow.

Delia did not speak.

A sullen booming began from the high balass door and the lenken bar in its steel sockets moved and groaned.

At that moment, with my Delia in so grave a peril, I think I can be forgiven if I say that had the four neemus been four leems they would have stood little chance. The first one sprang and I smashed the shield into its face and passed the thraxter through it, the sleek black fur clotting with blood, the claws grasping and scratching at the shield rim. On the instant I ducked and withdrew and slashed the sword in a flat arc that slit the second's throat as he sprang after his fellow. The third sprang, also, and landed on the shield; but I kept low so that his hind legs could not rake forward. The thraxter bit again. That left one. He circled, his tail lashing, his head turning from side to side, and he hissed and spat. And I charged him, and so took him, the shield smashing into his head and forequarters, and the thraxter sliding bloodily into his heart.

I stepped back.

Delia did not immediately climb down. I looked up at her and she lifted her right hand, and she said, "Hai Jikai!"

I laughed at her. "Rather, Delia, my girl, you should say as these folks here do—hyr-Kaidur!"

"Oh, they would, them and their debased arena."

She climbed down and I hugged her and then we prowled on toward the far end of that vast and shadowy chamber where the emerald idol of Havil the Green brooded through the centuries. The booming gong-notes from the balass door receded as we passed through the far opening. In this corridor I was completely at a loss. No one appeared. No guard, no courtier, no slave.

"The sacred precincts," Delia said, with her practical knowledge of palaces and fortresses and temples. "There must be a way out, if we can find it."

"We should be feeling like two trapped woflos," I said. "But I feel sorry for anyone who crosses our path. Lead on, my princess. After all, you are a princess—now let us see you put that elevated position to some practical use."

"You great shaggy graint! You, Dray Prescot . . ."

But I laughed and we went on, my thraxter and her dagger dripping bright blood, shining in a trail of red drops upon the priceless marble of the pavement.

We came at last to another vast chamber within the fortress of Hakal, which frowns down over Huringa, and now I stared about and whistled in admiration. We stood in Queen Fahia's trophy room. Almost all the collection gathered here referred to the Jikhorkdun, in weapons and armor and curious artifacts used in the arena. Delia was happy to throw down her curved dagger and take up an example of that long slender-bladed dagger in the use of which she is a master—or mistress, more accurately. I stopped. The hope had grown in my breast, but I would give it no credence, no room to burgeon—and now . . .

"Well, Dray, my shaggy Krozair, take it down and let us get on."

So I took down the great Krozair longsword.

This was the same weapon with which I had bested that silver-collared leem in the arena. My fingers felt the incised letters, feeling the power flowing from them, the miraculous magic of those simple letters KRZY pouring through me.

I threw down the thraxter, but I kept the shield and

176

pushed it back on loosened straps so that it sat high on my left shoulder. I strapped on the scabbard, but I held the brand naked in my fist.

We pushed on.

Delia said, "I think there will be no exits in this direction, Dray. The balass door protected all this wing of the fortress. There will be secret ways only, and we do not have the time to find them."

"Very well," I said, like any tomfool hero from a shadow-play acted out to the glow of samphron-oil lamps in the pink-lit moonlight of Kregen. "We will go back and make our way through these cramphs—"

"There is always a window."

"And the stones will be worn, for the fortress is old, and our fingers and toes have enough skin on them to see us down. Perhaps you are a princess, after all."

"You are a prince, my hairy graint, or had you forgotten?"

"I've not had the same practice at it that you've had."

"Well, you will go jaunting off on various mysterious errands. Little Drak and Lela are likely to grow up orphans if you carry on like this."

All the time we spoke thus to each other we ran swiftly through the deserted corridors. We both heard the distant booming thud, like a gong that is beaten so savagely it breaks from its chains and crashes to the floor. We both knew that the guards of Queen Fahia would be upon us with feral swiftness.

Delia found the right corridor and chamber beyond. Her instinctive familiarity with palaces grown with her from childhood did stand her in good stead now—aye! and me.

We ran swiftly along the corridor toward this room and now we could hear the clank of iron-studded sandals following us, beating a menacing tattoo upon the marble floor.

We burst into the room.

A narrow window in the far wall showed a pinkish wash of moonlight. The Twins would be up, forever circling each other, and I took heart from that, as a sign from Zair.

I stuck my head through the window.

The pink moonlight picked up the scene and showed me the trap into which we had blundered.

"What is it, Dray? Let me see!"

Delia wriggled herself by me to look out.

The angle of wall beside us dropped sheer in an unbroken line for six hundred feet, sheer to the fanged rocks upon which the high fortress of Hakal had been built. Just beyond the rocks terraces dropped away, one below another, to the northern face of the Jikhorkdun, its massive pile dwarfed as to height by the Hakal, its oval shape easily discernible.

"May Opaz smile on us now!" breathed Delia.

All along that precipitous drop the moonlight picked out crevices and chinks, but I doubted if they would serve us all the way. Then in that moonlight I saw the wide band of marble about the wall, a band smooth and slippery and carefully repaired, so that angle of marble fitted against angle. We would need a stout stake to drive in as a piton and a rope to negotiate that, and in this bare storage chamber with broken chairs heaped against one wall, a few brooms and buckets of bronze and wood against another, and dust everywhere, ropes and pitons were not available.

I looked along the wall.

A shadow moved there, and a shape humped around and a wing flickered up to be tucked more comfortably back, and I knew that Zair had answered my plea.

"Into the next room, Delia, and swiftly, before the cramphs spot us."

We ran from that dusty storage chamber along the corridor and into the next room. It was empty of life, although fitted as a sleeping chamber for a guardsman or courier. Judging by the perch-pole outside the narrow window, it was more probably the latter. With her neemus prowling, Queen Fahia had withdrawn all her people from this part of the fortress, ordering them to steal away down the secret passageways. Now that her pet neemus were slain—and would I ever forget the picture of my Delia facing with so great a courage the coming spring of the savage black beast?—and her guardsmen had broken through the balass door, we could expect mercenary guards to come streaming in from every direction.

I looked out the window. Here in the heart of Huringa, capital city of Hyrklana, where saddle-birds were common, there was little need even for the minimal anti-flier precautions they took in Miglish Yaman. As for the flier-protection of cities of the Hostile Territories, here in Huringa such things were unknown and—given that an attack

178

must cross the sea to reach the island at all, and then wing for dwaburs inland—unnecessary. A concession in the perch-poles was made so that they might in time of trouble be drawn inward. Feet clattered in the corridor outside and Delia swiftly closed the door.

I hauled in on the leather rope running from a brass ring in the wall. The flying beast out there stirred and flicked that wing again and gripped its claws into the perch and twitched around—and I cursed savagely.

The bird was a fluttclepper. It was a small high-speed racing bird, without the wide vane of the flutterell, and it was capable of carrying only one rider. One rider. Used in races, or as speedy mounts for couriers, the fluttclepper is a most desirable flying steed; for Delia and me, then, it was practically useless.

Surely, I thought, surely Zair would not disown me now? As for the Star Lords and the Savanti, I had written them off in situations like this a long time ago. To save myself, to save Delia, I must depend on my own strength and my own wits.

The jagged-edge rocks into which the foundations of the fortress were sunk grinned up at me, their edges glittering in the pink moonlight. Beyond them the terraces trended downward, most containing walled gardens of flowers or herbs or greenery, some set out as practice courts for the ball games of Kregen, others with butts for crossbow practice. Beyond them the wide patio surrounding the Jikhorkdun spread invitingly. But to reach it we must fly.

Must fly.

I hauled the strap in.

Delia said, "I do not think that small bird will carry both of us, my heart."

Blows broke upon the door, and the iron bolt groaned. An ax-head appeared through the wood, which was a smooth-grained yellow vone from southern Havilfar's pine forests. It would not resist like sturm or lenk; it would go down into long yellow splinters and ruin in mere murs.

The fluttclepper was in a bad temper, for he had been awoken from a sleep and his master, as he thought, was most inconsiderate to drag him on his leading strap like this. He dug in his claws and resisted. I cursed the fool thing, and hauled. I saw long splinters split from the perch. Then I realized the fluttclepper was no fool; he was smart. He had recognized I was not his master, his usual rider.

The door groaned and chips flew.

I threw the shield to Delia and she caught it deftly and swung with it facing the disintegrating door. The stones on the windowsill had been set only a foot above the level of the floor for ease of egress and ingress. I moved through the window, gripping the stone edge, and put a foot on the perch-pole.

The wind, unnoticed inside the building, now whistled about me. There were four long paces to reach the fluttclepper. I took a breath. My short half-cape billowed and I unfastened and let it slip from my fingers. It flew up and out like a monstrous bat, caught in the air currents, eddying about, twining in on itself, and finally falling long and long to the rocks below.

When I took a look back through the window into the room, still holding on to the stone architrave, I saw the door buckling away from the frame. A hand reached in for the bolt. Without even being fully conscious of what I had been about, for all I wanted to do was get that damned fluttclepper under my hands and set Delia upon him, I saw the way Delia was half crouched behind the shield, facing the door, and the long straight slender glitter of the dagger in her hand.

"Hurry, my princess!"

She turned to look up at me.

"You go on, Dray. The bird will carry you to safety—"

I never shout at my Delia—or not often. I said to her in a voice I thought was perfectly reasonable: "Get up here, woman, and do as you are told."

She stood up. Her eyes locked on mine, brown eyes staring into brown eyes. I could have drowned then. I took her wrist and hauled. She balanced easily on the sill.

The door across the room burst open as the hand at last slid the bolt. I took the shield from Delia and skated it across. Its bronze-bound rim gashed into the throat of the leading Fristle, and he screamed and frothed blood and toppled back into his comrades.

The leather strap hummed tautly as I hauled. I took those four steps on that narrow perch across emptiness and got my fingers into the fluttclepper's neck and I squeezed. I put a foot back on the perch, and braced myself. Beneath me gaped an abyss floored with jagged rock fangs. The wind blew. I shouted.

"Delia! *Now!*"

She made of those steps across that dizzyingly narrow

pole a superb dance of joy, a light skipping waltz that swept her effortlessly across and into my outstretched arm. My right fist twisted in the fluttclepper's white feathers. He tried to squawk and I kicked him, feeling my whole body sway.

"He will never carry us, Dray—but if we are to die, then I am glad we die together."

"Clack, clack, clack," I said. "Slide down and grasp his leg above the claws. And, my dearest heart—*hold on!*"

She slid down and gripped and, suddenly, looked up at me and I saw the anguish written on her beautiful face.

"Dray—oh, Dray, you will not send me away—alone!"

For answer I slid down by her side. My left arm encircled her slender waist, my right hand gripped fiercely into the legs of the fluttclepper. I yanked. The bird's claws scrabbled. He swayed. I jerked him again and the swing of our bodies overbalanced him so that he toppled screeching from the perch.

Angry faces appeared in the window and over the rush and batter of the wind I heard a high yell: "Crossbows!"

Much good that would do them in this wind and the hurtling pell-mell fall of the bird. He could not carry us both. That was true. But he had the instinctive reaction to and fear of falling and so he spread his white wings and beat frenziedly. We fell. But our fall was checked. The fluttclepper was acting as an animal parachute.

We plunged down and out and the edges of those fanged rocks whipped past us. We hissed down through the air. Now the terraces whirled away above. We were across the patio. We were nearing the ground, and the rustling shriek of the bird's wings tore the air about our heads.

We hit with a shock, but only enough to make us tumble head over heels across the edge of the patio and into a trellis of moon-blooms whose outer petals were greedily sucking up the moonlight from the Twins.

We scrambled up.

"You are all right, Dray?"

I looked at her. "As you are. We are out of that Opaz-forsaken place. Now we need a voller."

People on the patio and coming and going on the adjoining streets were rapidly left behind as we ran into the moon-drenched shadows. After a time we could walk as a normal couple, except for the chance I might be recognized. The great Krozair longsword I had unstrapped from my belt and carried bundled under my arm, a fold of cloth covering the hilt, where the fashionable cut of the sleeves permitted. For the rest of that magnificent scabbard, Zair must smile on its new owner.

The voller park we chose was not the same as that flierdrome from which, twice before, I had attempted to escape from Huringa. Again I went into a voller before the attendants were aware and sent the craft surging upward. Delia sat at my side as the wind slipped past our ears. Straight into the path of the Twins I sent the voller, and chance directed we would pass straight over the Jikhorkdun. That was cheeky, but safe, for I fancied Fahia would send her guards and her aerial cavalry searching the airlanes to the north. She might not believe my words on Delia and on Vallia, but she would act on them.

We had reached past the amphitheater and I was lifting the craft to attain a good height and maximum speed when what I could not believe, would not believe, occurred in all its horror.

Black clouds roiled in from nowhere. Lightning flashed from that abruptly jet-black sky. The wind velocity simply halted us in midflight and tumbled us back, like a dusty leaf, hurling us down with contemptuous colossal ease into the ground.

I remember yelling insanely, raving, almost incoherent with the scarlet, futile, frustrated rage burning within me.

"No! You who call yourselves the Star Lords! This is not possible! You cannot do this to me! Onkers—rasts, cramphs, yetches! Star Lords! Everoinye!"

The flier swung and swayed and in the supernatural gloom I gripped hard on to my Delia. If a hint of that hideous blue radiance swooped on me now . . . !

"Give me leave to depart, you Star Lords!" I bellowed. I was insane, then. I had won against fearful odds, and my Delia won with me, at my side, racing to freedom—and the stupid, vile, vicious, unspeakable kleeshes of Star Lords were driving me back, back to Huringa and the evil talons of Queen Fahia and the Jikhorkdun!

We crashed among the warrens clustering by the amphitheater.

My last conscious impressions were of the ground swooping up; of the warm and vibrant form of Delia clasped in my arms, and of her strong slender arms clasped about me; and of a crazed, upside-down vision of coys and apprentices and kaidurs running in the moonlight that, with a supernatural suddenness, burst through those roiling

182

diabolical black clouds. Lightning struck down, a ferocious earth-shaking noise burst up all about me—everything coming together like a volcano in my head.

Even as I knew I was being knocked senseless, I would not let go my hold upon my Delia. And she would not let go her hold upon me.

# Chapter Seventeen

## The Arena

Queen Fahia sat in her curule chair, flanked by the sinister shadows of her pet neemus, and she taunted me. She enjoyed that. She had left to her only two neemus, and that pained her. But, she had me, she had Drak the Sword, hyr-kaidur, who had caused her that pain.

She would not be kind.

I had, of necessity, to crouch. They had loaded me with so many iron chains I could barely walk. But walking was not necessary, for they had stuffed me into a tiny square iron-barred cage where I had to crouch in a doubled-up position. The cage was carried by sixteen massively thewed Brokelsh. I twisted my head up to look at this Queen Fahia, for she interested me. They had not tortured me. I knew why that was.

"You have done much mischief, Drak the Sword. And I was foolish and weak enough to think you were my friend."

Delia was not here. She was all I was concerned about. All this talk about friendship with this fat little woman who sat upon the throne of Hyrklana would have made Delia smile. I felt convinced, through my own agony and misery, that because I had not been harmed, Delia would not be either. I thought I knew the way Queen Fahia's mind worked by then.

"My name is Dray Prescot. I warn you, Queen—"

"Silence, you rast! I am the queen! You are no more than a yetch of a kaidur who presumes." She threw her head back and laughed, an unprepossessing sight, to be sure. "What! You call yourself Dray Prescot, Krozair of Zy?"

"Aye. But you do not know what that is. I am Pur Dray. But, also—"

She flicked her fingers and the Pallan Mahmud passed

her the scroll wherein was written my crimes. It was not paper, which would have interested me, thinking of far Aphrasöe, but a stiff parchment. She stabbed a jeweled finger down.

"You claim to be Pur Dray Prescot, Krozair of Zy, Zorcander, Lord of Stromber, Prince Majister of Vallia, Kov of Zamra and Can-thirda, Strom of Valka!" She lifted her head and stared at me with a jovial evil over the parchment scroll. "And you seriously expect me to believe this roll of rubbish? This tirade of tomfoolery? You yetch! Think of my neemus! Think of my guardsmen!"

"I have little need to think of them, for they are mostly dead. If only they all were."

She drew her breath. She stabbed the scroll again. "I know nothing of these impossible names—save Vallia and Valka. And Zamra. I once heard of a Kov of Zamra, for my stylors tell me his name appears in a secret document they brought from Hamal, where he visited. The Relts tell me his name is Ortyg Larghos."

I laughed.

"Ortyg Larghos was slain by many arrows, slain in foul treachery to his emperor."

"It is easy to claim a man is dead and take his name, when you are many dwaburs from his homeland."

I could see Fahia was enjoying this. She was working up to a great scene when I would scream and beg for mercy, and she could turn the screw tighter and tighter, until in the end I would admit all my sins. She licked her full red lips. Even then, I truly think, I pitied her.

So far no mention of Delia had crossed my lips. What I was absolutely certain was to happen would not be swayed, now, by what I said, and I wished to start the thing as soon as possible and so spare my Delia any further protracted agony.

We must have been scooped out of the wreckage of the voller after those damned Star Lords had brought all my proud plans of escape to nothing. I had awoken to find myself as I now was, loaded with iron chains and doubled up in an iron cage. I had been given food and drink. But I was in a foul state, for all the buckets of water had been hurled over me before I had been carried into the queen's presence. My clothes had been taken from me. I wondered where the Krozair longsword had gone, but forebore to ask. That would give one more item for them to crow about.

Presently the queen's taunts became cruder and cruder and there is no point in repeating them. She worked herself up into a veritable passion, her blue eyes flashing at me and her features twisting. She dribbled and slashed at her slave fifis who trembled and tried to wipe the spittle away with sensil cloths. She saw the way I looked at her, and I believe then she understood that if I could get my hands around her fat neck I would have had no compunction about squeezing her evil life out, for all that I pitied her, and had recoiled from that deed before, for events had moved on apace since then, by Vox!

"By the putrescent left eyeball of Makki-Grodno!" I roared at her. "You silly fat old woman! Get on with it, for the sake of that yetch Havil the Green. Or"—and I stared her full in the face as she flinched back—"may that hyr-kleesh Lem the Silver Leem devour your mangy body entire!"

She fairly exploded then.

Courtiers ran with whips to hit me, guards milled, a number of Horters fainted, and noble ladies leaned on their noble spouses' shoulders, shaking.

By the time the hullaballo had subsided Queen Fahia had left her audience chamber, and her black neemus padded balefully after her, twisting their rounded heads, their wedge-ears low, their tails lolling. I laughed.

The preparations within the Jikhorkdun for this greatest of great Kaidurs were made with thoroughness. Barriers around the arena were heightened and strengthened, and solid marble walls were erected before the queen's box, and many crossbowmen were stationed there. Her Chulik Chuktar still retained his place; but I knew it had been a near squeak for him when I had so impudently slipped and deflected his bolts and stuxes, and so barbarically hurled the bloody leem's tail in her face. Thinking back, I would not have dubbed that a high Jikai. More likely a little Kaidur!

They brought my iron cage to a small newly created stone enclosure I did not recognize. All across one side of the stone-walled space stood a line of mercenaries, all with their crossbows lifted, loaded, and cocked, and aimed directly at me. There were fifty of them. At the Chulik Chuktar's command—for he had taken personal control of this wild leem of a prisoner—fifty bolts would flash toward me, narrowing in a fan and piercing my heart.

There would not be a lot left of that heart by the time fifty steel-headed quarrels had bedded there.

Slaves wearing the gray slave breechclout unlocked the cage and the chains. The reasoning was, I suppose, that the slaves were expendable. As it was, the four of them shook so much their fingers made a sad hash of the locks, until I said: "Hai, brothers! I am not a slave-master. One day the light will reach this evil place of Huringa. One day slaves will be free."

They didn't believe me, of course. And, to my shame, it was a bravo's gesture, words out of an empty bladder of courage. They got the locks undone and then it was the old bloodstream twisting me about so that, for a time, I could not have faced a woflo, let alone a ponsho, and a quoffa might have had his way with me unmolested. When at last I could stand up, the guards with their crossbows aimed and their trigger-fingers white as death escorted me, all naked, through the far gateway.

Oh, yes, believe me, I can see that scene now, etched in acid on my retinas.

I stepped onto the silver sand of the arena.

Everything was the same and everything was different.

The terraces and boxes rose into the high blue sky. I was let out onto the sands of the arena exactly as the Suns of Scorpio reached the zenith. Shadows shrank small. Everyone would have a fine unobstructed view. The roar! The yells and shrieks in a bedlam of sound pulsed down from those thousands of throats. And I heard the tenor of much of that noise, the howls for "Drak the Sword! Hyrkaidur!" Oh, yes, they loved to see the hot blood spurting, and if it gouted from a champion, from a favorite, there were always new accolades to be won by kaidurs forcing their way upward in the Jikhorkdun.

The silver sand gleamed under the suns. The smell of caged beasts wafted in a streaming fetid breath down here, down on the blood-soaked sands of the arena, where the action was. There was, as usual, no wind. I looked up as a skein of mirvols with watchful patrolling aerial cavalry passed, and guessed they would find an excuse to wing around and so hover near, taking their fill of the sport below. They swung away, and a smaller, slimmer flying figure appeared, slipping in over the roof of the western stand and so disappearing in a twinkling. I had caught no sight of a flier upon the flying animal's back.

The beast roar smothered reason. Men and women—

187

apim and halfling—screamed and screeched and banged the benches and swung their rattles and beat their gourd-drums. The winesellers passed along the benches, and could not sell their wares fast enough to slake the throats that all this yelling turned into volcanoes of thirst. Young slave girls, apims, Fristles, Lamnias, sylvies, in particular, moved among the seated thousands carrying fresh paline bushes for sale. Their masters employed girls from those races which traditionally produced the most beautiful girls. I have not mentioned the sylvies before out of decency. But they were there, and doing a roaring trade with their palines and squishes and gregarians and all the exotic fruits of Kregen.

The royal box had never been more ornately decorated. It blazed with color and fire. Queen Fahia sat there, enthroned, and I could guess she would be sitting with her hand propped on her chin, absorbing all this pageantry of the Jikhorkdun with those blue eyes wide, her full lower lip caught between her teeth, mesmerized. If I say that I was to witness a similar spectacle that would surpass this Jikkorkdun of Huringa in Hyrklana, that is not to say that it was not a most impressive spectacle. Golden trumpets cut the air, shrieking their high notes above the din. A silence gradually fell, a silence of waiting, of lip-licking expectation.

I had been let out onto the sands, all naked as I was, from that special area near the queen's box from which her own Queen's Kaidurs—who owed no allegiance to any color—would march proudly forth to fight for her. They would halt and lift their arms in salute. There was nothing about the Queen's Kaidurs or their prospects in the arena to prompt them to cry anything about imminent dying and present saluting.

I walked out a little upon the sand. I had not been able—all the time I moved from that stone gateway onto the sand, all the time the corner of my eye had picked up that mysterious flier slipping over the roof of the amphitheater, all the time my senses had been drowned by the noise and smells—all that time, I had been quite unable to take my eyes from the stake positioned in the center of the arena.

I prayed she was unharmed.

Silver chains they had used to bind her. This was not because she was a princess, for Fahia did not believe that.

The silver chains, I guessed and felt the black rage in me, were a direct reference to the silver leem.

All naked she was suspended there.

Her glorious brown hair lay strewn about her shoulders and bosom. Her shape would set fire to any man. The silver chains draped her so that she could not move, and her arms were drawn up above her head and fastened with silver staples to the black balass of the stake.

She *was* a princess—and she looked more proud, more beautiful, more regal, than anyone there—*anyone!*

Soon, I knew, the horned bosks would be let out.

The thought of those long cruel bosk horns tearing into that slender form filled me with such horror, such rage, that I nearly allowed myself to go berserk and strive to climb that sheer unmarked marble wall to place my fists around the fat neck of that fat, evil woman.

I stood there, and I saluted her as her own Queen's Kaidurs might salute had they wished to die instantly.

There is on Kregen a gesture of such obscene connotation that I have made it a practice never to use, for I am squeamish in such matters.

Now I drew myself up and saluted the queen with this sign.

The sigh that rippled around the amphitheater might have been the sigh of the mourners around an open grave or gathered by the pyre.

I was naked and unarmed. I faced, as I expected, either a single bosk and his long horns, or two or three together. The Chulik Chuktar came to the edge of the arena and tossed me a djangir. The short sword, squat and fat and two-edged, landed in the sand at my feet. Being frugal in the matter of weapons, as you know, I bent and retrieved it. It was sharp. They wanted their sport, then, before I died. And with my death, the death also of Delia of Delphond, Delia of the Blue Mountains, fastened by silver chains to an ebony stake.

Once, she had said to me, "I wish to be known as Delia of Strombor."

But I had always thought of her as Delia of Delphond, Delia of the Blue Mountains. Now, perhaps in a few heartbeats, it would not matter.

Cunning are the ways of the managers of the Jikhorkdun of Huringa, which is the capital city of Hyrklana, in Havilfar. But, of them all, none so cunning or malefic as their queen, Queen Fahia, she of the blue eyes and golden hair and heart as black as the fur of her own neemus!

This time they did not wait until my back was turned to release the beast into the arena, as they had done when I fought the leem with the silver collar. This time they wished me to see at once the horror I faced.

One of the larger iron-barred gates swung up. Those bars were thick, and strong, and closely set. They had need to be.

I waited with the djangir in my fist, positioned halfway between the stake and the barred opening. I had not spoken to Delia. She had not spoken to me. We knew all there was to say to each other at a moment like this. I waited, then, poised and ready, for the first bosk to rush out, horns lowered.

A boloth emerged onto the silver sands of the arena.

A boloth!

Huge, impossible, sixteen legs, eight tusks, a massive monster of destruction, standing there with his bunch of whiplash tails swatting flies, staring, with his rapacious mouth half open so that its red darkness glistened and its rows of jagged teeth glinted in the Suns of Scorpio.

A boloth!

Impossible, inhuman, unstoppable.

And I—armed with a little shortsword!

There was only one thing to be done.

Without a shout, without a whoop, in a silent and feral rush I charged for the monster. I knew there was no hope; but then, my way is never to give up until they throw the grave-dirt upon me, and even then I'll likely as not claw up, cursing them all to the Ice Floes of Sicce.

The belly of the boloth, bright yellow, stood as high as my head. His green sides towered above that, and his gray rhinoceros-hide back lofted above. He just stood there, for they are slow beasts, savage when roused—and I was going to rouse him now!

I skipped aside as I neared him, away from the gravel-dredger mouth. The eight tusks formed a barrier of bristling ivory. I thought of the shorgortz and I thought of the ullgishoa, and then I thought only of this boloth.

My spring carried me past his lowered head, so that I could get a grip on his flap-ears, like those of an African elephant, if four times the size; but, unlike an elephant, there was no deadly weakness behind those ears where a thrust might do his business for him. And, remember, he had three hearts!

Up I clawed and lifted the djangir high and so plunged it down into his right eye.

The mess that spurted had no power to sicken me. It proved that fifty percent of his vision had gone. He reacted with a frenzied bellowing scream, for the boloths have no trunk and therefore he could not trumpet out his pain. But he screamed and bellowed and that massive head shook and I went up in the air and head over heels and so came down flat on my back. Only that old training in the disciplines of unarmed combat enabled me to break the violence of that fall.

The boloth stared about, shaking his head, stamping his feet, lashing his tails about. He continued to bellow. For him, the world had gone dark on his right-hand side. But—disaster—the djangir had remained firmly embedded in that vast ruined eye! I cursed by all the foulest Makki-Grodno oaths I knew; I had to get that djangir back, for, puny as it was, it had already served nobly and must do so again, before that left eye saw the slim form of Delia wrapped in her silver chains.

The bellowing ceased and the boloth turned his head in a peculiar and meaningful way. I saw his nostrils quivering, for he had four of them, and their blackly red edges shivered as he sniffed. Abruptly the whole amphitheater fell silent. The boloth could hear me well enough as I slid on the sand; but he could smell! And, in that silence, I heard the voice of Delia, lifted to me.

"Dray! They have smeared me with scented ointment!"

And I cursed most horribly that devil-queen of Huringa.

I might put out the other eye of the boloth with my bare hands, as I would—I would!—but still the beast would take the scent from my beloved and so charge full upon her. One gulp, one single snap of those gigantic jaws, and all I cared about or loved on two worlds would be gone forever.

And so, as I stood there on the sand, knowing that this vast beast must soon sniff that treacherous scent smeared upon Delia's naked body, I saw that I must express to her a final caress of love. I turned my back to the beast that threatened the lives of Delia and myself and ran away from it. I ran straight toward the balass stake. The uproar from the ampitheater changed into a shocked upheaval of disbelief.

Delia hung in her chains, glorious, desirable, and altogether wonderful. Gently, I reached up and caressed her naked body. I stroked her shoulders and arms and waist and thighs, and every now and then I rubbed my hands over my own naked body. The touch of her stung me through with a whiplash electric bolt of exquisite agony.

"Oh, my Dray. . . ."

"Remember what I have told you, my Delia. Remember the twins, Drak and Lela. But, remember, always, that I love only you of all women in two worlds."

Then I ran back toward the boloth.

He picked the scent smeared upon my body sniffing through those four nostrils and he charged. For that short mad dash a boloth runs faster than a totrix. At the last instant I skipped aside and he thundered past, his legs rising and falling in that smooth complicated rhythm. There was no chance to spring on his back. Next time, when he was slower . . .

The next time his charge carried him perilously near the central stake, and I had to race toward him, shouting and waving my arms, and all that battery of tusks nearly upended me. He had taken his breather with his three hearts pumping and he charged again. I leaped for his ear, got a grip, got my hand around the djangir hilt, but the pus and mucus slimed it so that I lost it and so fell, winded, to the sands of the arena.

This could not go on.

When I look back upon that brilliant scene what I have to tell you now never fails to straighten my spine, to make me relish the love and honor between man and man, man and woman. The crowd sensed the boloth was approaching the final kill. He stood obstinately shaking his head in which the djangir remained embedded, too short to do more than darken his eye, and his whiplash tails flickered ready for the next charge. Then . . .

The roaring from the benches now drowned reason. An abrupt and astonished howling tore from all those thousands of throats there in the tiered Jikhorkdun.

I stared at the red corner.

Four figures ran out onto the silver sand of the arena. I knew them all.

First ran Naghan the Gnat. In his hand he carried—oh, may Zair be praised over all of Kregen as I praised him in that moment! Naghan must have been there when we crashed in the voller. He ran on his spindly legs toward me and he carried high that great Krozair longsword all gleaming in the suns-light. The scabbard was belted to his waist, and he carried that magnificent Krozair brand all naked and ready.

Following him ran Tilly, my little golden-furred Fristle fifi, and with her ran Oby, that young rascal who dreamed of becoming a kaidur. This deserved the accolade!

And then, also, ran Balass the Hawk, clad in gilded iron of a kaidur's harness, with shield and thraxter and stuxcal, and his massive kaidur helmet was open so I could see his face.

Why?

I could guess the scenes taking place at that moment in the queen's box. Foaming, she would be shrieking her orders—and—here came the results!

Crossbow bolts hissed into the sand around the flying figures of my friends. My friends! It was impossible. I cannot recall that scene without the most painful surge of emotions, a feeling that of all men I did not deserve such friendship.

Tilly ran one way and Oby ran the other, making a wide circuit of the arena. They carried jars, and a liquid, rich and darkly purple, spilled upon the sand as they ran.

Naghan the Gnat checked, poised, hurled. The longsword flew through the air. I took it out of the thin air by the hilt. That hilt was Zair-guided into the palm of my hand, and it smacked there with a rich and satisfying thwunk of flesh and hide-grip. I sprang for the boloth. The great beast swung its head and its nostrils quivered.

"Get out of it, Naghan the Gnat!" I yelled as I charged.

He needed no second bidding. They had it all worked out. He took to his heels to run for cover and a crossbow bolt ricocheted up from the sand and sliced across that running heel and so laid him low. He lay, the wind knocked out of him.

I reared up to the boloth and dodged a vicious swipe of that battery of tusks and was able to slice off one of the nostrils. His lips were more darkly red when I had finished.

I sprang back and cast a quick glance back. Balass the Hawk had flicked his faceplate down, and the sheer mask of metal with its breaths and sights covered his dark eager face.

No time, no time for thoughts.

I swung to the beast and it was laying about itself, seek-

193

ing that scent, seeking to puzzle out in that sluggish brain what was going on. For Tilly and Oby were spilling lavish quantities of that alluring scent upon the sand of the arena, in wide circles, decoying the olfactory senses of the beast, confusing it. I breathed hard for the safety of the two as they ran so fleetly, the little golden-furred Fristle girl and the reckless scamp of a boy, running as the crossbow bolts sprouted and gouted from the sand. Truly, one does not have to be Krozair to dodge a quarrel!

"Hai Jikai!" I roared it out ferociously, joyously, as I leaped in once more upon that super-mammoth beast. Screaming his anger and fury, his outer tusk grazed past my leg as I leaped and curled the balanced longsword in and so took out another nostril, and sprang back. Now I knew I would not fail, and to the Ice Floes of Sicce what might come after!

This was a High Jikai! This made a hyr-Kaidur look the mean and base thing that is the heart and core of the Jikhorkdun as practiced then in Hyrklana. For the true Jikai lay with my friends, with Naghan and Tilly and Oby, with Balass.

The Krozair longsword sliced into the boloth and I leaped and sprang and so cut it to pieces, and the bewildering scents spread by Oby and Tilly worked most subtly and wonderfully upon the poor creature, for it merely pandered in its brute strength and hideousness to the evil hungers of the queen and her people. I saluted it as I took its other eye out. For now I thought the crossbow bolts would thicken about me into such a storm that a whole regiment of Krozair longswords could not keep them out.

I heard Delia yelling. She was not screaming. I was, at the time, leaping down from the boloth and hoping the poor beast would have sense enough to roll over, and not force me any further to hack it into pieces.

"Dray!" Delia shouted, her beautiful voice strong and firm and without a hint of panic. "Hurry, my heart! Hurry!"

I landed on the sand and whirled; the vast bulk of the boloth stood between me and the central balass stake. From below the queen's box files of her mercenaries were running out. The front ranks carried shields, high, and following them ran the crossbowmen. They had formed as though for battle, in ranks, and their shields formed that wall through which a wild and naked barbarian can seldom ever cut his way.

There was no sign at all of Tilly or Oby or Balass.

The oncoming guardsmen, precise in their dress, aligned, thraxters and stuxes ready, the crossbowmen following on, bore down on me.

Again I heard Delia's voice: "Hurry, Dray, my darling!"

I looked up. A voller from the Air Service of Hyrklana slanted down, and the faces of her crew showed over the side. With her flew a number of the queen's aerial cavalry astride their mirvols. I saw three mirvollers abruptly crumple up and fall in a wide spinning from the sky.

The mercenaries advanced. There was one quick way to get back to the central stake and there make the final stand, as Delia was calling me to do. I turned again for the boloth to jump up and claw my way over his back and leap down on the other side, for he was down on his knees now, his belly sagging, and there was no way under him. Then I noticed the guardsmen in their military formation, dressed for battle, were heading at a slant that would take them past the boloth and me. They were running with their military pace straight for the central stake, out of my sight, hidden beyond the boloth!

I yelled, then. I screamed at the cowardly assassins to fight me, and not bring all their armored might against a lone girl, naked and chained to a stake. The crowd noise was now so great that nothing else could be heard, even the sound of the armored men, the sound of my breathing, the hissing grunts from the boloth.

And then . . . !

And then I saw another wonder and, if anything, it was more wonderful than the first. But, no, that is not so. For the actions of Tilly and Oby and Naghan and Balass could have brought them nothing but death. And what I saw now came from men who wanted nothing to do with death—at least, with their own death.

For the neatly ordered ranks of the guards swayed, and writhed, and collapsed. Guards were falling in droves. And then I saw the sleeting rain of the steel-tipped clothyard shafts, and so I knew why Delia was calling to me to hurry.

I went up and over that poor old boloth like a steeplechaser at the first fence. I poised for just a second, looking down.

An airboat of a style unfamiliar to me hung a yard or so above the sand. But I knew the men who manned her! I saw their great Lohvian longbows bending in that smooth and precise rhythm, and the deluge of shafts that soared to pierce through with bodkin accuracy and penetration. I saw, also, the varters lining her sides angled upward, and loosing bolt after bolt toward the Hyrklanan Air Service vollers. And, the aerial cavalry astride their mirvols were not left out of that continuous pelting rain of destruction that sheeted from the airboat.

The voller was the largest I had seen up to that time. Her petal shape had been drawn out into a towering construction of terraced power, long and beamed, three-decked forward, four-decked aft. The varters spat and clanged and the bowmen loosed and she looked like a snarling demon of the skies. And—from every flagstaff floated the yellow cross on the scarlet field, that flag of mine warriors call Old Superb!

I roared out once, a mighty *"Hail Jakai!"*

Then I was leaping down from the destroyed boloth and feeling that familiar genuine pity for a noble beast done to death to please the debased whims of people who should know better. His three hearts pumped more slowly now as his bright blood poured out upon the silver sands of the arena, and he gave a last long mournful hooting, very distressing. But what else could I have done, there in the Jikhorkdun beneath the Suns of Scorpio?

Delia waited for me aboard the voller. I knew Seg and Inch and Turko had had adventures. Seg waved an arm to me, in between shooting. Inch flailed his Saxon-pattern ax about, cursing, I could so easily guess, that he could not get into close action. Korf Aighos, too, was there, jumping up and down, brandishing that monstrous Sword of War of the Blue Mountain Boys. He would be longing for a fast looting trip to bring him final satisfaction. Away up forward Tom ti Vulheim controlled his band of Valkan Archers, putting shaft after shaft down in the dense defensive pattern. I could have strolled up to the voller. Then I saw Obquam of Tajkent, that flying Strom who disliked the volroks, and I understood he had been that slender flying figure I had seen, and also how Seg and Inch had found me.

Nothing could be heard save the beast roar from the crowd. Not even the shrieks of the wounded and dying as those cruel steel birds tore into them and their crossbows and shields spilled into the blood-drenched sands of the arena.

I wondered what Queen Fahia was thinking.

Halfway there I stopped. Naghan the Gnat lay on the sand, his heel wet with blood. He waved at me and his lips moved. I guessed what he was saying, for a crossbow quarrel at random chunked into the sand beside us.

"Sink me!" I said aloud, although no one could hear. "I'll not leave Naghan the Gnat!"

I scooped him up and a bolt hissed past and so I did not walk, out of concern for Naghan, but raced to the voller and bundled him up onto the deck, where eager hands grasped him. I took a grip of the side, a brass-bound lenk coaming near a varter platform, and the airboat shot into the sky. For a lurid instant I hung there, dangling by one hand, for the other grasped the Krozair longsword which I would as lief hold on to as to the voller carrying us to safety. Wind whipped past. With a wriggle and a squirm, and with Seg and Inch hauling at my wrists, I came aboard.

As I stood up a shadow flicked over me, and I swung around, and there was Turko the Shield, at my back, and a last despairing try sent a crossbow bolt clattering harmlessly from the massive shield Turko lifted over me.

The noise diminished as we rose.

A Hyrklanan Air Service voller shot past, ripped and torn, her crew strewn across her decks with the clothyard shafts feathered into them.

"By Zim-Zair, my friends!" I cried. "You are most welcome!"

Delia clasped me and Korf Aighos cast a swirling scarlet cloak about her glowing nakedness and I laughed and drew her close beneath that flame of friendly scarlet.

Seg Segutorio smiled very merrily upon us, his reckless blue eyes and dark hair very dear to me. "We would have been here sooner, with the good aid of Obquam, but our airboat broke down. We had to take this fine new flier from some onkers who wanted to imprison us and take us to Hamal."

Inch was standing on his head, looking very serious, and we laughed but respected him and his taboos, and gave him room.

"Tom ti Vulheim!" I roared up at that massive foredeck. "Come down here and shake my hand!"

Korf Aighos produced golden goblets of refreshing wine.

"Seg and Inch, old comrades!" I cried. "Korf Aighos and Turko the Shield! Now we have an armorer with us in

197

Naghan the Gnat. And a hyr-kaidur in Balass the Hawk. And, also—"

"And also, dear heart, a saucy Fristle fifi!"

"Aye! And also a rascal who will now aspire beyond the kaidur dreams of the Jikhorkdun. Oby, you imp of mischief! Let go—" But with a screech and a clang the varter with whose mechanism Oby had been tinkering loosed. Everyone gave a great cheer.

"A parting shot to a rast's nest!"

Oh, yes, as we lifted high and higher and sped far and fast from that reeking blood-fouled arena of silver sand in the Jikhorkdun of Huringa in Hyrklana, I saw before me a great and dazzling future. One day, one day, Zair willing, I would return and perhaps, if the people were willing, cleanse the Jikhorkdun.

Now the future opened out bright with that promise. For no ominous clouds boiled about our path and no supernatural winds contemptuously hurled us back as they had done when I had previously tried to escape from Huringa. I knew why the Star Lords had prevented my going before, for then I had been in the past relative to the freeing of Migla, and had I returned I might have met myself—so that I had been forced to wait in the Jikhorkdun until my two presents once again merged.

No such impediment had caused the Everoinye to prevent Delia and me leaving together, and now the Star Lords were allowing us to go where before they had smashed us back to be captured. A task I had had no idea I must perform had therefore been carried out in the interim, and, looking at Oby as he joked and laughed with my good comrades, I fancied I could guess something of the Star Lords' purposes. Oby, in running with our friends into the arena, had saved me twice over!

And, too, no insidious blue radiance crept out to toss me four hundred light-years back across the void to the planet of my birth. Once again, so I fondly thought in my joyful ignorance, once again I was free upon the face of Kregen.

In my arms I held my Delia, my Delia of Vallia, mother of our twins Drak and Lela, and the Suns of Scorpio streamed their mingled opaz light and the sky remained clear and serene above.

# A GLOSSARY OF PLACES AND THINGS

## in the

# SAGA OF DRAY PRESCOT: THE HAVILFAR CYCLE

**A**

apim: Homo sapiens.

arena: See Jikhorkdun.

Astar: Group of islands midway between eastern Pandahem and Xuntal.

**B**

balass: A wood similar to ebony.

Barrath: An area of Hamal.

Beng-Kishi: These famous bells are said to ring in the skull of anyone hit on the head. This happens frequently on Kregen.

Bleg: A halfling with a face like that of a Persian leaf bat, without the large ears; fur and skin patches of green, yellow, and purple. The lower jaw hangs revealing row of thin sharp teeth. Two arms. Four legs arranged in a quadrilateral. Atrophied carapace on back.

boloth: A large animal from Chem with eight tusks, sixteen legs, a tendrilous mass of whiplash tails. The hide is hard and gray along the back, leaf-green along the sides, and yellow beneath. Normally slow, but fast in a short dash. Has an enormous underslung fanged mouth, keen scented; with three hearts.

bur: The Kregan hour, approximately forty Terrestrial minutes.

# C

Canopdrin: Island of the northwest Shrouded Sea, devastated by earthquakes.

Canops: Martial people of Canopdrin.

cham-faces: Nickname given to the Miglas.

chavonth: Powerful six-legged hunting cat with fur of blue, gray, and black arranged in a hexagonal pattern. Treacherous.

Chemzite Tower: Dominating structure of the high fortress of Hakal.

Chuktar: Highest of the four main military ranks. There are many subdivisions varying with country of origin.

Cnarveyl: A country bordering Migla in the northwest of the Shrouded Sea.

coy: Slave or volunteer fighting to become a kaidur.

Crimson Missals, the Battle of: In which the Miglas with the assistance of Dray Prescot and his comrades fought the Canops.

# D

Dap-Tentyrasmot: Town to the east of the Shrouded Sea.

db: Abbreviation of dwaburs per bur.

Deldar: Lowest of the four main military ranks.

deldy: Gold coin of Havilfar.

dermiflon: Blue-skinned, ten-legged, idiot-headed animal, very fat and ungainly, armed with sinuous, massively barbed, spiked tail. The expression "To knock over a dermiflon" is a cast-iron quarantee of effectiveness.

diff: A man-beast, beast-man. A halfling.

dilse: A species of maize, can be mixed with milk and water and pounded and served in a variety of ways. Grows freely needing little cultivation. Has serious nutritional failings.

Djanduin: Country of the far west of Havilfar.

Djang: Inhabitant of Djanduin.

djangir: Very short, very broad sword.

Djanguraj: Capital city of Djanduin.

dom: Kregish equivalent of English "mate" or American "pal."

dopa: A fiendish drink guaranteed to make a man fighting drunk.

dwa: Two.

# E

Everoinye: The Star Lords.

**F**

Faol: Island off the northwest of Havilfar, home of the Manhounds.

fifi: Saucy Fristle girl of exceptional liveliness and beauty.

fireglass: A crystal that does not distort or crack when used to hold fire for illumination and heating purposes.

flutsmen: Mercenaries of the skies, fierce and vicious, of many species.

fluttclepper: A small racing saddle-bird.

fluttrell: A strong saddle-bird with large head-vane, coloring beige-white and velvety-green, with powerful talons.

foofray satin: Expensive material often used to make slippers.

**G**

Gairnoivach: Capital city of Gorgrendrin.

Gdoinye: The giant scarlet and golden raptor, messenger and spy of the Star Lords.

Gorgrendrin: Land of Southwest Havilfar. Its inhabitants are often called Gorgrens.

green sun: Apart from Havil has many names: Genodras, Ry-ufraison, etc.

gros-varter: A larger and more powerful version of the ballista.

Gulf of Wracks: Gulf and channel in Southeast Havilfar leading to the Shrouded Sea.

**H**

Hakal: The high fortress dominating the city of Huringa.

Hakkinostoling: A remote province of Hyrklana.

Hamal: Empire in the northeast of Havilfar.

Hamish wine: A purple wine of Hyrklana.

han: Common suffix denoting son.

Havilfar: A continent of Kregen south and east of Loh.

Havilthytus, River: One of the main rivers of Hamal.

Hennardrin: A land in the north of Havilfar.

Herrelldrin: A country in the southwest of Havilfar.

Hikai: The unarmed combat equivalent to Jikai.

Hikdar: Military rank immediately above Deldar.

Hirrume: Kingdom in Empire of Hamal.

Horter: A gentleman of Havilfar. Feminine is Hortera.

Huringa: Capital city of Hyrklana.

hurm: A hard close-grained wood, similar to sturm-wood.

hyr: Great, renowned, high.

*Hyr-Derenqil-Notash*: "The high palace of pleasure and wisdom." A book of philosophy compiled by a Wizard of Loh two thousand five hundred seasons ago. Admits of many interpretations and analyses.

Hyrklana: An island realm off the east coast of Havilfar.

*Hyr-Lif*: A very important book.

hyrshiv: Twelve.

# I

inklevol: flying fox.

# J

jagger: In the syples of the Khamorros a kick with the feet delivered with both feet off the ground.

Jikai!: A word of complex meaning; used in different forms means: "Kill!" "Warrior," "A noble feat of arms," "Bravo" and many related concepts to do with honor and pride and warrior-status.

Jikhorkdun: The entire amphitheater, arena, and training and barracks areas. Sometimes slurred to "Jikordun."

jiklo: A Manhound of Faol.

jikshiv: Twenty-four.

Jiktar: Military rank immediately below Chuktar.

# K

Kaidur: Renowned gladiatorial feat of combat.

kaidur: Gladiator.

Kham, Khamster: A Khamorro.

kham: Levels of achievement within the syples of the Khamorros.

Khamorro: A man of Herrelldrin expert in unarmed combat.

Kharoi Stones: Ruins of a city of the sunset people in west Havilfar.

kitches: Midges of the marshes.

kleesh: Violently unpleasant, repulsive, stinking. An insult.

kool: An area measurement of land.

Koroles: Small group of islands off east coast of South Pandahem.

Krzy: Abbreviation for the Krozairs of Zy, a mystic and martial order of the Eye of the World devoted to Zair.

# L

laccapin: Ferocious flying reptile.

Lahal: Universal greeting for friend or acquaintance.

Lake of Dreaming Maidens, the: see the Wendwath.

Lamnia: Member of a race of halflings, gentle as a rule, with light-colored fur. Respected as honest and shrewd merchants.

Leaping Fishes, River of: Fast-flowing river to the north of Huringa.

Leem-Lovers: Insulting name for the reavers from the southern oceans.

leemsheads: Outlaws.

ley: Four.

lif: An important book.

liki: Small fly-catching spider.

Lily City Klana: Ancient capital of Hyrklana, now in ruins.

Llahal: Universal greeting for stranger.

lople: Deer-like animal of great grace and beauty.

*Loyal Canoptic, The*: An Inn in Yaman, renamed after the conquest.

*Loyal of Sidraarga, The*: Original name of *The Loyal Canoptic*.


# M

Mackee, Battle of: First battle of the Miglas against the Canops in which Dray Prescot was unwillingly engaged.

Magan, River: Wide sluggish river on which is built the city of Yaman.

Manhounds: Apims of Faol trained to run on all fours and act as hunting dogs. Extraordinarily vicious and predatory.

marspear: A crop plant.

Methydria: Ranching land east of the Shrouded Sea, sometimes known as Havil-Faril, sometimes Methydrin.

Migladrin: Land to the northwest of the Shrouded Sea.

Miglas: Simple, thick-legged, thick-armed, gnomish-headed people, with stumpy bodies and flap ears, of the northwest Shrouded Sea. Also known as Migladorn.

mirvol: Flying saddle-animal of Havilfar.

moons: Kregen has seven moons. The largest, the Maiden with the Many Smiles, is almost twice the size of Earth's moon. The next two, the Twins, revolve around each other. The fourth is She of the Veils. The three smallest moons hurtle rapidly across the sky close to the surface of Kregen.

Mountains of Mirth, the: A mountain chain in the west of Havilfar.

**Mungul Sidrath:** The powerful citadel and palace of Yaman.

# N

**neemu:** Black-furred, almost-leopard-sized animal with round head, squat ears, slit eyes of lambent gold, four legs. Their ways are amoral and feral, they are vicious, treacherous, and deadly.

**Notor:** Lord.

**nul:** Dismissive term for a person not of one's nation or creed or Order or Discipline.

**nulsh:** Term of abuse.

# O

**ob:** One.

**Ocean of Clouds:** A name for the ocean east of Havilfar.

**Ocean of Doubt, the:** Ocean to the west of Havilfar south of Loh.

**onker:** Idiot. Term of abuse.

**Orange River:** A river of Havilfar running westward into the sea opposite Loh between Ng'groga and Nycresand.

**ord:** Eight.

**Ordsmot:** Town on the Orange River divided into eight species sections.

**Outer Faol:** Island to the north of Faol.

# P

**paktun:** A mercenary leader; a notorious mercenary; a renowned soldier of fortune.

**paline:** Yellow cherrylike fruit with taste of old port.

*Paline and Queng, The:* An Inn in Djanduin.

**paly:** The easiest to catch of plains deer. The jungle paly has zebra-striped hindquarters.

**pastang:** A military company, often consisting of eighty men, infantry, plus ancillaries, commanded by a Hikdar.

**Pellow:** City of Herrelldrin.

**pimpim:** Tree of eastern Loh. The crushed fruits yield a brilliant green wine, thick and cloying, sweet and strong.

**prianum:** A cheap pine wood from forests in the south of Havilfar.

## Q

Quennohch: Island in the far southeast of Havilfar.

quoffa: Large draft animal, very mild and docile, powerful, shaggy, with a dogged head and a large patient
face. Has six legs and looks like a perambulating
hearthrug.

## R

rast: Six-legged rodent infesting dunghills. Term of abuse.

red sun: Has many other names besides Far and Zim.

reed-syple: Headband with symbols worn by Khamorros to
denote their syple discipline, their kham status and allegiances.

Remberee: Universal salutation on parting.

Rhaclaw: Manlike halfling with enormous domed head as
wide as shoulders.

Rivensmot: Town of a small kingdom within the Empire
of Hamal.

rofer: Very large multi-saddle-bird of Havilfar.

Ruathytu: Capital city of Empire of Hamal.

## S

Sava: Kingdom in continent of Havilfar.

Savanti: Mortal but superhuman people of Aphrasöe.

sensil: An extremely soft and fine form of silk.

sermine: A flower from which is processed a drug inducing
fighting fury.

Shander's End: Town connected by road to Huringa.

shebov: Seven.

shiv: Six.

shonage: A fruit of rich flesh and sweet juices, larger than
a grapefruit and as red as a tomato.

Shrouded Sea: Large inland sea running from the Gulf of
Wracks in the southeast in a northwesterly direction
into the heart of Havilfar. Is plagued by volcanic activity; dotted with islands.

sinver: Silver coin of Hyrklana.

six: Common suffix denoting daughter.

sleeth: Saddle-dinosaur running on two legs used by the
more sporting rider in races; an uncomfortable ride.

smot: Town.

so: Three.

stux: The Migla vosk-hunting throwing spear. Used as javelin by soldiers.

stuxcal: Device for carrying eight stuxes.

**syatra:** A corpse-white man-eating plant, with spine-barbed leaves and many thick fleshy tentacles sprouting from a central trunk. Venus's-flytrap-type growths larger than coffins grow around the trunk. Likes hot, damp gloomy climates. Chem is choked with them, according to Prescot.

**syple:** A training and mystic discipline of the Khamorros.

# T

**Tajkent:** Mountain aerie of flying men of Havilfar opposed to volroks.

**Thothangir:** Region in farthest south of Havilfar.

**thraxter:** The straight-bladed cut-and-thrust sword of Havilfar.

**totrix:** Close cousin of the sectrix and nactrix. Six-legged saddle-animal, blunt headed, wicked eyed, pricked of ear.

**Triple Peaks:** A mountain aerie of the volroks.

**Tungar:** A vadvarate south of the Orange River.

**Tyriadrin:** A country bordering Migla to the south.

**tyryvol:** Large flying saddle-animal.

# U

**ulm:** Unit of measurement, approximately 1,500 yards.

# V

**veknis:** Scramasaxlike hunting knife used by Miglas.

**volclepper:** Fast, small flying saddle-animal.

**volleem:** The flying form of leem.

**voller:** The Havilfarese name for fliers, airboats.

**volrok:** One species of flying men.

# W

**week:** On Kregen the week is usually six days, although it is seven days in Zenicce. Six-day week associated with Opaz.

**Wendwath:** Known as the Lake of Dreaming Maidens. With its associated sea inlets and fens cuts off the western promontory of Havilfar from Herrelldrin and the northwest.

**wersting:** A vicious black and white striped four-legged hunting dog.

**whistling faerling:** One of the kinds of Kregan peacock.

**White Rock of Gilmoy:** A tremendous pillar of white rock

standing on the northwest coast of Havilfar opposite Faol.

wo: Zero.

woflovol: Bat with large membranous wings.

Wraiths, River of: River of Djanduin.

# X

Xaffer: A race of diffs remote and strange; when slaves they are usually employed in domestic and light duties.

# Y

Yaman: Capital city of Migladrin.

Yawfi Suth: Dangerous and difficult fen area of western Havilfar.

yetch: A term of abuse.

# DAW≡sf BOOKS